DAY'S END

Garry Disher titles available from Text Publishing

Garry Disher has published over fifty titles across multiple genres. With a growing international reputation for his best-selling crime novels, he has won four German and three Australian awards for best crime novel of the year, and been longlisted twice for a British CWA Dagger award. In 2018 he received the Ned Kelly Lifetime Achievement Award.

garrydisher.com

DAY'S END

GARRY DISHER

TEXT PUBLISHING MELBOURNE AUSTRALIA

The Text Publishing Company acknowledges the Traditional Owners of the country on which we work, the Wurundjeri people of the Kulin Nation, and pays respect to their Elders past and present.

textpublishing.com.au

The Text Publishing Company
Wurundjeri Country, Level 6, Royal Bank Chambers, 287 Collins Street, Melbourne Victoria 3000, Australia

Published by The Text Publishing Company, 2022
Reprinted 2022

Cover design by Text
Cover image by iStock
Page design by Jessica Horrocks
Typeset in Garamond 13.25/18.25 by J&M Typesetting

Printed and bound in Australia by Griffin Press, an accredited ISO/NZS 14001:2004 Environmental Management System printer

ISBN: 9781922458827 (paperback)
ISBN: 9781922791078 (ebook)

A catalogue record for this book is available from the National Library of Australia

The paper in this book is manufactured only from wood grown in sustainable regrowth forests.

For Sue Turnbull and Graeme Blundell

1

OUT IN THAT country, if you owned a sheep station the size of a European principality you stood tall. If you were a rent-paying public servant, like Hirsch, you stood on the summit of Desolation Hill.

Not much of a hill—but it was desolate. It overlooked patches of saltbush and mallee scrub and a broad, red-ochre gibber plain that stretched to the horizon; wilted wildflowers here and there, deceived by a rare spring shower.

It also overlooked an image of Wildu, the spirit eagle, carved into the plain: spanning three kilometres from wingtip to wingtip and poised to strike. And Desolation Hill was one of the last places Willi Van Sant had visited before he disappeared.

'The urge to launch oneself,' Willi's mother said, hugging her daypack to her thin body, 'is irresistible.'

Hirsch agreed and they stood silent at the guardrail for a while, that Thursday morning in spring. The urge to launch oneself and ride the air currents above the plain— as an actual wedge-tailed eagle was doing just then, along with a distant, buzzing ultralight plane that Hirsch guessed was photographing the geoglyph for some calendar or post-card publisher.

He was reading a sun-faded sign bolted to the rail— *Wildu is a Ngadjuri word referring to the stars of the Southern Cross, their arrangement here represented by the tips of an eagle's talons*—when Dr Van Sant gave a dismissive sniff and pointed to the carven eagle below them. 'Appropriation?'

'Sure is,' he agreed cheerily, wondering if her son had expressed that thought in an email home.

He gazed again at the geoglyph—or artwork; or graffiti, homage to the Ngadjuri or instance of cultural appropria-tion, depending upon your point of view. Some hero with a grader had scored the eagle into the ground in the mid-1980s. No one had ever said who; the overseer, station hands and absentee property owner denied all knowledge. When Hirsch first noticed it, on one of his long-range patrols of the rain-shadow sheep stations, it was obscured by decades of sand drifts, desert shrubs and the churning tyres of hunters' four-wheel drives. Then last year a grazier named Russ Fanning had bought the place, restored the motif with a pair of GPS-guided excavators and created the lookout on the peak of Desolation Hill.

Strange guy, Fanning. Contradictory. He wasn't after sightseeing dollars, just wanted to acknowledge the Ngadjuri people, and had met with some of the local elders, intent on getting the mythology right. They'd had reservations, but he'd gone ahead anyway. Hirsch wasn't sure if that made Fanning a bad guy or not, but elsewhere on his property, where the soil was less marginal and enjoyed a better chance of rain, he'd set up revegetation and conservation programs, installed solar panels and batteries; he conserved and recycled water. A guy who liked to yarn with Hirsch, show him around the property. Who admitted one day that he voted Labor.

And twice in the past month he'd called Hirsch to ask if he was any closer to identifying who'd shot his merino stud ram, valued at forty-five thousand dollars. A high-powered long-range-rifle bullet to the head. Hirsch clenched with guilt. Short answer, no. He'd knocked on doors—a round trip of three hundred kilometres out in that country—and got nowhere. Maybe 'roo shooters, someone suggested. Maybe wild-goat shooters, said another. Maybe mischievous, maybe malign. And maybe accidental, the ram resembling a goat if he'd been caught in the tricky shadows of a saltbush twilight.

Hirsch shook off the guilt and turned to Janne Van

Sant, dismayed to see tears, a twist of sadness or anxiety. He tried a smile. 'Shall we move on?'

'One moment please, Constable Hirschhausen.'

She dug in the front pocket of her tan canvas pack and retrieved one of the photographs she'd shown Hirsch ninety minutes earlier, in the front room of the little brick building that housed the Tiverton police station. Printed from a message sent by her son, it showed a tall, slim kid with blond dreadlocks, smiling for the camera, Wildu the eagle spread behind and below him. Twenty-one years old. Backpacking around Australia, taking a job here and there.

It occurred to Hirsch at that moment: the photo was not framed like a selfie. Someone had been with the kid, here on the summit of Desolation Hill.

As to who, he thought—that was a question to ask the station owners Willi had been working for.

He watched Dr Van Sant hold the photo at head height with both hands, adjusting until she knew exactly where Willi had been standing all those months ago. She was a slightly shorter and less tanned version of her son. A cap of cropped fair hair. A similar smile—what Hirsch had seen of it in the past hour and a half.

And hours to go yet: another thirty minutes over chopped and powdery back roads to reach Dryden Downs; a conversation with the Drydens; the trip back to the police station and her rented Camry.

She had dumped the daypack on the bonnet of the SA Police Toyota. A handful of other photographs spilled out.

'May I?' Hirsch asked, gathering them up.

Her response was a shrug that he thought of as very European. It said: 'If you must.' And so, with some hesitation, he neatened the photos and flipped through them. Warm from the Toyota's duco, it was almost as if they were straight off the printer.

Willi on a horse; Willi swimming in a dam; Willi with a sheepdog, on a claypan, pointing down at the tracks of a solitary sheep; Willi beside a Cessna marked *Dryden Downs Pastoral*; Willi crouched next to a gravestone, gesturing comically at the inscription: *Here lies Tom Sewell, who shot himself accidentally on purpose, 25 September 1923.*

Hirsch got a kick out of it, too. He shoved the photos back into the daypack and checked his watch.

'Yes, yes,' Dr Van Sant said, her tone at odds with her air of containment.

Hirsch steered the rattling Hilux down through the switchback bends, then left at the T-intersection at the base of Desolation Hill and onto a corrugated dirt track named Manna Soak Highway.

'Irony,' Dr Van Sant said.

'Yes,' Hirsch said, accelerating. Drive too slowly on these roads and your teeth shook out; too quickly and you might lose traction on a curve, roll your vehicle, lie pinned in the wreckage for hours, even days, before another vehicle happened along. You needed skill with a dash of nonchalance. Hirsch had been making these back-country ventures for three years now and was getting better at it.

Right now he was concentrating on the road, not Willi's mother, who was saying, with an air of carefully testing her words and pitching her voice above the rattles: 'A national trait, do you think? A reluctance to take anything seriously?' She'd been in the country exactly four days: two in Sydney, then the drive to Tiverton, in wheat and wool country halfway between Adelaide and the Flinders Ranges.

Hirsch decelerated for an eroded incline washed free of topsoil; more the spine of a stone reef than a road. He topped the rise at walking pace, slowly increased speed on the downslope and said, 'Yes, partly that.'

Slim and straight-backed in the seat beside him, and perhaps testy that he'd taken so long to answer, Janne Van Sant said, 'And the other part, or parts?'

She's picturing her son out here, Hirsch thought; how he might have fared—how he might be faring—in a land where no one took anything seriously. 'Isn't being ironic a sign that you take something seriously? You're trying to stop it swamping you?'

Dr Van Sant gestured beyond her window at the salt-bush and mulga struggling to survive on the red dirt plains. 'Manna Soak, is that irony, too? The bread of heaven?'

Hirsch braked gently and pulled to the side, letting an oncoming Land Rover with Western Australian plates pass by. His mind raced, distracted from answering by the presence out here of an interstate vehicle with two averted faces on board.

Dust roiled; tiny stones pinged along the flank of the Toyota. The air cleared and he drove on. 'The naming isn't always ironical. Some names are quite frank.'

'Mm,' Dr Van Sant said. 'They trace the faltering march of white progress. Hope Hill,' she added, a name they'd seen on a signpost on the road from Tiverton. 'Mischance Creek—what mischance, and why did it matter enough to name something? Desolation Hill.'

Hirsch pointed to where a couple of acres of red dirt surrounded a lone chimney amid a pile of stones. 'We're in a rain shadow,' he said. 'People came out here in the mid-1800s, saw running creeks and spring grasses, and built a house. They didn't know they might wait twenty years for the next rainfall.'

'One hopes,' Dr Van Sant said, 'but suffers misfortune—and so is desolate.'

This isn't really about the place names, Hirsch thought; she's thinking of Willi. The journey he may have made from hope to despair. Not wanting to say anything trite to buck up her feelings, he lowered his side window. Dust lingered, but so did perfumed traces of plants, soil released by the attentions of sun and wind.

He said, 'Manna Soak is an actual place. That photo of Willi pointing at the sheep tracks? A big, dry claypan most of the time but a shallow lake when there's been rain. You should see the birds when that happens,' he added brightly. He wanted her to take some goodness with her when she left this place.

'And now?'

'Dry, I'm afraid.' Not that Hirsch had ever seen the birds flocking at Manna Soak, only the photo on the Tiverton general-store calendar, which hung in the police-station waiting room.

Twenty minutes later he slowed, turning off the track and rumbling over a stock ramp between a pair of massive stone pillars. An old sign on one pillar, sun-faded and dust-abraded, read: *Dryden Downs, est. 1865, 560,000 acres, please close gates after you.*

Hirsch had called in at the property once before. Crime waves permitting, he made two long-range patrols every week, the first taking in areas east and north of the Barrier Highway, the second west and south. Mostly it was responding to reports—of stock theft, for example—and welfare checks: a farming widow here, teenage kids with a bedridden mother there.

A place like Dryden Downs, with its own plane and airstrip and a large, capable staff, could cope without a regular visit just so long as they knew he was around. The Drydens—Sam and Mia—had been out the day he'd dropped in, but he'd left his card with the station cook and that evening Sam had called him, apologising, apprecia-tive, his voice a soft, precise rasp.

The sign on the other pillar was new: *Unvaccinated visi-tors welcome here,* and, in smaller type, *We refuse to enforce unlawful directions from a government that would microchip its people.* As Hirsch accelerated along the immaculate white-gravel driveway, passing a third sign—*Homestead 15 km*—and a fourth indicating a fifty k speed limit, Dr Van Sant said, 'Vaccinated visitors, on the other hand, are not welcome?'

Hirsch barked a laugh. 'You strike it in Belgium, too?'

'Oh yes.' She paused. 'A government that would microchip its people. It's age-old, isn't it, the fear that powerful, malicious figures are working against us through invisible means? Like witches.'

'Yes,' agreed Hirsch, thinking: *who are you?*

Dryden Downs was large enough to encompass a range of soil types, from gibber plains to undulating bushland and grazing country. The homestead driveway took them through grassland with Angus cattle on the left, black-faced Dorper sheep on the right. At the fourteen-kilometre mark, the track climbed a low rise. Visible on the other side was a broad, shallow depression spread with as many rooftops as an English village: main house, overseer's house, cottages, implement sheds, workshop, shearing shed, stable block, hayshed, hangar and station hands' accommodation. Scattered among these buildings were stockyards, lawns, extensive gardens, concrete water tanks and a horse-riding enclosure.

'The hope doesn't seem quite so faint here,' Dr Van Sant muttered.

Hirsch pulled the Hilux onto a turning circle beside the main house, a long, elegantly proportioned structure built of local stone and deeply shaded on all sides by verandas hung with grapevines. He parked in the shade of a massive ghost gum, switched off and got out, closing his door with a soft click, feeling oddly that a slam would be out of place.

The silence after the bone-shaking drive was a blessing, and the spring sun was balmier here than up on Desolation Hill. A deep stillness, too: the airstrip windsock limp and no one gunning an engine, shearing a fleece or yelling at a sheepdog. The only movement was a woman on a black horse circling the riding arena intently, as if the world consisted solely of her, her horse and this small, hoof-churned yard. Mia Dryden, guessed Hirsch, hooking his face mask on.

Dr Van Sant joined him, also masked. 'Willi told me that she is horse mad,' she murmured.

As they were about to cross to the enclosure, the rider dragged on the reins, walked her horse to the railing fence and called, 'Hello, there. Sam's inside, doing the books. Give him a shout at the front door. I'll join you as soon as I've cleaned up.'

Then she wheeled away and made for the gate closest to the stable block. Dr Van Sant had insisted on an unannounced visit—an old cop's tactic, and fine by Hirsch—but if Mia Dryden was unsettled or curious, there was no sign of it. A practical, horsey blonde in her forties, a little heavy, full of smiling good-neighbourliness, that's all. But that sign at the driveway entrance...

Hirsch turned to Dr Van Sant, who was looking at

him flatly. He tried to read her: *Almost as if she had been expecting us.* Or maybe: *The effortless grace of the very rich.*

He gave a whisper of a smile and a nod, and together they crossed a lawn to the main entrance of the station homestead. The inner door was open, revealing a long, broad corridor hung with paintings and light sconces. Hirsch knocked on the external screen door. It rattled feebly. After a few seconds he knocked again and called, 'Mr Dryden?'

A distant scrape and thump, as of a desk chair on a wooden floor, and a tall man stepped out of a doorway halfway along the corridor. 'Yes?'

'Police, Mr Dryden. We met your wife; she said it was okay to knock.'

'Police?' Dryden said, ambling towards them. He stepped out onto the veranda, a lean, ramrod-straight man in his late forties, wearing khaki cargo shorts, a baggy blue polo shirt and cracked leather sandals: weekend or day-off mucking-around gear. Beneath it lay a hard authority. He was a man poised for action, generating in Hirsch an absurd desire to snap to attention. Ex-military?

He stuck out his hand. 'Paul Hirschhausen, from the Tiverton police station, and this is Doctor Van Sant.'

'Janne,' she said, offering her hand. 'Willi's mother.'

Dryden shook, gravely courteous, even bending slightly at the waist, before stepping back, head cocked, his frown a little knot between his brows. 'I'm afraid Willi's not here, Doctor Van Sant. Janne. He left us two or three months ago.'

She stepped towards him impulsively, about to speak, and he breathed in and stood straighter. 'I suggest you talk to my wife. She knows more than I do. Here she is now.'

Thinking, *That was quick, she must have got a stable-hand to take the horse*, Hirsch turned and watched Mia Dryden approach the house.

Still wearing jodhpurs and a perspiration-damp black T-shirt, she called, 'Darling. They found you, I see.'

Where her husband's energy lay coiled, hers vibrated. Her eyes were bright; her teeth flashed; she was a ripple of movement; her words poured out as she skipped up the steps in an eddy of hot-day and horse-riding odours. 'Give me five minutes to change, would you? Darling, how about cold drinks on the veranda? Or if either of you would prefer tea or coffee? And you may remove your masks, you know.'

'We'll keep them on, thanks,' Hirsch said, but she was already through the screen door, touching her husband's wrist on the way. She's still not curious, he thought, shifting his attention to Sam Dryden, who was regarding Dr Van Sant: preoccupied but not unfriendly.

Then Dryden snapped out of it, gesturing along the veranda to a gathering of cane chairs around a glass-topped cane table. 'Please do make yourselves at home. What can I get you?'

They asked for mineral water and shortly after that an aproned man appeared, carrying a tray of glasses and bottled San Pellegrino, with Sam Dryden in his wake. Hirsch recognised the station cook from his first visit. Shorter than

Dryden, with cropped hair and the same military bearing. 'Barry, is it?' Hirsch said. 'Barry…McGain?'

McGain nodded; left silently.

When he was gone, Sam Dryden filled each glass, then sat. 'I expect you cover a lot of ground in your job, Constable Hirschhausen?'

Hirsch nodded. 'Quite a lot—two patrols a week. Call me Hirsch, by the way.'

Dryden tried it: 'Hirsch. You're familiar with everything by now?'

'There are still a few out-of-the-way properties I'm yet to call at, but I'll get to them eventually.'

'The face of the law.'

'Sort of.' Hirsch shifted uncomfortably. He didn't want to get into it, his twin roles, law-upholder and welfare worker.

'If it's any help,' Dryden said, 'you've reached the end of the road here. Nothing but scrub and semi-desert beyond my driveway.'

Hirsch wasn't sure how to take that, detecting an edge to Dryden's tone. The weight of age and privilege, as though the pastoralist were issuing an order, not offering advice. Hirsch said, 'Fair enough.' Fully intending to venture further along Manna Soak Highway one day.

'Did you know my son well, Mr Dryden?' Janne said.

Dryden turned to her; seemed to study her. 'Sam, please. Not well. I'm often away, you see—business. My wife can help you.'

As if answering a signal, Mia Dryden stepped onto the veranda. She'd had a hurried shower; her hair, heavily damp, had darkened a sleeveless, collarless blue cotton shirt. With bare feet striding and a filmy knee-length skirt swishing, she approached on a tide of delight, as if no one had visited the homestead for months, before pausing behind her husband, a hand on each shoulder and brushing his neck with her lips. Dryden closed his eyes; his whole body relaxed.

Mia straightened again. 'I see my grouch of a husband has been looking after you! Cold drinks, just what the doctor ordered,' she said, stepping away from Dryden and swivelling neatly onto the fourth chair. She reached across the table and touched Dryden's wrist. 'Darling, I know you're super busy.'

He stood, nodded gravely, strode along the veranda and vanished into the house. Watching him go with the clear gaze of a young girl in love, Mia turned her attention to Hirsch and smiled. 'Now, what brings you to our door?'

'I'm stationed at Tiverton,' he began.

'I thought it might be you.'

'And this is Doctor Van Sant. She's very concerned for the welfare of her son, Willi. I understand he worked here?'

'Willi!' Mia said. 'Such a lovely boy, always smiling, a pleasure to have around.' She leaned towards Dr Van Sant. 'You know, you needn't wear your mask here. And I would so love to see your face. Already I can see a resemblance to Willi around the eyes.'

'It's best if I keep it on,' Janne said. 'Omicron-riddled Europe, two long flights, airports, you know...'

'As you wish,' Mia said, erect again. 'Willi. As I said, a lovely boy. There was nothing he couldn't do, if he put his mind to it.' She leaned forward. 'Did you know we had him mustering sheep like a pro by the time he left here?' She sat back. 'Everyone loved Willi. Our one and only jillaroo was head over heels.'

The person with the camera, Hirsch thought.

'That is as may be,' Janne Van Sant said crisply, 'but he stopped contacting me four months ago. Quite suddenly. One day there he was, on his bunk bed, talking to me on Viber, and the next day, nothing.'

Mia was troubled. 'I don't know what I can tell you,' she said with a helpless gesture. 'He and the girl he was seeing just packed their bags and drove off into the sunset. It left us in quite a pickle, work-wise. But, you know, young ones...'

Dr Van Sant eyed her stonily. 'My calls and emails have gone unanswered.'

'As I said, he's young, in love...he's probably still in Noosa, living it up.'

'My calls and emails to *you*,' Janne said.

Mia sat back with a pretty frown of concern. 'To me?' Her hand went over her chest. 'Are you sure? I mean, we are very remote out here...'

Hirsch glanced across the yard at an impressive antenna array. He said, 'Willi and his girlfriend went to Noosa?'

'Well, yes,' Mia said. 'Stay there, I'll be right back.'

15

She returned with a postcard. Addressed to Sam and Mia Dryden, it showed a curve of beach dotted with swimmers and sunbathers, with a biro scrawl and an arrow: *Us in the shallows!*

On the other side, in a looping, breathless hand: *Hi Sam and Mia! Just to let you know we're missing you—kind of!—and thanks so much for the experience! Love, Eve and Willi xxooxx.*

'When did this arrive?'

'Oh, ages ago. Weeks. A couple of months, at least.'

'Do you have contact details for this Eve?'

Mia took a phone from her skirt pocket and scrolled through her contacts. Turned the screen to Hirsch. He saw the name Eve Tilling and a mobile number.

Using his own phone, he called it. It rang out. 'Did either of them leave anything behind?'

'Not a skerrick.'

'Do you know where Ms Tilling grew up? Has her family been in touch?'

'In touch? With us? No. She grew up in Sydney, but where, exactly, I couldn't tell you.' Mia shifted uncomfortably, as if reluctant to let a cloud dim her sunniness. 'She didn't get on with her stepfather though, I do remember her saying that. An old story, as I expect you know.'

The story suggested abuse, and Mia Dryden seemed to struggle against the image until her smile burst out again. She said, 'You must be so *worried*, Janne. But I'm sure the Department of Foreign Affairs will be of some help.'

'Idiots,' Janne Van Sant said.

'Oh,' Mia said. She seemed to think about it. 'A government bureaucracy,' she said darkly.

Hirsch said, 'If we could have a quick word with the people Willi and Eve worked with day by day? The other station hands?'

Mia put a hand over her heart again. 'Oh, I'm sorry, spring is a busy time for us. They're all out mustering.'

'Maybe on another occasion?'

Mia said nothing. She shifted her gaze to Janne. 'I shall ask each and every one of them for information when they get back tomorrow. Do you have a card?'

Janne Van Sant reached for Mia's phone. 'May I enter my details?'

'Of course.'

Hirsch watched Janne's fingers fly over the screen, and then she was tugging down her mask, draining her mineral water and saying, 'Thank you for your hospitality,' and heading for the Toyota.

She was halfway there before Hirsch could gather himself. He stood, nodded to Mia Dryden, and said his thanks, his hand extended.

She shook it hard, a jolly up-and-down. 'I understand you're fond of the term "Covid moron", Constable Hirschhausen,' she said with hostile relish. 'Tell me—do you think I'm a Covid moron too?'

2

HAD SHE OVERHEARD him last month? At the medical clinic, arguing with that guy trying to stop his wife getting vaccinated? Hirsch thought it was just as well that he'd said 'Covid moron' and not what he'd almost said: 'Too stupid to live.' He was badly rattled as he picked up speed on the long driveway, and did not at first register what Dr Van Sant was saying, except that it sounded like an observation. 'Uh-huh,' he replied, hoping he'd struck the right note.

'You noticed it, too?' she said. Snorting, she added, 'A

double act. He disarms with his air of elegance and polish, and she with her, what's the word, airhead routine. I cannot quite work him out, but she wears the trousers. Deep down she is not a silly woman.'

'I agree,' Hirsch said.

They had reached the gateposts. He turned left onto Manna Soak Highway and so they began the long drive back to Tiverton.

The Hilux pitched, tilted, juddered and sometimes rolled along smoothly, but the variations seemed not to bother Dr Van Sant. Gazing out of her side window, head pillowed by the headrest, she spoke more about her son, her tone mild, wistful and reflective. Soccer mad. Popular, with a mutually supportive group of friends. Adventurous: loved camping, climbing, rafting. Belonged to a garage band. A racing cyclist almost good enough to enter the Tour de France. A BA in hotel management from a college in Bruges—and this backpacking holiday was a hiatus between study and career and possibly a drawcard on his CV.

'*In Bruges*,' Hirsch said. 'One of my favourite films.'

Dr Van Sant slumped a little, as if she'd heard those same words from every English-speaking numbskull she'd ever met. 'Is that so?'

'A beautiful city.'

She turned to him, still disappointed. 'You have been?'

'Yes.'

He'd travelled through France, Belgium, Germany

and Italy with Wendy and her daughter Katie—Kate, as she expected to be called now—a few weeks before Covid hit. 'Briefly,' he added.

Dr Van Sant looked away. 'A beautiful city. But Willi grew up in Brussels, where my home is.'

'What do you do?'

She looked at him searchingly, as if to assess how deserving he was. 'A public servant, like you.'

They fell into a troubled silence now, as they turned onto the Tiverton Road and eventually broke through the rain shadow into better country, with vivid yellow canola crops spreading along shallow valleys and over hillslopes, threaded here and there with dirt roads lined with equally vivid springtime weeds and grasses. Loftier, better nourished gum trees. Farmhouse cypress hedges. Wildflowers.

Pointing to a patch of purple, Dr Van Sant said, 'What plant is that?'

'A weed,' Hirsch said, 'called Salvation Jane.'

Kate had shown him how to pluck the little flowers and suck the base; taste the honey.

With a grin in his voice, he added: 'Also called Paterson's curse in other parts of Australia.'

Eyes triumphant, Dr Van Sant swung around on him, ready with another quip about naming practices; saw his face, and subsided. If she'd been a friend, he might have said, 'Gotcha: you smiled.'

Tiverton was ten minutes away now. He said, 'I've been thinking about your next moves. If you like, I'll contact the police in Noosa and ask them to check hostels and Airbnbs. And the police in Sydney, to see if they have anything on the girl Willi's travelling with. Otherwise, try social media appeals.'

'Thank you,' Janne Van Sant said, just as Hirsch's mobile rang. The phone, in a cradle on the dash, showed that the caller was Bob Muir.

'Where are you?' Bob said.

'A few minutes from town,' Hirsch said.

'We've got a little fire. The Cobb kids were flying a drone, and Laura says they saw something burning near the town paddock.'

The town paddock was twenty-five acres of wheat on the northern approach to Tiverton, between the Barrier Highway and a vast lucerne property. Once a segment of an old stock route—its width allowed for the turning-around of bullock teams and the droving and overnight penning of sheep and cattle—it was now ploughed, sown and harvested by volunteers, the profits benefiting the town's primary school, sporting clubs and annual strawberry fete.

'Which side of it?'

'The access track. I told them to stay away.'

'Good,' Hirsch said. 'Thanks.'

Laura Cobb and her older brother, Daryl, were the sole carers of their mother, who had bipolar disorder. Or rather, sharp-witted Laura cared for them both. Daryl was a big, floppy kid, easily led, and he'd have been drawn to the flames. Likely to burn himself or post phone footage

21

on Instagram or trample over evidence that might explain the fire.

'I'll be there in five,' Hirsch said.

It was more like four. As Tiverton's rooftops, gum trees and grain silos appeared in the distance, he turned left onto a side road and then right onto the town paddock's narrow, rutted access track, wondering if he should have delivered Dr Van Sant to her car first.

He could see smoke now. It was coming from the ditch at the base of a deceptive rise in the track that briefly concealed the town from view. Just a wisp of smoke. Something was smouldering. Not the springtime grass— too moist and green.

Pulling closer, he realised that the source of the smoke was down in a culvert. Saying, 'Please stay here for your own safety, Doctor Van Sant,' he got out, and had barely stepped away from the Hilux when he saw the district's Country Fire Service truck come over the rise, Bob Muir at the wheel.

Muir, an electrician and Hirsch's friend, was alone, which probably meant he'd been on a job in town when the call came, and the other volunteers were unavailable.

Now Bob stepped down from the cabin, leaving the motor running, and they shook hands in the middle of the road. Bob, a quiet, burly, practical man in grey overalls and cracked tan work boots, tipped his head to the side, looking past Hirsch. 'Who's your passenger?'

Hirsch turned: Dr Van Sant was heading towards them. He made the introductions helplessly and said again, 'It would be best if you waited in the car, Janne.'

'I have experience,' she said, marching off to view the fire.

Bob exchanged a glance with Hirsch, shrugged and returned to the truck, calling, 'I'll get the pump going.'

Hirsch joined Dr Van Sant and together they peered down into the ditch. A massive old canvas suitcase, bulging here and there, with a weak creep of smoky flame in one corner. Tossed in, Hirsch guessed, and the sudden jolt had caused the contents to shift, and strain the zip or the fabric so that a pale, hooked, tubular shape was exposed.

And just as realisation hit Hirsch, Dr Van Sant got there first. 'A human elbow.'

'My first body in a suitcase,' Hirsch said, but it fell flat.

Dr Van Sant scowled. 'Diesel fuel,' she said.

She was right: he could smell it now, a dense layer under the weak acridity of the smoke.

Hirsch turned, saw that Bob was trotting over with the hose. 'Ah, good.'

Alerted by his tone, Dr Van Sant turned also, and promptly stepped into Bob's path, both hands up, pushing at the air. 'No! No, please, Mr Muir.'

Bob halted, confused, the metal nozzle dripping water and heavy in his hands. 'What?'

'Evidence,' Dr Van Sant said. She turned to Hirsch. 'Fetch our water bottles, please. We apply one cupful of

23

water at a time, to preserve the evidence. This is not a fast or a dangerous blaze, but it will destroy evidence over time—as a powerful jet of water will do in a very short time.'

She spoke with such assurance that Hirsch found he'd let her into his crime scene—for surely that's what it was—with barely a second thought. He stood with Bob on the lip of the culvert and watched her grow flushed and grimy as she flipped little gouts of water onto the flames, until they were extinguished. Satisfied, she swiped her hands on her thighs and climbed out, and Hirsch reached for her when she slid on the slick grass.

'Thank you. Diesel has been splashed everywhere,' she said. She narrowed her gaze at the two men. 'Diesel is combustible, not flammable, and not a good fire source in cases of arson. You may even extinguish a cigarette in diesel fuel.' She gestured: 'And so we have here a fire retarded by its very accelerant. The suitcase is saturated in diesel, but there is evidence'—she pointed to the scorched corner —'that your culprit realised his mistake and employed a secondary source, a rag soaked in some other substance, possibly lighter fluid. Either there was not so much diesel in that area, or the two fluids combined to effect a better flash point.'

Hirsch cocked his head. 'You are some public servant, Doctor Van Sant.'

She made one of her impatient gestures: first things first. 'Your crime-scene officers will now have a better chance of obtaining useable evidence.'

'Thank you.'

'The body is that of an adult male. I cannot determine the age, but I did glimpse a faded forearm tattoo.' She looked intensely at Hirsch, and he saw there deep sadness. 'I conclude therefore that it is not my son.'

He winced internally. He should have anticipated her hopes and fears. He reached out, in his own sadness, and reflexively touched her forearm.

She swayed towards him, as if for an embrace, then recovered and said, 'I am employed by the National Institute of Criminalistics and Criminology in Brussels.'

'Forensics.'

'I am attached to two working groups,' she said. 'Paint and glass, and fire and explosions.' She paused. 'Of course, the two are often linked.'

Hirsch nodded. He'd attended his share of house fires, hit-and-runs and cars wrapped around trees. Paint, glass, smoke, destructive forces. He looked at her again, this time professionally sad. 'I'm afraid I'm going to be stuck here for the rest of the day—and most of it will be waiting for detectives and crime-scene officers to arrive.'

She put up a hand to forestall him. 'Of course. My being here would not be appropriate, and nor will I be needed.'

She was looking up at him searchingly. He saw in her face regret, respect, a day of shared adventures. 'Good luck,' he said, shaking her hand. 'Bob will take you to your car. Do you have somewhere to stay tonight?'

'The Woolpack Hotel in Redruth. After that...?' She shrugged eloquently.

'If I learn anything from the police in Noosa or Sydney, I'll let you know.'

'Thank you,' she said, striding towards the truck, at the last moment veering right as she remembered which was the passenger side. That made Hirsch even sadder for her.

He called it in and daydreamed through the next ninety minutes. The sun, high in a cloudless sky and tipping towards mid-afternoon, baked the interior of the Hilux, even though the temperature was only twenty-six degrees, so, after checking the on-board computer, he chose some meagre shade and sat in the dirt for a while, his spine against a tyre. He monitored his phone, checked the suitcase a couple of times, watched a sleepy lizard waddle across the road.

And he listened to the hum of the universe, drawing in the odours of warm soil, lucerne and spring grasses. He itched to open the suitcase. He got no further with thinking he should study for the sergeant's exam. He was looking forward to tennis starting again—so long as he wasn't the club treasurer this time. On that note, did wanting tennis to start again make him a local now, or still only a city guy trying to be a local? Which led to thoughts of Wendy Street, and love, and the future, and—so far—steering a deft course with Kate, her daughter. There were complicating factors. Kate had saved his life within a few months of his posting to Tiverton; he'd started going out with her mother; she didn't resent his presence in their lives; they'd developed a mutually pleasing code of wisecracks and teasing; and now she was at high school and outgrowing all of that.

And she was a target of online bullying, and she wanted to deal with it herself. Wanted Hirsch and her mother to butt out.

Hirsch had offered to call in a cybercrimes specialist, but Wendy had scotched that idea: 'We're just talking about other kids,' she said. 'We need to be supportive, that's all. She's got a good head on her shoulders. We teach her how to be strong and avoid engaging with these bullies, and how to wean herself off Instagram and so on.'

Thinking about online matters led Hirsch to thinking about Mia Dryden, and he was about to google her on his phone when he heard a vehicle tearing towards him from the direction of the town. A crime-scene van? Detectives from Port Pirie? Going too fast, anyway, and likely to plough into the Toyota, so he stepped out into the middle of the road, ready to intercept the driver. Then realised it was a poorly tuned motor he could hear. A loose or badly holed exhaust.

A sun-faded white Holden station wagon breasted the rise. Braked abruptly, its rear end twitching in the dirt, and Jacob Maher was gaping at him through the windscreen.

The kid hunched, grinned in embarrassment, waved, made a panicky five-point turn and trundled back over the rise.

Idiot, thought Hirsch. Maher and his mother had arrived in Tiverton with a handful of other people shortly after Easter. They said they'd been priced out of the Adelaide housing market by Covid, and bought a wreck of a place near the grain silos. Then they'd immediately attracted the attention of Hirsch and his colleagues down in Redruth: possible shoplifting; a dog barking all day; car hooning; loud music at 2 a.m. Their high achiever was Jacob. Arrested for stealing a car, he'd arrived at his magistrate's hearing in a car he'd stolen to get himself there.

Hirsch hadn't seen the station wagon before. Also stolen? If not, perhaps unregistered? Unroadworthy? He made a note to call at the kid's house as soon as reinforcements arrived to release him from the scene.

Meanwhile other motorists might decide to use the track, so he set about placing traffic cones at the top of the rise and around the culvert. Then he drove the police Toyota into the paddock, wincing to think of the delicate new wheat shoots being crushed. Finally he waited in the meagre shade again, checked his phone, watched an eagle, wished, selfishly, that he could chat with Wendy, who'd be fronting a maths class.

And so time passed, and presently his sergeant arrived, followed by a crime-scene van, followed by a Port Pirie detective named Comyn. One of that motley crew even said, 'What have we got here?'

3

HIRSCH STOOD BY with Comyn and Sergeant
Brandl as the crime-scene officers debated the pros and
cons of examining the body in situ or transporting it,
undisturbed in the suitcase, to the lab.

Comyn rode over that, in his stolid way. He was squat
and humourless as a beer barrel, and always apparently
irritated by Hirsch's very existence whenever they met.
He said, 'Clearly there's been a crime of some kind. But
was the victim scraped up off the road by his friends after
an accident, or was he murdered? If somebody offed him

I need to get onto the Homicide Squad right now. So let's have a look.'

'You're the boss.'

Not quite; Sergeant Brandl outranked him. But she wasn't a detective, and she settled in with Hirsch to watch as the crime-scene officers photographed the case, made two shoeprint plaster casts—a left heel and a right toecap barely apparent in the soil—and finally teased open the suitcase's main zip and folded back the lid.

The dead man was skinny, heavily inked above and below a pair of blue boxer shorts. His face was an unrecognisable pulp, his hair stiff with blood.

He could still have been an accident victim, until one of the crime-scene officers said, 'We have lacerations and cigarette burns.'

'Okay,' Comyn said, fishing out his phone.

The other officer had leaned her face close to the blood-matted hair. She swung back, fetched a pair of tweezers from her evidence-collecting case, leaned in again and plucked out a chip of something terracotta-coloured. 'Maybe bashed with a house brick,' she said.

'Lovely,' Comyn said. 'Okay, seal it up again and take the whole thing, as is, to the lab.'

He walked a short distance up the road, phone to his ear. Calling Homicide, Hirsch thought.

Meanwhile Sergeant Brandl was looking at him with pity. 'You're in for a circus tomorrow.'

'If not tonight,' Hirsch said glumly. Media. Carloads

30

of suits. 'With any luck the guy was killed in the city and carted up here.'

'A long way to cart a body.'

'Yeah.'

'How did it go this morning?'

It had been the sergeant's idea that Hirsch take Dr Van Sant out east. He knew the area; Brandl and the young Redruth constables she called 'the children' didn't. But she would take care of the missing-person paperwork.

'Good and bad,' Hirsch answered. He told her about Willi Van Sant's photographs, the Drydens, the Noosa postcard.

And Janne Van Sant's gentle dousing of the suitcase fire.

'Really?' Brandl said, stepping back as if to examine Hirsch for exaggeration. She was lean, no-nonsense, with fuss-free hair.

'Yep. And lucky for us,' Hirsch said.

'Huh.'

She stood beside him again and they watched the loading and driving-away of the suitcase. Comyn joined them and said Hirsch should expect a team of detectives by late afternoon. 'Where can they set up?'

Hirsch thought about it. 'The CWA meeting room. In the Institute.'

'Who do I talk to?'

This year the Country Women's Association president was Nan Washburn. Hirsch gave him the details.

31

'Okay, I'm off,' Comyn said.

Then Sergeant Brandl left. 'Good luck for tomorrow,' she said as she got behind the wheel of her car.

There was a tinge of worry in it. She didn't mean his day with detectives and media hounds; she meant his Zoom bollocking from Inspector Alwin.

Hirsch spent a moment planning the next few hours.

Follow-up calls on behalf of Dr Van Sant. Check the town's CCTV, what there was of it. Talk to the Cobb kids. Ascertain if suspended-driver's-licence-holder Jacob Maher was driving around in another stolen car. First, though, preserve the town's little wheat crop from the churning wheels of police, media and stickybeak vehicles.

He found a padlock and chain in the crate of odds and ends he kept in the Toyota—towrope, hatchet, rubber boots, hand tools, evidence bags—and secured the paddock gate. Then he drove south along the track, around the oval and down First Street to the Barrier Highway. Just as he reached the intersection, the Redruth High School bus rolled past, heading north on the highway with a last handful of farm kids. Lifting a hand in greeting to the driver, Hirsch turned left and drove two blocks to the police station.

Almost on autopilot, he took stock of that stretch of the town. Dr Van Sant's rental car was gone; the primary school across the road had finished for the day; a few of Tiverton's Redruth High kids were slopping around

32

beneath the general store veranda. Huge kids, with Cokes, crisps and mobile phones in their hands, massive backpacks at their feet. Ed Tennant, the shopkeeper, was torn: they spent their money in his shop; they made a racket and other customers had to step around them. Hirsch's response had been, 'It's only a few minutes a day,' which was greeted with the disdain that Ed thought it deserved.

Both men knew that these kids would eventually graduate and head for the big city, though. A country-town story. Other town kids, like Daryl and Laura Cobb, were trapped—Daryl because he wouldn't do well on his own and Laura because she couldn't abandon him or their mother. The kids' father, a beer thug with the vicious bloat of ignorance, had abandoned them long ago.

They lived a hundred metres from the police station, and it was Laura who answered Hirsch's back-door knock—no one much used front doors in this town. Pale, with long dark hair falling around thin cheeks, she wore an apron over faded jeans and a yellow T-shirt with a misshapen neck. Shy, guarded, she had a curious white flash half a centimetre wide across one eyebrow. Hirsch had asked her about it once, chit-chat to ease the tension after one of her mother's manic episodes, but he'd misstepped badly. She'd touched the eyebrow and said, in a dead voice, 'Mum did it when I was ten. Seven stitches.'

'Hi, Laura,' he said now.

Barely meeting his eye, she whispered, 'Come in,' her back against the wall, one arm holding the screen door open for him. 'Making spag bol for tonight,' she added.

Her days would be like this, Hirsch thought. She had completed Year 12—top marks—and now worked odd jobs around the town, sometimes at awkward hours, meaning she might cook up a big pot of something in the middle of the day, do the laundry at night, grab sleep when she could.

She took him into the kitchen, a cramped region of chipped appliances and scuffed cupboards. The chrome and laminate table might fetch a few dollars at a retro place in Adelaide, but you'd need the time, the energy, the transport.

'Sit,' she said, turning away from him to stir the sauce in a pan on the stove.

'Smells great.'

She swivelled around, looking pleased. Maybe praise was scarce in her life. 'Would you like to take some home with you?'

'Actually,' Hirsch said, 'that would be great.'

The alternative was frozen crumbed fish fillets from the shop. Baked beans on toast. He watched her bend neatly, ferret in a drawer beneath the bench for a takeaway container, fill it and plonk it at his elbow. 'You might need salt and pepper, or try a dash of sugar. I always find tomato paste sharpens the flavour too much.'

'Thank you.'

She checked the sauce again and sat opposite, still shy with him. 'I guess you want to know about the drone.'

'Didn't know you kids had one.'

She looked worried. 'It's Daryl's. Mrs Washburn gave

it to him for his birthday.'

'Great present,' Hirsch said, realising it was true. Anything to get Daryl off his console and out of the house.

Laura flicked him an anxious look. 'Are we in trouble? Are there like regulations about flying a drone near houses? We weren't, really. We were on the oval.'

'You're fine,' Hirsch said. 'I just need to know what you saw on the video feed—it's got a camera, right?'

Laura nodded. 'We took it in turns and I saw what looked like smoke—not much smoke, though—so I sent it over to have a look.' She shrugged. 'There wasn't much to see, just this thing smoking in the ditch. Then Daryl started losing it, you know how he gets.'

Hirsch guessed. 'He was worried the smoke might get into the motor or something?'

'He thought it was going to catch fire, so I flew it back again and called Mr Muir.'

'Did you see anyone there? Parked car? Or driving away?'

'Nothing.'

'How about earlier, when you were walking towards the oval?'

She shook her head. 'Wasn't really looking.'

'Could I have a quick word with Daryl?'

'He can't tell you anything more than that. And he's in with Mum, reading to her.'

And that sad little loving picture undid Hirsch for a while.

—

Now to tackle Jacob Maher.

Hirsch walked back to the police station, climbed into the Toyota again and headed to the southern edge of the town. The westering sun blazed on the ram's head painted on one of the silos, the structure itself throwing a thick band of shadow across the highway. Right turn onto Wirrabara, a side street that took him over the railway line and in a return sweep past disused stockyards to three cowering stone cottages set about fifty metres apart. The smaller two, ruins now, had housed linesmen back when the rail system was flourishing. The larger had housed the stationmaster. A shearer had been living in it when Hirsch first arrived in the district. Since he'd died it had sat unoccupied, neglected and open to the sun and the rain until six months ago, when Jacob's mother and a mob of relatives and hangers-on had moved in.

They hadn't improved the place. Weeds thrived in the drooping veranda gutter and choked the surviving shrubs and rosebushes. Lichen bloomed on the rust-fringed corrugated iron of the roof. Cobwebs hung from the eaves. A listing grey VW diesel van was parked in the driveway and a car rested on blocks on the front lawn.

Somehow, motor vehicles were at the heart of everything this crowd got up to. Hirsch had proof they drove unregistered, unroadworthy, stolen and speeding vehicles—with or without the benefit of a licence—and suspected that these same vehicles sometimes transported stolen goods.

This crowd…Hirsch still hadn't quite worked them out. Apart from Jacob, there was his mother, Brenda, and her boyfriend, a weedy guy named David Hillcock, who had brought his stepdaughters with him to the menagerie and had had a baby with Brenda. Toby, about eighteen months old, something like that.

Hirsch parked beside a defeated-looking wrought-iron gate in a low, collapsing wall, locked up and stepped onto the veranda. Rapped his knuckles on the door and waited. Did it again.

No answer, so he headed around to the backyard, reasoning that Jacob, banned from driving for six months and knowing he'd been seen on the town paddock road, would head home and hope for the best. The Holden station wagon would be behind the house.

Hirsch rounded the back corner and there was the car, along with a battered old caravan and a kind of white-trash-mountain-people-zombie-apocalypse tableau. Brenda Maher, lavish and vast, was lolling topless in a brand-new vinyl recliner, the baby boy suckling at one pillowy breast; David Hillcock, in oil-stained biker boots, jeans and T-shirt, lay on an adjacent recliner, holding her hand. No sign of the younger stepdaughter but the older one, Alice—McNamara, was it?—skinny, inked and pierced, was draped over the station wagon, watching Jacob. He was kneeling at the front bumper with three numberplates and a screwdriver.

'Guys,' Hirsch said. 'Lovely day for it.'

Hillcock's eyes slid away. Then the man himself slid away, swinging his boots to the ground and sidling into the house. Brenda, watching him go, shrugged and turned a lazy, off-colour smile on Hirsch as she briefly adjusted the unsuckled breast.

'Knock it off, Brenda.'

She covered herself, cackling, and set the baby down on a blanket, where it sat wobbling and trying to outstare a rottweiler that was straining and choking on a kennel chain. Hirsch squatted beside the blanket. 'How's it going, Tobes?'

Rewarded with a gummy smile from the baby, he beamed back, creaked upright again and approached the station wagon. 'Guys.'

Alice McNamara shied away. 'Wasn't doin' nothin'.'

'I can see that. Jacob, on the other hand…'

Jacob on the other hand had kicked the numberplates under the car and seemed to be tossing up between flight and fight. He turned a wondering look at the screwdriver in his right hand. Let it fall onto the weedy dirt.

'Fucken bought this car,' he said.

A skinny kid with meth-hollow cheeks who affected a trademark black glove on one hand, along with ripped jeans and the grimy Megadeth T-shirt he'd worn to his car-theft court appearance a month earlier—only to be told by the magistrate to go away and reappear in a mask, and clothing that showed 'respect for the court'. Seeing Jacob at an utter loss that day, Hirsch had taken him down the street

38

to the Redruth Emporium and forked out sixty dollars for a polyester shirt more yellow than white and a pair of gabardine trousers. Sixty bucks he wouldn't see again.

'I can show you the papers,' Jacob went on.

'That would be good, thanks, Jake.'

Jacob jerked his head at Alice, and Hirsch had to step aside so that she could slide past him and climb into the caravan. A moment later she reappeared clutching a slip of paper and proffered it to Jacob, who said, 'Not me, him.'

Hirsch took it from her. The sum of $999.99 had been received from Jacob A. Maher on 10 September, according to Martina Golos of 6 Bundaleer Street, Muncowie.

Muncowie was a depressed collection of mostly empty fibro houses half an hour north of Tiverton. Hirsch had the contact details of every mid-north publican stored in his phone—along with doctors, ministers of religion, school principals, mail carriers and busybodies. He stepped away from the car and called the Muncowie pub: there was a Bundaleer Street, but as to who lived at number six, 'couldn't tell ya'.

Next Hirsch photographed the rear numberplate and called it in, then knelt to fish the plates out from under the car. Two were a pair; the third matched the rear plate. He ran them.

The rear plate belonged to the Holden station wagon, but the registration—in the name of Martina Golos of Bundaleer Street in Muncowie—had recently lapsed. The other plates were from a written-off Kia Cerato.

Watched glumly by Jacob and Alice, Hirsch walked around the car. A broken tail-light. Rust. Bald tyres. Cracked windscreen. And, as if to offset the misery, a shiny new dashcam unit.

'Jacob,' he said, 'I don't know how you got this car—at least it's not stolen, or I hope not—but it's unregistered and unroadworthy, and you've been driving it around without a licence. What if you'd hit a Rolls Royce? What if you'd run over a kid?'

'Haven't been driving it around.'

'I just saw you an hour ago.'

'Nup.'

Hirsch didn't want to get into it. Putting his phone away, he said, 'You know I'll have to write this up. Give me the keys and I'll fetch the paperwork.'

Jacob jerked his head again. Alice fished the keys from the ignition, and...something in Jacob's eyes.

There are spare keys, Hirsch thought.

He pocketed the keys, saying, 'Thank you. I'll arrange the tow in a minute. In the meantime I—'

'What fucken tow?'

'Jacob, I'm impounding this car.'

'You can't fucken do that.'

Behind them Maher shrieked, 'Leave him alone ya prick.'

Hirsch turned, said, 'Stay out of it, Brenda,' wondering why he'd let himself engage with her, and turned back to the son who, emboldened by Brenda, was shaping up now,

40

feet apart, fists raised, chin jutting.

'Wow,' Hirsch said. 'Warrior chook pose.'

Jacob flushed. He flung a weak punch and the clenched black glove sailed past Hirsch's jaw. Overbalanced now, Jacob recovered and ducked back, fists up, feet dancing.

'Oh, for fuck's sake.' Hirsch stepped in and clapped his hands smartly against the kid's ears. Not hard.

Jacob reeled back. 'Fucken do that for?'

'Police brutality,' shrieked Brenda, echoed with less conviction by Alice.

'As a police officer in the execution of my duties,' Hirsch said, 'I perceived a clear and present danger to my person and took swift, appropriate and non-injurious steps to defuse that threat.'

'Clear and present danger' was pure Hollywood, but maybe this bunch would swallow it. Or maybe, thought Hirsch as he removed the station wagon's distributor cap, I've stepped in it again.

He found Alice studying him. 'You doing Jake for assault?' she demanded, and he saw a hard intelligence in her eyes. She's smarter than the others, he thought.

'Frankly, I'm just too tired,' he replied. 'But he needs to stop being an idiot.'

A helicopter passed overhead: Channel 7. And so it starts, Hirsch thought, returning to the Hilux to call a tow truck. Passing a side window of the house, he saw the glow of a massive wide-screen TV. Hillcock was watching it from the corner of a sofa, beer in hand.

4

ALMOST 5 P.M. now, Hirsch gearing up for a few hours of mind-numbing paperwork as he drove back through the town. First, though, he checked the culvert—the forensic team had finished—then the CWA clubroom at the institute, a fine colonial-era stone building on the highway, with a World War II field cannon and a memorial to the war dead at the front. Here Comyn and another Port Pirie detective were installing computers, desks and phones, and told Hirsch to piss off, he'd be contacted in due course. Finally, the police station. He'd barely pulled on the handbrake when the Channel 7 team raced across the road from the shop, bristling with cables, camera and microphone. Trotting out his 'Can't comment on an ongoing investigation' line, but helpfully pointing them to the institute, he unpinned his mobile number from the front door—thank Christ the media hadn't found it—and went in. They'll be frustrated, he thought. No help from me, no help from the suits. And probably no help from the good folk of Tiverton, who'd endured a couple of 'country town, dark secrets' stories in recent years.

Making his way through to his living quarters, three poky rooms at the back, he made a mug of tea, scrabbled around in the jar for the last Tim Tam and put his feet up for a while, making himself switch to pleasant, end-of-the-day thoughts. Usually these thoughts involved Wendy and Kate Street. He liked to kid himself that he was bound to them telepathically, even as he recognised the more prosaic reasons for the tingles in his skin. He'd spent all day jarring over back-road corrugations, for example; or, after three years with them, he pretty much knew where they were and what they were doing at any hour of the day.

And right now, as he forced himself to relax on his lumpy sofa, he began to visualise their house on Bitter Wash Road. Their car pulling in. Homework in Kate's backpack and lesson plans in Wendy's briefcase. And then his mobile phone was ringing, and—telepathy?—Kate was whispering to him frantically.

He sat upright. 'Say that again?'

'There's a man and a lady and they're scaring Mum and I'm scared the man's going to hit her. He already punched the wall and kicked a hole in the flyscreen.'

Hirsch plonked his mug down and climbed out of the sofa. 'Coming now.'

Her next words were torn away, a mix of *Stop it* and *...hurt her...* and *...police*, with a man's shouts, a woman's pleading.

Then the phone went dead.

Hirsch ran outside to the Toyota—then put a brake on that, not wanting to alert the media, standing a hundred metres away outside the institute. He strolled around to the driver's side door, slipped nonchalantly behind the wheel, backed out onto the highway and rolled past the shop, gradually picking up speed. He was flooring it by the time he reached the broad, shallow farming valley to the south of the town. Yellow canola and green cereal crops on either side; a glimpse of cypress hedges and farmhouse roofs tucked away at the end of long driveways.

He made the Bitter Wash turnoff in three minutes, heading east now, into undulating foothills, the dirt road shaking his bones, gravel smacking around inside the wheel arches. Stone-wall fences from the colonial days. Fat merinos ready for the clippers. Windfarm turbines stretching along a ridge of hills and the Toyota's rear end twitching in treacherous sand drifts on the bends.

At Wendy's driveway he braked and turned in with a shudder, almost burying the nose of the Hilux in the canopied rear of a Holden Colorado twin-cab ute. He piled out, ran along its flank—giving his knee a painful knock on the bull bar—then past shrubs to the small house with its faded red roof and warped veranda decking. Here a youngish guy with a woman tugging futilely on his arm was towering over Wendy, who had her back to the wall. She was a heartbreakingly small figure to Hirsch's eyes just then.

He couldn't see Kate—and then she was darting to his side from the shadows of the garage and Wendy's car. 'Mum had the handbrake on too tight.'

Hirsch realised that she'd started the engine of Wendy's Golf. Plucky kid, he thought. He advanced on the house now, calling, 'Break it up' and 'Sir, you're frightening Mrs Street' and other things like that, hoping his uniform would work, even if the actual words didn't.

The man swung around in mid-tirade, and slumped. 'Ah, fuck.'

He spotted Kate and snarled, 'Whatcha call the cops for?'

She bristled. 'Take a wild guess.'

'Ed.' The woman tugged on his arm, which was a slab of white flesh hanging, too naked-looking, from a tight grey singlet. Mirrored sunglasses perched on his brow; two-day stubble more slovenly than designer; beefy white legs squeezed by the cuffs of faded cargo shorts.

'Ed, calm down,' continued the woman, a brunette as heavyset as her partner, wearing black leggings and a baggy yellow T-shirt.

When the man named Ed jerked his arm away, her eyes flared briefly. 'No need to be an arsehole about it.'

'Arsehole? Who's the arsehole?' the man said. He gave Hirsch a mulish look and gestured at Wendy. 'You need to arrest this bitch. Fraud. She ripped us off.'

'The only one getting arrested will be you, sir, if you don't control your anger.'

Ed was outraged. 'Me?' He hunted tremblingly for the expression he needed, settling on: '*Righteous* anger, it's righteous anger. What this bitch did to us is what you should be looking at.'

'Let's all take a deep breath, be respectful of each other and sort out what the problem is,' Hirsch said.

He started by introducing himself, learning that their names were Ed and Elly Kline. He couldn't help himself— Ed 'n' Elly, Ed 'n' Elly—and caught Wendy's gaze. Slight, dark-eyed and small-boned like her daughter, with a consummate resting bitch face, she twinkled very faintly at him. Reading me, he thought.

He saved himself by turning away to grab three faded deck chairs. He set them in a half-circle facing the veranda, and ordered everyone to sit. 'Let's work this out,' he said, perching himself on the veranda edge.

Then he felt a whisper of movement: Kate had slipped beside him, barely touching. He felt some of his tension ease.

'Mr Kline, you first.'

'Yeah, well, this bitch—'

Hirsch put on his resting bastard face. 'What did I just say?'

Kline subsided. He blinked, not tears, and swiped at his face as though tormented by flies. Not good with words or emotions, Hirsch thought. 'Mrs Kline, perhaps you could explain?'

Elly Kline flashed him a grateful look. 'Last month me and Ed both got jobs up at the windfarm place and we been living in a caravan behind the pub while we look for somewhere to rent.' She waved a helpless hand at Wendy's house. 'This come up on Facebook.'

'I didn't post it,' Wendy said quietly.

'A local marketplace page?' guessed Hirsch.

Ed Kline said, 'Yeah.' He was huge in the deckchair, a mass of muscle and softness, with small eyes in a fleshy, juvenile face.

'With photos?'

'Well, yeah. We probably wouldn't've been interested otherwise.'

'You answered the ad. Did you actually speak to anyone or—'

'It was all Messenger,' Elly Kline said with an apologetic grimace at Wendy. 'Far as we knew, we were texting with the owner who signed everything "Wendy" and said she was working in New Zealand for a year and couldn't show us around. Anyway, we applied and the next day she approved it and asked for bond money and a month's rent up-front.' Pause. 'Which we paid.'

47

'Into a bank account?'

'Western Union.'

'Almost three grand,' Ed Kline said, squirming in his chair. 'She said we'd find the key in the fuse box on the back veranda, so we rock up here just now and hello, here's Wendy, and she's pretending she doesn't know what we're talking about.'

Slow to twig, thought Hirsch. Or he does twig but can't admit it. 'I think you may have been scammed, Mr Kline.'

Kline gestured at Wendy. 'Yeah? How do we know she hasn't ripped off other people? How do we know she even lives here?'

'Can I speak, Mr Kline?' Wendy said.

He slumped. 'Whatever.'

'This is my home. I've lived here with my daughter for several years now. I teach at Redruth High, where I'm vice-principal and head of maths. I don't need to rip anyone off and I'd never do that anyway. I'm really, really sorry it happened to you, but Senior Constable Hirschhausen here is a good sort, he'll help you in any way he can.'

Hirsch put his trust-me face on, even as his mind raced. It was an easy scam to set up and run, and it tapped into a sad trend: too few rural houses for rent and too many desperate renters. But how were the scam properties selected? Pulled out of a hat? And here the fraudsters had used Wendy's name. Coincidence? Hirsch didn't often run into it.

'The name of the marketplace group?'

'Mid-North Rent, Buy and Sell,' Elly said. She began tapping at her mobile phone. A moment later she slumped. 'They've taken the listing down.'

'Any other places listed?'

Elly Kline proffered her phone. 'These, but they're either falling down or too expensive.'

Hirsch crossed the lawn, took the phone from her and scrolled through the four listings shown. He knew only one of the houses. It was beside the Redruth police station and legitimately for rent. Still, he'd monitor the site for a while.

'I'm sorry,' he said, returning the phone and perching on the edge of the veranda again.

Wendy said, 'There are agencies you could contact. Consumer Affairs, for example. And if you need financial help or emergency accommodation, try Mid-North Families and Financial Services.'

Ed stirred. 'We look like charity cases to you? We got jobs. We just need a proper place to live, not a caravan at the back of the pub.'

Wendy retreated with a little shrug. But Elly, touching her husband's forearm warningly, shot Wendy a smile. 'Thank you.'

'I'll report it to the Fraud Squad,' Hirsch said. 'They might have other cases they're aware of, they might even have someone in their sights. Meanwhile, try contacting the website, they might have ways to track these people down or ways to stop them posting again.'

And pigs might fly, everyone's face said. Ed climbed to his feet, looking sheepish. 'Sorry I yelled.'

'Vanished from my mind,' Wendy said.

Now they were all standing, and Hirsch asked, 'Before you go, Ed—is it possible you and Elly have been targeted specifically in some way? Has anyone got it in for you?'

'How would that work? Anyone could've answered that ad. The answer's no, anyway.'

They targeted Wendy, Hirsch thought; made a few bucks at the same time.

Ed, looking helplessly at the screen door, said, 'I'll pay for the damage.'

Hirsch saw that Wendy almost told him to forget about it, but she said, gently, 'Thank you, that would be good.'

The Klines drove away, and Hirsch stayed for an early dinner, the atmosphere more sombre than usual, Kate withdrawn, picking at her food, hurrying off to her room. Hirsch helped with the washing up, then said he had homework of his own to do, and mother and daughter followed him out to the Toyota and stood there as he wound down the window and turned the key.

Kate leaned in, kissed him distractedly, said, 'Thanks, Aitch, see you on the weekend,' and shuffled back to the house.

'She all right?'

'If she isn't, she's not telling me,' Wendy said, leaning in.

50

5

IT WAS THE light of early evening by the time Hirsch had parked in the driveway of the Tiverton police station again. The town looked quiet, only a token media presence. He went in, sat at his desk, booted up his computer and started on a string of landline calls. Missing Persons, the Noosa police station, New South Wales police headquarters, the Fraud Squad. A fruitless hour later—but at least with information logged into various creaky systems—he began googling 'Dryden Downs', 'Sam Dryden' and 'Mia Dryden'.

He skimmed the property hits, a mix of puff stories and photographs of merino rams in the *Stock Journal* and other rural publications. Mostly they amounted to saying that Dryden Downs had been in the same family for several generations, and that everything operated on a large scale—acreage, stud prices, output, infrastructure, the pioneering of new crop-growing and animal-husbandry methods.

The results for Sam were more interesting. Now a full-time grazier, he'd been a defence department analyst when he inherited the property on his father's death in 2013, and a Special Air Services captain in Afghanistan before that. Not squeaky clean in civilian life: his name had been mentioned, in passing, in a *Sixty Minutes* investigation into the activities of a bankrupt property developer in the Barossa Valley and a *7.30* exposé of a mid-north Liberal Party powerbroker who was convicted of obtaining money by deception and influencing local council planning decisions.

But nothing had stuck to Dryden, and he was later touted by Liberal Party heavyweights as a potential candidate for a mid-north seat—except that two election cycles had passed and he wasn't nominated. In Hirsch's experience, not even full-out corruption, drink-driving or MeToo scandals had ever come between a politician and glory, so was something else going on?

Dryden—said to be reserved, gracious, highly intelligent—had no social-media presence and had given few interviews. But there were reports that an address he'd given at a conference had possibly rubbed the party faithful up the wrong way. Most members of parliament, Dryden had said, were guilty of betraying Australia's sovereignty. 'We are losing our freedoms bit by bit. Our whole social structure is being destroyed; our national survival is under threat.'

Now for Mia Dryden. She proved to be significantly more prominent and forthcoming, with a scattergun presence across Instagram, Facebook and Twitter, along with mentions in lifestyle glossies and newspapers. Active in student politics at Adelaide University, she had been critical of feminism, student-union fees and left-wing academic staff, and behind a Women for National Socialism group within the Young Liberals. Then—herself the child of a pastoralist—she'd hooked up with Sam at a Liberal Party conference in 2013. Society wedding. Children.

Nothing overt while the children were very young, but in 2019 she'd started posting about 'the importance of re-exploring the almost forgotten bonds between humans and their natural environment'—which boiled down to a defence of shooting goats and kangaroos. She was all over Instagram, posing beside her kids on a dusty hillside with a dead goat at her feet or draped around her neck, a disturbing mix of long tanned legs, cleavage, blood-stained shirt and high-powered rifle in the crook of one arm.

Hirsch made follow-up notes: Where are the kids—boarding school? And: how many guns does she own; are they registered; are they properly secured?

He read on. Mia Dryden defended hunting because factory farming involved pumping meat full of hormones and antibiotics—'Which we eat!' she wrote. 'Much more sustainable for my family and me to hunt our own meat! Better for Mother Nature, not to mention our tummies! And my children gain an understanding that the animal we kill has led a good life and we honour the animal by utilising it to feed ourselves.'

Hirsch was with the anonymous poster who expressed their hope that the animal world would one day turn on her. But Mia wasn't bothered. 'Your ignorance is not my burden to bear,' she'd replied.

Her latest interest—no surprise—was Covid-19. Here she was less clear, if more fervent. The virus didn't exist, or, if it did, was no worse than a bad cold. Inoculation didn't work and the vaccines were full of unknown and risky chemicals. And mandatory vaccination went against the sovereign right of ordinary citizens not to have government agents inject poisons and microchips into their arms.

All of that was easily traced via the internet. Hirsch wanted to know more about her. How had she learnt of his 'Covid moron' comment, for example? Would it play a role in tomorrow's Zoom reprimand?

He found little more than repetitions. But then, buried deeply in the web, he came upon sceptical responses to a claim she'd made to the media. Apparently, in her first year of marriage to Sam she'd headed into the wilderness, got lost, and staggered out two weeks later, the heroic survivor of a terrible ordeal, grateful for her well-honed bush skills.

Mid-north locals with their own bush-survival skills had been sceptical. Hirsch phoned the only one he knew.

'Her!' Bob Muir said. 'Media whore.'

'Don't sugar-coat it.'

'She couldn't have survived for two days where she said she'd been. It was like a furnace out there. No shade, no water—or if there was, it was barely drinkable. Either she was somewhere else all that time—like her sitting room—or she had supplies dropped in. Why?'

'Met her today.'

'Ah.' Bob was silent for a beat or two. 'Careful there, Paul.'

6

HIRSCH'S MORNING WALK was non-negotiable, in the same basket as sleep, food, love, life. Thirty minutes, that's all he needed—all he had time for—starting at 6.30 and getting back in time for the 7 a.m. ABC news of the world at peace. Sometimes he merely walked right around the town, which was a narrow strip of houses nestling under gumtrees, the silos at one end, the football and cricket oval at the other. Or he strode up and down the side streets randomly, the town waking around him: kitchen radios, a shower running, a car backing out of a driveway in the dawn light. The town didn't change but the seasons did. And nor was Hirsch constant: this particular daybreak was of the benign, slow-moving, good-to-be-alive kind, warmth creeping into the overnight coolness, the atmosphere laden with dew and blossoms and songbirds. At the same time, he was fretting about this morning's Zoom conference.

Or rather, the fact that he was in trouble again had brought back memories from three and a half years ago, when he'd been turned inside out by Internal Investigations and labelled a dog and a maggot. He was neither corrupt himself, nor a dobber, but he'd discovered only weeks into his first posting as a detective constable that the rest of the CIB squad was falsifying evidence and stealing drugs. He tried to protect himself by recording his interactions but still—some of the mud stuck. Hence his demotion to uniform and subsequent posting here, a little one-officer police station in wheat and wool country three hours north of Adelaide. Hirsch, a city boy: a fish out of water, mistrusted by the locals and despised by his fellow cops in the neighbouring stations. Working slowly to decipher not only this strange new place but the crimes that germinated here.

Like a body in a suitcase beside a wheat paddock.

The world had mellowed around him since then. The towns, farms and arid back country had become more familiar. He'd found companionship—love. But his sense of belonging was tenuous. His home—three poky rooms on which he paid rent to the department—was only his until such time as a clerical pen stroke assigned him to some other far-flung corner of the state.

It occurred to Hirsch, as he walked up and down the side streets that Friday morning, that the town's streetscapes had altered overnight. A flyer about a hard-rubbish collection had been slipped under front doors and into letterboxes a few days ago, and he'd been seeing household goods heaped on the nature strips: unwanted mattresses and bed-bases, plastic garden furniture, lamps, bookcases and kitchenware. He himself had added a card table to Bob and Yvonne Muir's set of heavy old suitcases and a dented twin-drawer filing cabinet—not a good look to leave it sitting outside the police station. And now most of the nature strips were clear again—except, he noticed, for a dented saucepan here, a VHS player and a warped tennis racquet there. Picky rubbish collectors?

Hirsch paused twice to assure a couple of early garden-waterers that the man found in the suitcase had no connection to the town, then turned into Goyder Street. He was halfway down it when Bob Muir said, 'Howdy.' He was sliding a toolbox out of the rear compartment of a gleaming white Mercedes van in the driveway of Rose Elliot's sun-faded transportable home.

'New wheels?' said Hirsch. 'Nice.'

Bob's old workhorse had been a battered Holden ute, on its second or third engine and gearbox: 475,000 km on the clock, he'd told Hirsch one day. Now Bob rolled his shoulders uncomfortably. 'Yeah, well, the time had come.'

Country people, Hirsch thought. Suspicious of display of any kind. You didn't show off your new tractor, phone, diamond necklace, artistic talent or Mercedes van. He nodded at the house. 'What's the job?'

'Rose reckons she can smell smoke if she leaves one of the halogen lights on too long.'

Hirsch nodded. 'Cody isn't with you?'

Cody Morton was Bob's apprentice, Bob doing his bit for rural youth unemployment after working alone for most of his life. 'Yeah, well, we parted ways.'

'Oh.'

Bob looked vaguely wounded. 'He's a kid, you make allowances, but I couldn't get him to wear a mask around the clients half the time. And he tried to show me a video of the Christchurch massacre.'

Hirsch shook his head, visualising Cody, a skinny, pimply, vacant-eyed kid with a mullet. 'What you might call cloth-eared.'

Bob snorted. 'Wanted me to join some mob called Antipodean Storm.' Shook his head and adopted a declamatory pose: *Be part of a single beating heart*, or some crap. Plus, the little shit wouldn't get vaccinated.'

Hirsch stopped himself from saying it again—'Covid moron'—even though there was no one to film or record him.

At 8:50 a.m. he was walking his open laptop around the cramped confines of the police station premises, testing

59

the Zoom video function for the optimum play of light on his face. He didn't want to look washed out, he didn't want to lurk in the shadows. The best spot was behind his desk after all. Now for optimum elevation so that Inspector Alwin wouldn't be looking up his nostrils. A pile of statute books did the trick.

Then he stuck a note on the front door—*Unavailable until 10 a.m., please call 000 in case of emergency*—and, hoping his dressing-down would take five minutes rather than sixty, he locked up and settled himself in the cubbyhole between the inside wall and the counter that separated him from the waiting room.

At 8:59, Inspector Alwin's face filled half the laptop screen, unreadable and perfectly lit. 'Sir,' Hirsch said.

'I can hear you, Constable Hirschhausen, but not see you. Turn on your video...That's better.'

'Sir.'

The Port Pirie inspector wore a loosened striped tie and a rolled-sleeves white shirt. He was balding, with tufts of carroty hair above his forehead and each ear. He was a brusque, take-charge, clipped-sentences man but, Hirsch thought, ultimately fair. He must have known Hirsch's back story but hadn't let it influence their prior encounters. His was an equal-opportunity brusqueness.

'You know why we're having this meeting?'

'Sir.'

'The Internals wanted to haul you over the coals, but I convinced them we could handle this at a local level.'

'Thank you, sir.'

'The audio clip has been taken down—it was muffled to begin with—but not before a few hundred Covidiots heard it. And it may surface again.'

Covidiots. Was that a good sign? 'I'd like to apologise for momentarily losing my cool, sir. No excuse.'

'Talk me through it.'

Hirsch took a deep breath. 'Doctor Pillai from the Redruth Medical Centre has been holding a Friday clinic here in Tiverton for the past couple of years, and last Friday she called me to a disturbance.'

She had sounded tense—'There's a man here shouting and tearing off people's face masks'—and Hirsch, on his way out to a fence dispute between neighbouring farms, had U-turned at the silos and raced back to the clinic in the old Adelaide Bank building across the road from the shop.

'Mostly, sir, she just consults on everyday stuff,' Hirsch continued, 'but that day she was also offering Pfizer boosters.'

'Someone objected?'

'Yes, sir.'

'Go on.'

Just then Hirsch's mobile pinged beside his elbow. Irresistible: he glanced down. Janne Van Sant had texted him: *Thank you so much for your assistance yesterday. You will be kind to keep me informed of new developments. J.*

Then, wincing, he looked up at Alwin again. 'Sorry, sir, I should have turned it off.'

'Leave it on. You might be called away suddenly. So might I. The disturbance at the clinic?'

'Sir,' Hirsch said. He explained that he'd found ten people stretched in a line along the footpath, standing on strips of black gaffer tape 1.5 metres apart—both Cobb kids and their mother, Ed Tennant, Nan Washburn and a handful of others. More in the waiting room, presumably. A board outside the front door had been kicked over— *COVID-19 inoculations today 9 a.m–5 p.m.*—and a QR code check-in sheet sticky-taped to the window had been ripped in half.

Nan was trembling. Her hand to her mouth, she'd said, 'He ripped my mask off. Screamed in my face, "Scared of catching cold?" Stuff like that.'

'Who?'

'Wes Stragan. His wife's in there.'

Stragan, aged in his fifties, was an all-purpose rural delivery driver: hay to outback New South Wales, wool to Adelaide, a new tractor to Streaky Bay, wild-goat meat to Greek restaurants in Melbourne. That's all Hirsch knew about the guy.

But he was easy to find: just follow the shouts. Hirsch had opened the clinic's front door and stepped straight into the waiting room.

Five people seated along one wall, looking frightened, and Stragan, a thin guy in blue work pants and chunky yellow boots confronting Dr Pillai at the far end. She was in the doorway of her consulting room, one arm raised as if to ward off spittle or keep Stragan out, or both.

'Wes, don't, you're scaring everybody,' she said.

She spotted Hirsch striding down the room. That alerted Stragan, who whirled around and said, 'Oh, marvellous.'

'Wes, calm down.'

Instead, Stragan seemed to inflate. Taking a step to one side, he stabbed a finger at Pillai, then Hirsch. 'You, you—you're both agents for the government. It is actually not your privilege or power to infringe on my sovereign rights and my wife's sovereign rights. I am powerful and I will return, and you have not heard the end of this.'

'Paul, you talk sense into him. I give up,' Pillai said, stepping into her room swiftly and closing the door with a gentle click.

'Bitch!' shouted Stragan at the door. 'You're sticking a needle in her, right? You have no right to do that without my permission.'

'Wes, calm down,' Hirsch said. 'I don't want to arrest you, but I will if I have to.'

'Arrest?'

'Shouting at people, menacing them, ripping off face-masks,' Hirsch said patiently. 'I could do you for assault and threatening behaviour.'

Stragan sneered. 'Government agent.' He ducked past and strutted along the row of waiting patients, saying, 'You, Pfizer? You, Pfizer? You, you, you? You know what that causes, right? You start shedding spike proteins and

63

you endanger the health of the people you live with and the people you work with.' He raced back, dodging Hirsch's forestalling arm, and screamed at Pillai's door: *Just like my so-called wife's endangering the kids and me.*

A small woman emerged from Pillai's consulting room. About fifty, tired, worn-looking, Jill Stragan wore a sleeveless dress and had a scrap of cotton wool taped to her upper arm. 'Wes, sweetheart, don't. Just don't,' she said, all the world's weariness in her voice.

Stragan raised both hands to ward her off. 'You're sleeping in the spare room the next few nights, okay? You can fucking eat in there too, till you stop shedding.'

'Wes, let's take it outside,' Hirsch said.

'Fuck off.'

Dr Pillai emerged. 'Wesley, please. Jill is perfectly safe to be around.'

'I might be, but my dear husband isn't,' Jill Stragan said. She turned to Hirsch. 'He needs to be vaccinated for his job.'

Hirsch knew where this was going. 'Okay.'

Stragan tried to muscle in. 'Shut up, bitch.'

She retreated to the open doorway. Looked at Hirsch and said, 'He's got a fake certificate.' Turned to her husband and said, 'Sorry, sweetheart, people have to know. It's just too important.'

Stragan had shot Hirsch a slippery look, then swelled again. 'Yeah, get injected with poison, get injected with microchips.'

Hirsch paused in his narrative at that point, giving his inspector an apologetic shrug. A moment later, Alwin nodded. 'And that's when you called him a Covid moron?'

Hirsch shifted in his chair, even more relieved that he hadn't said *Too stupid to live.* 'Yes, sir.'

'Who heard you, do you think?'

'Don't know, sir.'

Hirsch thought he'd merely muttered the words, but clearly someone had taped it. He'd only known one person in the waiting room, Yvonne Muir, and she was the last person to make trouble for him. The others had been strangers. Maybe one of them was in a mandated occupation, but reluctant to get the jab? Or was looking for a dodgy exemption?

'What happened next?' Alwin asked.

What happened next was that Stragan had marched up to Hirsch, announcing: 'As a citizen of the people, I am arresting you for crimes against humanity,' prompting several in the waiting room to shout, 'We don't want you,' and 'You're no citizen.' Apparently bewildered by this, Stragan had stifled a sob and fled the clinic.

'Mr Stragan ran out of steam eventually,' Hirsch said now. 'He had a delivery to make, so I let him leave.'

'Wise, if he's hot under the collar. But we need to follow up on his vax certificate. Leave that to me, all right?'

'Thank you, sir.'

'But Senior Constable Hirschhausen, did you check in on them afterwards? Did it not occur to you that Mr

Stragan might take it out on his wife?'

'I did. He hadn't. And I also checked with Mrs Stragan before she went home.'

He'd taken Jill Stragan to the tearoom at the rear of the building filled with dusty file boxes—possibly old bank records. There was a chipped white table and two chairs against one wall, a grimy sink and an urn against the other. He'd looked for teabags or coffee but couldn't find any.

'Water will do,' she'd said.

'Does he ever hurt you, Mrs Stragan?'

'He's never laid a finger on me. He's all piss and wind.' She paused. 'He's afraid, that's all.'

'But scary when he gets worked up. People were badly frightened just now.'

'He's fallen for all this rubbish that floats around on the internet.'

'You came in for a booster?'

'Yes.'

Understanding clearly for the first time that it wasn't only society in general fracturing on the issues of Covid and getting vaccinated, but also families and friends, Hirsch had asked, 'What about your children?'

'They're vaxxed. He didn't like that, either.' A pause. 'Look, he's the father of my kids and I love him. I don't want to divorce him. But people need to know he's a danger—to them and to himself.'

Alwin cut into Hirsch's recollections. 'You will keep monitoring the situation?'

'Sir.'

'Meanwhile, you can't take sides, Constable Hirschhausen.'

'No, sir,' Hirsch said, thinking of the two sides that mattered: us and the pandemic.

'It's exhausting and stressful dealing with Covid, on top of our everyday duties.'

'Sir.'

'You can't show any kind of partiality. You can't even roll your eyes.'

'Sir.'

'You can't be *seen* thinking someone's stupid. First, it's not the right thing to do; we are above that. Second, these days everyone has a mobile phone with a video camera in it.'

'Sir.'

'If you *do* get into it with someone like Mr Stragan, the advice is to question them gently and respectfully about their views. Don't challenge, don't mock; try to sound genuinely interested. Then perhaps ask them politely where their information has come from; perhaps wonder aloud if their sources are reliable. That's about all you can do. If you're lucky, one in a thousand might stop and think.'

'Sir.'

'And most of them aren't stupid, they're just scared, or feel the vaccines were rushed into production or whatever.'

Hirsch shifted in his chair again. He knew that. He

should have known that the moment he saw Wes Stragan ranting and raving.

'Okay,' Alwin said, looking down and apparently gathering notes together, 'enough for now. I'm recommending that no further action be taken.' He looked up at Hirsch again. 'In all other respects, you're doing a fine job.'

Could have gone worse. Hirsch felt drained. 'Thank you, sir.'

7

THE TROUBLE WITH most Saturdays was that busy locals, taking a breather after racing around all week, might discover that a hole had been cut in the top paddock and thirty sheep were missing, the toolshed had been stripped bare or pub louts had keyed the Mazda. But Hirsch was spared any of that this Saturday and managed to catch up on his reports, emails and phone messages.

At noon there was a knock and Comyn, the burly Port Pirie detective, walked in and leaned on the counter wearing his perpetually unimpressed expression. 'Hard at it?' It was exquisite courtesy by his standards.

'Catching up,' Hirsch said, waiting for some tedious request or general bastardry.

Comyn jerked his head, indicating the world outside the police station. 'The Homicide boys are packing up. We'll be out of your hair in half an hour.'

Hirsch nodded. It made sense. He'd given his statement and, in a place the size of Tiverton, it was possible to doorknock the entire population in just a few hours. 'Find anything?'

Comyn shook his head and picked at an old gouge in the countertop. 'But if you could keep your ear to the ground? Strangers, strange cars.'

'Will do.'

The detective got to the point finally. 'Prints came back on suitcase man.'

'Yeah?'

'Damien Pierce, thirty-six, possession, possession with intent to supply, assault, destruction of property.'

All of which suggested that Pierce had a messy line of acquaintances, victims and known associates. 'He wasn't doing any of that around here, or I'd have known.'

'Elizabeth. Born and raised.'

Elizabeth, named incongruously after the queen, was a depressed satellite city to the state's capital, a place of struggle, especially since the General Motors plant had shut its doors. 'And yet he was found here.'

'Working theory?' said Comyn. 'He fucked up

somehow, pissed off the wrong people. They dumped him up here, barbecued, thinking he wouldn't be identified.'

'Beautifully put.'

'You got another theory?'

'No. But dumping bodies up here is hardly new,' Hirsch said, thinking of Snowtown, the bodies in the barrels.

Comyn nodded gloomily. 'Anyway, it's not my case, I was just helping out.'

'But now they have a place to start.'

'Yep,' Comyn said. He slapped both palms on the counter and took a step back. 'That's it, I'm off.'

There was a very faint question in the man's voice and manner. Hirsch didn't quite trust it—normally Comyn was scornful verging on hostile—but he found himself saying, 'Quick pub lunch before you go?'

That stopped Comyn. He blinked, checked his watch. 'Raincheck? I have to take my kid to footy. I've missed the last few Saturdays, and the wife...'

Family life. Hirsch's main sense of it came from Kate and Wendy, and his involvement in their lives was part-time; maybe even tenuous. As for his parents, he rarely saw them. They were vigorous retirees living in the Adelaide Hills, more than three hours away. 'Loving but distant' best described that relationship. But what was a family these days? Blended families. Same-sex families. Single-parent families. Two teenage kids caring for their mentally ill mother. Brenda Maher's menagerie. Not to mention

71

the legions of families like Comyn's: husband, wife, and kids who needed to be carted to Saturday sport. Hirsch felt a powerful sense of the divides in his life just then: he and the man standing on the other side of the counter; the police and those they policed; family life and a single person's life.

'Raincheck it is,' he said, wondering if the old stink that had been clinging to him was starting to dissipate.

Hirsch had a hit of tennis with the Cobb kids and Nan Washburn after lunch, then packed an overnight bag and reached the house on Bitter Wash Road at 5.30. The plan was an early dinner, then drive down to Redruth, where the new—to Redruth—James Bond was showing. The cinema, a recently converted stone building that had once housed a wool-broking firm, seated forty and showed films at 8 p.m. on Saturdays and 2.30 p.m. on Sundays. Hirsch had never been. Hadn't been to a cinema for a year and a half, he realised. Covid, and the fact that cinemas were not thick on the ground in the mid-north.

Wendy was preparing a stir-fry of chicken and vegetables, her focus intense, her movements about the kitchen a swift, economical juggling of timing, flame heat and slicing and dicing, so Hirsch perched on a stool at the end of the main bench to watch and chat. She liked it that he did that and didn't get in her way. You make accommodations in a relationship; you muddle along; you learn.

Then he set the kitchen table and Wendy walked down

the little hallway to Kate's door and knocked. 'Dinner's on the table!' No answer. She knocked and called again, and Hirsch heard a muffled bark in reply.

'Just about got my head bitten off,' Wendy muttered, returning to the kitchen, sliding into a chair opposite Hirsch. She poured water into her glass, smoothed a napkin over her lap and said, 'She's been in such a bad mood lately.'

'Something at school? The online stuff?'

'Both, feeding into each other,' Wendy said. 'I think some of the extreme behaviour is post-pandemic fallout— if you can say that about something that's still going on. We've got kids vaping, going home at lunchtime and not coming back, acting out in class. And some of them are into some pretty alarming social media activity, including bullying. Plus, their social skills are rusty. So, yeah, stuff at school. But remember that boy she was keen on earlier in the year? Tony Pitt? He dumped her in a really shitty way last week.' Deepening her voice, letting her face go slack, becoming a dickhead teenage boy, she said, '"I'm not feelin' it." That's what passes for a break-up conversation these days.'

'She still wants to go to the film, though?'

'She does. Some of her friends will be there. It's just, I don't know, it could simply be moody teenage stuff. I must admit I didn't think it would happen to me.'

'She seemed distant the other day.'

'Distant, hardly speaks to me, storms out of the room at the drop of a hat.'

'Talk about me, why don't you,' Kate said, appearing in the kitchen and taking her seat with the barest disturbance of the air. She shrank into her grey hoodie and picked at a strip of capsicum. Wendy opened her mouth, shut it again.

Hirsch heard a soft buzz, then another. Kate's shoulders hunched and she had her phone in her lap. She shoved it back again, looking bleak.

'Kate,' Wendy said, 'turn your phone off, please. Check it when you've finished your dinner.'

'Tell us about your day, sweetheart,' Hirsch said, like an idiot.

She turned a snarl onto him: *'You're not my father.'*

Dismayed, Wendy said, 'Kate, please.'

Kate shoved her chair back. 'Not hungry.' She stomped from the room.

Wendy's eyes were moist. 'That's what it's like.'

'Maybe I could talk to her.'

'And say what? I know she likes you. She loves you. You're terrific with her. But she's right, you're not her dad and I don't think you can stand in for him in this instance. I don't know. Anyway, I have to live with her all the time, you don't. That's not a criticism.'

'Of course. But that business with her phone…'

'I know. It's as if she wants to check it but she's dreading what she'll see if she does.'

'She looking thinner?'

Wendy was frustrated. 'Picks at her food. And then she'll binge on Tim Tams.'

74

'Is she sleeping?'

'Well, look at her. She looks exhausted. But you know I sleep like a log—she could be up half the night for all I know. A couple of the other teachers have hinted her marks are suffering. She acts like she's shutting herself away to do homework, but maybe she's not doing it, or only half-heartedly.' She opened her arms wide, as if to underscore the hopelessness of their situation. 'And does any kid want their mother teaching at the same school? It makes them a target.'

The Redruth Cinema was a husband-and-wife operation. Gordon Mannix sold the tickets and Heather Mannix was on choc tops, Maltesers and soft drinks. 'We're film mad, the pair of us,' Gordon had said once when Hirsch was helping the short-staffed Redruth police investigate a break-in. 'Always wanted to run a bughouse. Didn't think it would be out here in the sticks, though.'

Aged in their sixties, they'd made a mint in Adelaide real estate and could afford to buy and refashion the old stone building—and withstand the drop in income, since Hirsch doubted they were making a mint in the cinema business. They were happy though. Had plans for a weekend film festival, a short-film competition and a film-review prize for local schoolkids.

Hirsch, Wendy and Kate arrived at 7.45, pushing their way into the crammed foyer. A heightened atmosphere, with cinema patrons excited to be out and about and eyeing each other, the buzz palpable.

Look at her, done up like a dinner. You could scrape that makeup off with a knife. Haven't seen that family before. Who's she? He's only been divorced five minutes.

Or maybe they weren't thinking anything. Hirsch edged through to the ticket counter, and at 7.55 the crowd surged up a dim, carpeted incline and through the door that opened onto the back row.

Hirsch checked the tickets: row D, too close to the screen, in cracked, lumpy seats that had been stripped out of an Adelaide drama studio undergoing a refit. Hirsch was in D7, Wendy and Kate on either side of him. When they were seated, Wendy leaned to peer across at her daughter. 'All right?'

Kate was texting with fixed intensity as the lights began to fade, her thumbs flying, almost punishing her phone. She ignored Wendy, who slumped back in her seat and leaned her shoulder against Hirsch. He took her hand; they moulded their forearms and fingers together on the armrests.

A run of local ads—Redruth Motors, Tiverton Lucerne Seed—and the film started. Hirsch settled back to watch. Beside him, Kate continued to work her phone.

Risking another outburst, he leaned in. Murmured, 'Kate, love? Maybe turn it off?'

She seemed to wake from a trance. 'Sorry.' She pressed the side button and shoved the phone into her hoodie pocket.

But Hirsch knew there'd soon be a buzz announcing

yet another irresistible message. 'Maybe all the way off?'

Behind him someone hissed, 'Shush.'

Kate seemed to blink awake. 'Pardon?' He didn't see surprise or outrage; more like incomprehension, as if he'd proposed something profoundly alien.

'Off,' he whispered. 'Just enjoy the film.'

She seemed paralysed for a moment; then she fished out her phone as it lit up with a new message. She peered at it and sobbed abruptly; shot a look over her shoulder and back to the phone. Struggling, switched it off.

Curious, Hirsch glanced around at the rows of seats stretching to the back wall. The people immediately behind him looked pissed off. Three teenage girls further back caught his eye. They were laughing, high-fiving.

He returned his gaze to the screen, to the spurt and scuttle of a chase scene, and checked his watch. It was 8.40 and intermission wouldn't be for another thirty minutes at least. At that moment, Kate stood, whispered, 'Loo,' and slipped away into the darkness. Hirsch craned his head again: the girls behind were also edging out of their row, heading for the exit.

Whispering, 'Back in a tick,' to Wendy, he stepped past knees and pulled-in feet to the aisle and headed for the foyer, which was empty. A note on the refreshments counter, weighed down by an empty Fanta bottle, said: *We're off home now. Help yourselves to drinks and lollies, leave money on the counter. Last one out please lock up.*

Taking a moment to think, *Only in a country town,*

Hirsch heard a scream and a thump in the women's bathroom on the other side of the foyer. He trotted across and pushed the door open a short distance to reveal a quadrant of floor and wall tiles.

'This is the police. Out, all of you.'

Immediate silence. A young voice called, 'Bullshit you're the police,' and another whispered harshly, *Her mum goes out with a cop,* and the room was silent again. A moment later, the three back-row girls filed out, not looking at him but scowling pettily, full of attitude.

Hirsch watched them disappear, then stepped further in, calling, 'Kate.'

She was in one of the stalls and he sensed, more than knew, how desolate she was. 'Sweetheart? Safe to come out now.'

Nothing.

'Do you want to go home?'

After a while she said, 'Don't know. Maybe.'

'Will you feel safe here while I fetch your mum?'

She considered it. 'I think so.'

Hirsch would know if her enemies doubled back anyway. He said, 'Won't be long,' and headed up the carpeted incline again.

The trip home was wordless under stars and a fingernail moon, along the unwinding highway, the high beams casting tricky shadows and spotlighting a fox trotting across the road, glass shards glittering like ice in the ditches.

78

They were in bed by 10 p.m., and Hirsch, pressing warmly against Wendy, as close as he could get, almost ministering to her, murmured. 'Did she say anything just now?'

'Told me to leave her alone,' Wendy said. 'Not in a bitchy way—as if I wouldn't understand. But she agreed to talk about it in the morning.'

'Good.'

Hirsch slept fitfully. At 2 a.m. he dragged on shorts and a T-shirt and tiptoed to the kitchen, intent on making camomile tea, and saw a strip of light under Kate's door. He heard her voice, sounding wretched: 'Why are you doing this to me?'

He tapped and entered and she slammed her laptop shut. She was caught between misery, shame and indignation. 'You can't just…'

He crossed the room and sat on the edge of her bed. 'Come on, you need to stop. It's the middle of the night.'

She wailed and toppled away from him, her head in her arms. 'I can't!'

Hirsch opened the laptop. Whoever she'd been messaging had signed out and disappeared. He turned it off, shoved it under the bed and rested a tentative hand on Kate's upper arm. He said nothing.

Time passed and she was crying and he let her cry. She cried until she was cried out and, painfully slowly, expending the last of her reserves, she pushed down on the mattress to lever herself upright, her back against her pillows again. 'Sorry.'

'No need to apologise. It's okay to be upset.'

'I thought I could handle it but the more I try to, the more I get dragged in and I can't stop, and I can't fix anything.'

'Who is it, do you know?'

'These days it's kids at school, like the ones at the film tonight.'

'What are they saying?'

'Stuff like, "Your mum's a slag, a good gangbang will set her right" and "Don't come to school, no one likes you" and "Do us all a favour and top yourself" and "You're an ugly lezzo and we're going to burn your house down and you and your lezzo mother in it." Stuff like that.'

'Have you saved any of these messages?'

'Yes. Just in case.'

Her mind had been working even as it stopped serving her, Hirsch thought. 'Good, we can use it to—'

'But a lot of it's to do with Mum!'

Hirsch understood. 'You don't want to make her more of a target.'

'No!'

Treading carefully, Hirsch said, 'Is it just messages, or...?'

She shrank. 'No. I can't show you, please don't make me.'

'Okay, give me a general idea.'

She searched for the words she wanted. 'It started a while back with someone sending me links to porn shots with my face superimposed. Sometimes Mum's. And there's this Instagram sex-rating site where people make comments about my body or brag about sleeping with me.' She looked at Hirsch: 'I've hardly even kissed anyone!'

He nodded. 'You said *these days* it's kids at school. Do you mean the earlier stuff was someone else?'

She shrugged. 'It felt…different? Kind of more sophisticated, I guess. Lately it's all stupid and bitchy and more about school. You know, "teacher's pet" and "think you're so great because your lezzo mum's a teacher". Plus there's this TikTok video of me at a party where I'm asleep and my skirt's rucked up a bit…' She cast him a worried look. 'I had too much to drink, but I didn't, like, *do* anything.'

Had the kids at her school picked up on material that was already online? Hirsch would like to get one of them into an interview room…

'You might have to set up new social media and email accounts. And be more careful about who you give the details to.'

She snorted bitterly. 'I did all that, but I must have told one person too many. I can't even trust my friends.'

'You could turn off your notifications at night.'

She winced, ashamed. 'I tried that, too. I've tried blocking and muting, but I can't help it. I have to know what they're saying.'

Wendy was in the doorway. She came in, crouched, took her daughter's hand and said, 'Come to bed with me.'

—

On Sunday morning Hirsch walked for a couple of kilometres along Wendy's narrow grit and gravel road, with only a few magpie warbles for company, but when he got back to the house, dust on his toecaps, he smelt coffee brewing and saw Wendy contemplating the percolator, half awake, shoulders drooping.

He wrapped her up and kissed the back of her neck. 'You're awake early.'

She tilted back her head, scraped it against his chest, merged with him. 'Couldn't sleep. She was restless all night.' Turning in his arms she added, 'Sorry you got banished to the spare bed.'

'That's fine.'

She wriggled free and poured the coffee, adding frothed milk, and they sat at the little table. 'What do we say to her? How do we do it?'

'The trouble is,' Hirsch said, 'I think *you* were the main target at first.'

'Me?'

'The rental scam, for example. Not something a schoolkid dreams up. And Kate says the trolling started out more sophisticated, hurting her as a way of hurting you.'

He told her about the slut-shaming and sex-rating posts, the photoshopped nudes. 'It's possible that whoever posted this material copied in kids at school or they stumbled onto it somehow, and it snowballed.'

'But why would they?'

Because your daughter's whip-smart, perceptive, a bit bolshie, Hirsch thought. 'She's a brainy kid and her mum's a teacher, which is bound to rub some kids up the wrong way. And maybe you pissed a kid off one day, called them out for bad behaviour...'

'I'm not a tyrant, Paul.'

'With some people it doesn't take much.'

'Maybe.' Wendy wasn't convinced.

'Anyway, when Kate's awake I'll take some screenshots of images and texts and report the abuse. There's a police cybercrime unit, and a federal outfit, the Cybersecurity Centre.'

Wendy was troubled. 'Federal? If some outsider's set all this up, I'd happily see him—or her—charged. But schoolkids? For a few bitchy texts?'

'It's more than that, though,' Hirsch said. 'When some kid in Year 9 continually texts Kate to go kill herself, or circulates photoshopped nudes of her, any online activity like that, she's breaking the law.' He began to paraphrase the statutes: 'Using a carriage device to menace, harass, stalk, cause offence, manufacture child porn, engage in image-based sexual abuse...'

Wendy grabbed at the hair above her ears. 'We need to get the school involved. There's a bullying policy, but, you know, little country high school, a hundred and thirty kids, it's hardly ever activated. The main issue's always been the town kids–farm kids divide.'

83

'Would you like me to talk at assembly one morning? The legal and police perspectives?'

She shook her head. 'Too many of the kids know I'm involved with you. It would put Kate in the spotlight.'

'Sergeant Brandl?'

Wendy thought about that. 'Hilary would be good.'

'And if the principal could have a few quiet words in the ears of a few kids...'

'Oh, God. They'll know immediately who gave them up.'

'It'll be hard for Kate for a while. But she's strong.'

'Is she? Kids have been known to commit suicide...'

'I don't see Kate—'

'She's changed, though, Paul. She's clearly depressed, shutting herself away for hours on end. But I don't want to limit her time on her laptop or...or make her do her home-work at the kitchen table. I don't want her thinking I don't trust her.'

'At the moment,' Hirsch said, 'it's like an addiction. She knows it's bad for her to check every incoming text or image, but she can't stop herself.' He paused. 'Is the school counsellor any good?'

Wendy shrugged. 'Supposed to be okay.'

Time passed and Kate appeared, sleepy, dazed, creased, withdrawn—but, Hirsch thought, maybe a bit better? Somehow looser and less wired. She walked up to Wendy, fell against her and said, 'Sorry I've been such a bitch.'

Wendy patted her on the back in desperate relief. 'Oh, lovely, you haven't.'

Then Kate broke away and loped over to Hirsch. The embrace was brusque, fierce. 'No matter what people say about you, Aitch, you're a man of quite average emotional intelligence.'

The old Kate, almost.

'Yeah, right, great, good to know,' Hirsch said.

Later, freshly showered, comb tracks in her hair and looking very young, open and vulnerable, Kate sat with Wendy and Hirsch in a sun-drenched stretch of the back veranda, her phone and laptop on the slatted outdoor table there. She showed them a flood of messages and images, some of it new to Hirsch, all of it new to Wendy.

'Now and then a week can go by, and nothing happens,' she said, 'then it starts up again. You're ugly. Don't bother coming to school, no one wants you there. Everyone hates you, even your mother. Why don't you cut your wrists? I ask why they're doing it and they say because it's fun and I'm worthless anyway.'

She grabbed Wendy's hand. 'I couldn't show you, some of it was *about* you. I thought you'd get all heavy with them. I thought you'd take my phone and laptop away.'

Wendy said nothing, smiled sadly.

'And I thought I could handle it by myself. But I couldn't. I had to keep looking.'

She tapped at her laptop and turned the screen to the

others again. 'This is the first thing I got. I don't know who sent it. All the later stuff has been from kids at school.' She shrugged. 'Most of them are too dumb to hide who they are, or they don't care. But *this*…'

The site was Mid-North Men's Network, the post an image of a naked woman, with Kate's face superimposed, using a vibrator, and captioned: 'Who has other nudes of this chick? I hear she throws it around.'

'You learn someone's shorthand way of messaging and posting after a while,' Kate said. 'Kind of their style, their voice. This guy'—she tapped the screen—'did a lot of posting about me, on this site and a couple of others.'

Another possibility occurred to Hirsch: someone was getting at mother and daughter to get at *him*.

'Pathetic,' Wendy said in disgust. 'All they want is a reaction. Can't relate to anyone in real life.'

More to it than that, though, Hirsch thought. Narcissism. A sense of power, of invulnerability through anonymity. A very real desensitisation to others. And for all that trolls might be compensating for feelings of insecurity or victimhood, some were vicious and dangerous. Whether or not they hid behind a keyboard.

He looked at the sparrows flitting in and out of the side hedge and a pair of swallows building a muddy nest on a rafter at the end of the veranda. 'You seem a bit better this morning, like some of the weight's come off your shoulders?'

Kate looked at him assessingly. 'Maybe. What do you mean?'

'Your mum and I can help, but is there anything you can do yourself?' Hirsch said.

He could feel Wendy's critical scowl. He turned and looked at her steadily: *trust me*. She stared back hard. And then her face began to relax. She turned to Kate. 'We'll be behind you every step of the way, but some of it has to come from you, sweetheart.'

'Yeah. Yep.' Kate took in a breath, held it, breathed out. 'You want me to stop looking at my phone and laptop all the time.'

'Easier said than done,' Wendy said. 'And it's not so much about what we want—you have to want to do it.'

In a little voice, Kate said, 'I'll try. What else?'

'Well, what else do you think?' Hirsch said.

As if it was a huge bother, Kate heaved a sigh and rattled out: 'Turn off notifications and stick to it this time, change all my settings and passwords and logins again, set up new accounts, watch who I tell, yada, yada, yada.'

Still got the attitude, Hirsch thought, but she's listening.

Wendy leaned across the table to clasp her daughter's forearm. 'And if you do see texts or pictures, you need to know it's not personal. Even if it feels like it at first.'

Hirsch nodded. 'To a troll, it's just business, hurting someone.'

'Okay,' Kate said, folding in on herself.

'Take away their power,' Hirsch said. 'Block and mute and report. Don't respond—it's what they want. And keep us in the loop.'

'Be self-aware,' Wendy said. 'Ask yourself, why am I dwelling on this? Is it helpful? What can I be doing instead?'

For a moment—swiftly there and gone again—Kate stuck out her mutinous, victimised bottom lip.

'Too much?' Hirsch said.

Kate gave him a look and replied, with indolent charm, 'Kind of a bit preachy.'

That was more like the Kate he knew.

They smiled faintly at each other and were a little better prepared to face the day.

8

A TYPICAL WORKING week generally began with Sergeant Brandl's Monday briefing, and so, after his morning walk and the news, Hirsch pinned his mobile number to the front door and headed south on the Barrier Highway, slotting in a CD, the third compilation of Old Fart's songs that Kate had burnt for him. He tapped skip until 'Badge' filled the cab of the Hilux. So far this month, the old Cream number was his nominated best song of all time. God knows how Kate had sourced it, but it was apt in the circumstances. There was always a badge somewhere in his life: on his uniform, on the doors of the SA Police Toyota, on the legions of disapproving senior officers in his life. He'd once asked her to account for 'Badge,' 'Gimme Shelter' and a handful of other old songs, given that they were from his parents' generation, not his. 'Them,' he said. 'They're the old farts not me.'

'Oldish,' she said. 'Fartish.'

'I'm pretty sure that's not a proper word,' he'd said at the time. A time before things started to get so hard for her.

The highway passed through the little town of Penhale and then between canola crops again, and—new to the area—a vast paddock of legumes. A landscape imprinted by history, Hirsch thought. A farmer might dig up a Ngadjuri grinding stone when he planted his legumes. Meanwhile the legumes and the canola represented a new kind of agriculture in the mid-north, and Hirsch had heard more than one old wheat cockie mutter gloomily about that.

Then he was on the outskirts of Redruth, a town of pretty stone houses with steep-pitched roofs and elegant stone colonial-era public buildings folded over and around seven small hills. Old structures dating from the mid-1800s, with shiny new SUVs parked in the driveways, antenna dishes on the roofs, a Qantas jetstream overhead.

He passed a sign to the copper mine. Now a pastoral centre—merino sheep and cereal crops—Redruth had been settled by Cornish copper miners in the 1840s. The mine, long since defunct, was now a tourist attraction with sheds, crushing batteries and stone chimneys dotted on the slopes around a bottomless pool of water—variously dark blue or dark green according to mineral sediments and the angle of the sun.

He drove on, past the hall and the Ngadjuri cultural centre, down into the town square, a patch of lawn with a tiny rotunda at one end and a statue to the war dead at the other, overlooked by shops and a couple of pubs. Decelerating as he approached the square, Hirsch headed out along the Adelaide road for a short distance to a narrow side street and the Redruth cop shop, a modern, purpose-built building with a proper front office, conference and interview rooms, a small lockup and a roomy rear yard.

He parked at the kerb and entered by the front door, pausing to greet Petra Osmak, the new auxiliary support staffer. Her job was to keep an eye on the split-screen CCTV monitor, answer the phone, file and hunt out reports, deal with the walk-ins. She was mid-twenties, with chemical-auburn bristly hair, discreet nose and ear studs, inked forearms and a warm, setting-the-public-at-ease manner. Hirsch had only met her twice, the past two Mondays.

'Settling in okay?'

She smiled. 'Everyone's really nice.'

'The others here yet?'

Petra jerked her head. 'Go on through.'

A door in the wall behind her led to a short corridor and several rooms, the largest of which was the briefing room: chairs around a long table, a whiteboard and a video screen on one wall, local-area maps on another, a line of filing cabinets against a third, a window overlooking a hedge on the fourth. And right now also containing a pot of coffee, coffee mugs, a solitary Danish pastry on a chipped plate and the three Redruth police officers: Sergeant Brandl and her two newly minted constables, Jean Landy and Tim Medlin.

Medlin's hand was hovering over the last Danish. 'Uh-uh,' Hirsch said.

'The quick and the dead, Constable Hirschhausen.'

'That's senior constable to you.'

'Profound apologies,' Tim Medlin said, withdrawing his hand. He was awkward, earnest, still finding his way.

Hirsch shot a grin at Jean Landy and sat at the end of the table. Small and wiry, her dark hair in an unravelling ponytail, she was older than Medlin and, after five years as an ambulance officer, more experienced at dealing with extremes of human behaviour. She grinned back; looked theatrically at her watch. Hirsch took the bait. 'I have further to come than you.'

'The week that was,' Sergeant Brandl said, bringing them to order, tapping a small pile of folders together. 'Paul, you first.'

The main function of the Monday briefings was to air recent incidents, tease out any possible links and offer suggestions and theories. Hirsch, mid-bite of his pastry, chewed hurriedly, swilled it down with coffee, coughed and said, 'Three main things...'

Dr Van Sant's search for her missing son; Jacob Maher's

car; the investigation into the suitcase stiff.

'Maybe don't say "suitcase stiff" outside this room,' Hilary Brandl said. 'It's entirely possible that someone loved him. But good to know that Homicide's shifting their attention elsewhere.' She glanced at them all in turn. 'That doesn't mean there isn't, or wasn't, a mid-north connection, though. Keep your eyes and ears open.'

'Sergeant,' they chorused.

'Jean?'

Landy had worked mostly with Tim Medlin all week. The usual: a couple of domestic disturbances, kids doing burnouts in the town square, a handful of drink-driving and speeding charges, some minor thefts.

'And Auntie Steph was in on Friday,' she said, 'reporting a break-in.'

Auntie Steph was Stephanie Ingram, a semi-retired social worker who ran the new Ngadjuri drop-in centre for Indigenous people seeking legal, health and welfare advice or simply someone to talk to. School groups visited sometimes. Dr Pillai held a Monday clinic. Hirsch barely knew Auntie Steph, but found her to be kind, patient, philosophical—and tough when she needed to be. She was the main elder consulted by Russ Fanning before he resurrected his eagle. As Fanning had described their meeting to Hirsch, Steph had merely expressed some reservations while explaining the significance of the eagle and the Southern Cross. Steph's version of their meeting was somewhat different. 'I bloody well pointed out that gubbas

93

carved that thing into the plain, not my mob,' she'd told Hirsch. 'We were never consulted. We had no attachment to it then, and we don't now. You might say it's symbolic of our ongoing displacement. And get this, all the time Russ was trying to sweet-talk me, he'd already got the district council on side.'

'A break-in at the Wurlie?' Hirsch said now.

The Wurlie was Steph Ingram's name for the cultural centre. As she'd said to Hirsch, with one of her not-quite-straight faces: 'Otherwise known as the Redruth and District First People's Art, Cultural Heritage, Education and Welfare Centre.'

It wasn't the first time the Wurlie had been targeted. There had been resistance before it even got off the ground, with accusations of taxpayers' money down the drain, and last month slogans had been spraypainted on the walls of the building, a small stone annexe to the town hall.

'Graffiti again?'

Jean shook her head. 'They threw rotten eggs around inside.'

'CCTV?'

Landy shifted uncomfortably. 'The electrician keeps giving her the run-around. He's installed the cameras but they're still not connected.'

'On it,' Brandl said darkly, scribbling a note on her pad. 'Is she feeling better?'

'I called at the centre yesterday morning,' Landy said. 'She seemed fine.'

Seeing Hirsch's questioning look she added, 'Epilepsy. She had a seizure when she came to report the break-in.'

'In the station?'

Landy shook her head. 'On the steps outside. Someone called Doctor Pillai.'

Hirsch pictured it. 'Poor Steph.'

'Moving right along,' Brandl said. 'The stolen explosives. Tim, you caught that.'

Medlin rolled his shoulders as if to order his thoughts and went on to describe how a mining transport driver named Scott McInnes, carting a supply of explosives to a mine east of Broken Hill, had stopped in Redruth and spent Wednesday night at the Woolpack Hotel. When he was about to get going on Thursday morning, he discovered that the van had been broken into and the contents were gone.

'It's called Tovex, an alternative to dynamite. Safe to transport and handle,' Medlin said. 'You'd need blasting caps to detonate it, and he wasn't carrying any.'

'A few questions spring to mind,' Brandl said. 'Why didn't he make the load more secure? Did he break company protocol by overnighting somewhere when he had a load of explosives on board? And have there been any blasting-cap or detonator thefts reported recently?' She paused. 'I'll look into all that. The Woolpack's CCTV: show anything?'

'Nothing, sergeant.'

'Okay. Now, in other news...'

Brandl pulled her laptop towards her, dimmed the

lights and started projecting a short, poor-quality clip onto the video screen beside the whiteboard. 'I'd like to know who these bozos are.'

The CCTV quality was poor and the camera positioned too high, showing mostly the tops of people and objects, but after a few seconds Hirsch understood that he was looking along a section of passageway separating the Redruth supermarket's cash registers from the rows of shelving. An elderly woman carrying a shopping basket emerged from an aisle at the far end and disappeared down another. Then there was no movement for half a minute—the IGA was rarely busy—until, at the bottom of the screen, the backs of two heads appeared, followed by another two. Young men dressed in black T-shirts, camo pants and baseball caps, marching away from the camera, two by two, in tight formation. Unable to see their faces, Hirsch tried for body-language clues. But this was artificial language. It looked as though they had learnt how to move from watching North Korean military parades.

'Wait for it,' Sergeant Brandl said.

The four men reached the far wall, about-turned clumsily and returned, marching towards the camera now. Still unrecognisable, their features all but obscured by the peaks of their caps. But the symbol above the left breast of each T-shirt was clear enough: a bastardised Celtic cross.

Brandl paused the video. 'Recognise anyone?'

They shook their heads, but Hirsch was uneasy. The shape of a former jawline, the bushiness of the hair bunched behind the ears…was it Cody Morton, Bob Muir's former apprentice?

He felt only a faint tingle—a long way from probability, let alone certainty—so he said nothing. But he'd find out where Cody lived now.

'Could be anyone; sorry, sergeant,' Landy said.

Brandl pressed play again. Soon the four men were under the camera and then out of sight. 'Any other CCTV?'

Brandl shook her head.

'What were they shouting?'

'According to the cashiers, a bit of everything. Waltzing Matilda and "We are the lads", things like that. Apparently they were laughing and high-fiving like naughty kids as they went out the door, so it was almost not reported to us.'

'Where did they go when they left the shop?'

'There was a Jeep waiting for them in the street. They piled in and it took off.'

'Plates?'

Sergeant Brandl smiled tiredly. 'Too much to hope for.' She shrugged. 'Could be boys mucking around, could be something more serious. Heaven knows, the nutters have been coming out of the woodwork this year.'

9

'SO WE WONDERED,' Hirsch said, when he was alone with the sergeant, 'if you could talk to the school. About the legal ramifications.'

A flicker in Brandl's eyes, almost of panic. She's going to refuse, he thought. 'Sorry, I know you've got a lot on.'

She flapped both hands at him. 'It's okay, it's important, happy to do it.'

'We thought it would have more weight if you did it rather than me.'

She gave him a don't-bullshit-me look. 'It would make

Wendy and Kate less of a target, you mean.' Then she flapped her hands again. 'Sorry, they might cop it either way. Anyway, I know the principal, we run together sometimes—but I'll have a word with Kate and Wendy first.'

'Thanks, sergeant,' Hirsch said, nodding goodbye to Petra Osmak as he left the police station. Some wag had written 'wash me' across the dusty rear window of the Hilux, which was hot inside, so he wound down the windows and sat for a while, planning his day. He reached to turn the ignition key a couple of times; had second thoughts; sat back.

Check in with Dr Van Sant, he thought finally, starting the engine. Say hello to Steph in the cultural centre. Study for the sergeant's exam.

He trundled back to the Redruth town square and the Woolpack Hotel, a squat, two-storey building wrapped in deep verandas. Big, fading old West End beer signs on either side of the front door, smaller Coopers signs between the frosted-glass main windows. It was mainly a peaceful lunchtime schnitzel and after-work beer kind of pub, with a couple of poker machines, a small lounge populated by club chairs on dense Axminster, highly polished wood panelling and pressed-tin ceilings. Cool, airy, not very beery inside. The upstairs consisted of two vast function rooms and four travellers' suites. Sometimes Hirsch got dragged up there for one of the Sunday-afternoon Celtic music sessions Wendy loved, and he'd once attended a lecture, given by a Flinders University cultural geographer, that tied the insecure Indigenous, Cornish-miner and small-farmer tenancy in the mid-north to corresponding global forces, but otherwise he rarely visited the first floor.

And not today, either: according to the woman setting tables in the dining room, Dr Van Sant had checked out.

He climbed behind the wheel again and headed back around the square to the car park behind the town hall. Locked up and walked around to the street entry for the little stone building that housed the Ngadjuri cultural centre. Here he found an elder known as Uncle Doug supervising the rotten-egg clean-up, his back against the corridor wall, arms folded, watching a teenage girl on her hands and knees with a mop bucket and a scrubbing brush, a teenage boy chipping with a spatula at something congealed on the wall.

'I love hard work,' he said, the moment he spotted Hirsch.

'You can watch it for hours,' Hirsch said, finishing the old joke.

'Good one, Uncle Doug,' the girl said.

The boy shot Hirsch a complicated look that he was all too familiar with. It was in the air, in the water, in stories told at the knee and passed down in kitchens and school playgrounds: the cops hassled you. Hassled you for being black on the footpath, in charge of a car, in a shop or a train. For even existing.

Noting the boy's edginess, Doug said, 'Not to worry son, this bloke's okay.'

He's harking back to Redruth in the recent past, thought Hirsch. The old sergeant and the thugs who'd served under him. Not that long ago.

'Is Auntie Steph in?'

She heard him. Stuck her head out of a doorway at the end and said, 'Paul. Come on through. Excuse the mess.'

With a nod to Doug, Hirsch continued along the corridor, into her office, which had evidently been cleaned first: fresh damp sponging here and there; a gleaming patch on the wall between her social work degree and an Aboriginal Languages map of Australia; dirty rags in the wastebasket; the air laced with disinfectant.

Hirsch could see a clump of egg yolk still clinging to the leg of her desk that made him itch to pick at it. He pointed. 'There's—'

Still standing, she said, 'I know. It can wait. What can I do for you?'

She was about sixty, a dark vigour and humour in her face, which was fringed by curly, mostly black hair. Tortoiseshell hoop earrings. Comfortable in black jeans and a grey top. 'I heard you've been in the wars,' he said.

She gestured minutely, a kind of rolling of the eyes that said, *You think?*

'Sit,' was what she did say.

Hirsch checked both visitors' chairs. Chrome frames, hard plastic seats and back supports, all egg free. He placed one across the desk from her. The moment he sat, so did she.

'I can only give you a few minutes. Some of the old ladies need reassurance the first time they see Sandali.'

Hirsch remembered: Dr Pillai's Monday-morning clinic. He thought about that sadly. Old Aboriginal women and a young Sri Lankan doctor tiptoeing around each other, trying to chip away at their differences. 'I won't keep you,' he said. 'Just checking in.'

Steph tilted her head, a look that said she'd been too long in the world for nonsense like his. 'I'm all right. I'm one of the lucky ones, I don't often get seizures. But I was a bit stressed the other day.'

'Sorry.'

'Don't give me sorry, I'm sick of gubbas giving me sorry,' she said, with a touch of heat. She paused. Grinned. 'Sorry.'

He returned the grin. But an idea had been nudging him, this past week, and now it kicked him in the shins. 'Has the centre been getting online threats? Harassment?'

She just looked at him. 'Does the pope shit in the woods?'

She showed him and it was as vicious and predictable and misspelt and uncoordinated as expected. He tried to stitch everything together as he drove away—the tactics used on Kate and Wendy; the supermarket stormtroopers; Bob's apprentice—but had barely reached the phone tower on the outskirts of Redruth when movement caught his eye: hurried, with a spurt of dust. An old white Pajero that had been parked beside the tower, which sat on two hectares of sloping dirt and weeds beyond the saleyards, had suddenly sped up the slope and out of sight. He could chase it, or he could see what its occupants had been doing.

Nosing up to the locked gate in the perimeter fence, Hirsch saw that the wires had been cut, stakes flattened. He drove in, careful of sharp wire ends, and idled at the base of the tower. Staked slogans had been driven into the dirt: *Combat 18* and *5G=Deep State microchip activation*.

No brushes or spray cans, no CCTV, only boot and tyre prints in the dirt, so he kept going, speeding up the low incline behind the tower. The Pajero must have crashed straight through the fence on the far side and disappeared. The Barrier Highway was clear in both directions, but it gave access to plenty of nearby side roads and Hirsch could spend half a day venturing up each one and back again, doorknocking at farmhouses.

He returned to the tower, took photographs and called the sergeant.

'That's the second time this month,' she said. 'Telstra had to get in a graffiti-removal crew from Port Pirie. Did you get a plate number?'

'Sorry, no. Tinted windows, too.'

'Old white Pajero. Only about a million of those in the bush.'

When he was halfway to Tiverton, Hirsch called Bob Muir,

103

who sounded faintly terse: 'Mate, I was up a ladder.'

'Sorry mate. Just wanted to see if you've got an address for Cody.'

There was a pause. 'No. I had the impression he was couch surfing.'

Bob was too tactful to ask why Hirsch wanted to know. But then he said, 'I understand a few idiots have been goosestepping up and down the IGA in Redruth.'

Hirsch guessed, 'It's on YouTube?'

'Apparently.'

'Do you know who Cody is staying with?'

'Can't help you there.'

Hirsch knew he was stuck. There weren't many young people left in the mid-north, where job opportunities were scarce and working as a glorified farmhand for your old man held little appeal. And there were not many young people who owned a couch, let alone a place to put it.

Agreeing to catch up for a meal later in the week, Hirsch finished the call and continued along the long, broad valley. No clouds today, just unfiltered sunlight, the yellow canola on either side blazing in it. A curious wheat-and-wool country colour, Hirsch thought. Almost artificial. Almost civilising, like a cushion on a sofa. He played 'Badge' again—twice—and rolled into Tiverton.

Leaving the Hilux at the kerb, Hirsch went around to his yard and in through the back door, straight into his poky kitchen. He ate a mandarin—an item rarely spotted in Ed Tennant's shop—as the kettle boiled, then took a mug of green tea through to the office.

A half-dozen topographical maps with curling edges rested across the tops of two adjoining filing cabinets. He dug out the one that showed Desolation Hill and the nearby farms and stations, placed it face up on the desk and traced Manna Soak Highway to its end point forty kilometres past Dryden Downs. Sam Dryden hadn't been entirely accurate when he indicated there were no properties beyond his front gate—there were no *functioning* properties, but someone had struggled and failed there in the old days. The highway dead-ended at a small track winding between low hills to a tiny notation, *Ruins*, set in a big, oddly shaped place that curved around behind Dryden Downs and Desolation Hill.

It was late morning now. Wendy would be teaching, so he sent her a text: *Hilary's on board re the cyber lecture, talk later*, and checked emails and then forthcoming events on his phone. Even though he entered these assiduously as they cropped up, it was his special fear that he'd one day miss a vital appointment.

Wendy returned his call at lunchtime, and they chatted until she said she was due back at the chalkface, and he said he should probably swot for the sergeants' exam.

His eyes were glazing over at 4 p.m. when he was saved by Brenda Maher banging in through the front door. Wearing a billowy black T-shirt, fraying tights and a face full of malicious glee she said, 'You know Eileen Pitcher?'

'Fine thanks, Brenda. How're you?'

Brenda clenched as if she wanted to punch him. 'Eileen Pitcher, I said. You know her or not?'

Eileen Pitcher and her daughter, Gemma, lived in a cottage near the tennis courts. Gemma worked in the shop, and it was Hirsch's hope that she'd find new horizons one day. She was unschooled but smart, and he feared the smartness would grow dull as her horizons shrank if she stayed in the town. Where Gemma was large, Eileen, her mother, was small and wizened with a jaundiced take on almost everything. A flinty soul. Hirsch shuddered to think of a clash between Eileen and Brenda.

'What about her?'

'The bitch only went and dumped her rubbish on our front lawn last night.'

'Lawn' was a stretch: dead grass and a dead car on blocks. 'Did you actually see her do it?'

'Didn't have to,' Brenda said, fired up and enjoying herself.

'So how do you—'

'Stupid cow left this.'

Brenda slapped down an unopened Salvation Army envelope addressed to Eileen—the kind soliciting a donation, to which Eileen's generosity was unlikely to have responded. It was smeared with dark, moist, pungent-smelling matter of some kind. Rotten banana. Gravy. Hirsch hesitated, loath to pick it up. Such a small envelope, such a rich stench. 'This happened last night?'

'Yep.'

'Have you had any run-ins with her?'

'Don't even know who she is. I drove past her place just now, ready to give her a serve, but I thought, nup, do the right thing, report it.'

Citizen of the year, Hirsch thought. 'Okay, leave it with me.'

Self-satisfaction turned to scorn. Brenda stepped back from the counter, wiping her hands on her shiny black shrink-wrapped thighs, and said, 'Not going to do anything, are ya. Just because my boy made a mistake. Youse cops are all the same.'

All Hirsch really wanted to do was open a window. 'If a crime's been committed,' he said, 'I'm obliged to act on it.'

Grudgingly mollified, Brenda marched out. When the door slammed behind her, Hirsch grabbed an evidence bag and ushered the dirty envelope into it with the tips of his fingers. Washed his hands in soapy water. Returned with a rag and a spray cleaner and scrubbed the countertop.

Then, leaving the police station, he made his way across to the tennis courts and Eileen Pitcher's house. Eileen was in her customary spot, a subsiding club chair behind grapevines draped around her front veranda, drawing hungrily on a cigarette. She eyed him as he stepped through her listing gate and up onto the veranda.

'Eileen.'

She muttered something that approximated his name.

'Gemma's at the shop, if that's what you're after.'

Hirsch shook his head. 'A word with you, actually. A complaint.'

'Oh, yeah, what kinda complaint?'

'That you dumped rubbish on someone's front lawn last night.'

'Correction,' Eileen said, stabbing the red coal of her cigarette at him. 'I didn't *dump* rubbish, I *returned* rubbish from whence it came in the first place. There is a difference.'

From whence it came, thought Hirsch. 'An item with your name on it was found in among the rubbish, Eileen.'

She granted him that. 'Yeah, well, it's possible I added a bit of my stuff to the mix. But so what? Them...*lowlifes* dumped rubbish on my place first. So I gave it back to them.'

'Why would they do that?'

'Gemma caught one of the kids, that girl Alice, shoplifting.'

'She didn't report it.'

'Not worth the effort. It was only a Mars Bar and she grabbed it off her and told her to piss off and not come back.'

This was a nightmare. A tedious bad dream at least. There was nothing in the rulebook which, in Hirsch's experience, wasn't unusual. 'But do you know for sure who dumped rubbish in your yard?'

'Got a photo. That do you? I was just going to bed and saw Fatso through the window.'

She fished a phone from her pocket, poked at it and turned the screen Hirsch's way. He peered: the lighting was dim, the image small, but he recognised Brenda Maher's shape. 'Send me a copy?'

He gave Eileen his number. She poked laboriously at her phone again. The image arrived. He sighed inwardly, tried to think what his next step might be. Throw a scare into Eileen—pointless—then throw a scare into Brenda—pointless—and hope that sound police work of this nature would win the day?

10

TUESDAY, PATROL DAY.

It would take up the whole day, too—as many as ten hours on the road, out in the back country, calling on the lonely, the troubled, the troublesome. It was routine for Hirsch to cover a few hundred kilometres on patrol day.

He headed north-east first, deep into rain-shadow country, but skirting Desolation Hill this time, turning south onto the Mischance Creek road as he made his way to his first stop. Passing the Mischance Creek ruins—and reminded again of the fatal home invasion he'd stumbled upon two years earlier—he came to a side road and turned left, coming to a stock ramp and a sign reading *Wildu Station Merino Stud*. Russ Fanning's driveway was much shorter and less well-maintained than the Drydens', rutted in several places where spring rains had overflowed from blocked ditches on either side of the track. He drove for three minutes, through scrubland and in and out of dry creek beds where flecks of gold might linger among the rounded, ankle-twisting, water-tumbled stones and pebbles.

Then to the farmhouse, a modern, insulated corrugated-iron and wood-panelled structure a hundred metres from the original stone house, where Fanning's farmhands bunked down. A windmill, water tanks, a dam, sheds, orchard trees, ghost gums and a small paddock of solar panels. Money had been spent here, but not on the Drydens' scale. And thoughtfulness, not ego, had directed the spending.

Hirsch parked, got out, and heard a shout: 'Over here.'

Fanning was in a nearby implement shed, tinkering with a battered all-terrain vehicle. Hirsch hated these contraptions: he'd attended too many rollovers, with farmers, or their kids, pinned underneath, broken up inside or bleeding out on stony soil.

Fanning wiped his oily hands on a rag. 'Won't shake, too mucky.'

He was blockish, balding, weather-seamed and always genial, the kind of man who sought out and embraced any distractions that his day might deliver—Hirsch turning up, for example. He beamed; Hirsch sketched a little wave that stood for a handshake. 'Engine trouble?'

Fanning gazed gloomily at the ATV. 'Dirty spark-plug—I hope. Tea? Coffee?'

'Sure.'

They headed for the house and went inside, Hirsch as usual expecting a blast of furnace heat from the corrugated-iron exterior, but the air in the huge, open-plan living area was cool. The walls, painted an off-white that further cooled the atmosphere, were hung with Fanning's late wife's watercolours. She'd specialised in rusty windmills, collapsed barns, old tractors with fretting tyres at rest in a collar of dead grass, distant blue hills smudged by trees and stone reefs, and gum trees split by lightning or bent by the winds of all the years. Not national gallery quality but better than any art-show offering, and treasured by Fanning.

Hirsch did what he always did and wandered from painting to painting while Fanning boiled the kettle. It occurred to him that just as there hadn't been much cinema in his life lately, there also hadn't been much art.

He stopped at his favourite, a smudge of blue hills in the background and one end of a collapsed barn in the foreground, with a crooked little peppertree poking its head around the corner as if shy or inquisitive. Then Fanning was standing with him, a mug of steaming tea in each hand. 'You always stop at this one.'

'They're all good,' Hirsch said inadequately.

With a nod at the painting, Fanning said, 'Shed and tree, both gone now. A storm. Broke my heart.'

His wife's death had broken his heart, Hirsch thought. He followed Fanning through to the room's only table, a long, broad, solid affair notched and carved by life. A refectory table, imported from England and bought by Fanning's wife in a Barossa Valley winery's clearing sale.

The table was beside a window that looked out onto a rose garden. The roses needed deadheading, and Hirsch thought that it was probably a struggle for Fanning to keep alive every memory of Janet Fanning.

Then Fanning was breaking into his thoughts. 'Any closer to finding out who shot my ram?'

'Sorry, no.'

Fanning waved that off. 'A stretch, we both know that. You did your best.'

Hirsch wondered how to ask his first police question of the day. He didn't want to plant a seed, but found himself saying, 'What can you tell me about Mia Dryden?'

But Fanning was quick. He cocked his head, smiling and wry. 'Likes to hunt. Likes to shoot.'

'Yes.'

'Don't go thinking she hasn't passed through my mind. But Jesus, it's not as if she lives next door to me. We barely know each other. We're poles apart in our political views, but so what? You don't shoot a bloke's livestock to make a point—and why would she make a point to me?

113

I've never had a go at her about her views. And if she was just out hunting, she'd never have mistaken my ram for something else, not with a good telescopic sight, which I assume she uses.'

'Okay. You didn't hear the shot?'

'No. I've told you that, Paul.'

'Do you ever hear shots?'

'Not often. If you do, you don't pay much attention. Someone after foxes or wild dogs. Eagles, maybe.'

'Eagles are protected, Russ.'

'Fair enough.'

As they were talking, a teenage boy wandered disconsolately past the far end of the rose bed. Shorts, a T-shirt, neat fair hair. Noah Fanning, guessed Hirsch. His father's solid build.

Before he could inquire, Russ Fanning gave a little head jerk. 'A spot of bother at school, so he came home halfway through term.'

'Boarding school?'

Fanning nodded. 'Prince Alfred.' He paused. 'Misses his mother. Well, we all do.'

The men looked at the tabletop awkwardly and then Fanning seemed to turn shy, but with a need to unburden himself. 'Look at him. He's miserable. I don't know what to do with him. I don't even know how to talk to him, and he hardly opens his mouth to me, so we just stay out of each other's way. You need a woman in these situations. You need the mother. And that's the whole point, she's gone and we're both lost without her. Sorry.'

'Mate,' Hirsch said. He searched for a more adequate response. 'School holidays are coming up. Maybe he could invite a friend to come and stay? A couple of friends?'

'I don't even know if he has friends. Presumably he does.'

'What happened at school? If you don't mind me asking.'

'Stuff.' Fanning put his head on one side. 'You suggesting I send him to Redruth High? I would if there was a bus out this way.'

Clutching at straws, Hirsch asked, 'Are there any aunts who could talk to him? Or your mother, or Janet's mother?'

Fanning turned down the corners of his mouth in surprise and contemplation. And said, with growing appreciation, 'My sister. She'd get through to him. I should have thought of that.'

'Give it a try,' Hirsch said. He drained his tea. 'Better push on.'

And he drove away, realising yet again that he could never fully help people, never fully tackle or solve the headaches that came his way.

Next, he called on a shearer, crippled with back pain, who lived in a transportable home on five stony acres north of Mischance Creek, followed by a whisperingly shy sharefarmer's wife who couldn't meet his eye through her flyscreened front door, and a gas pipeline crew running trenches across a gibber plain east of Muncowie.

Mid-afternoon now, the final part of his broad loop taking him to meet the Barrier Highway at a point thirty minutes north of Tiverton. Singing along with Leonard Cohen about lousy poets, he turned left and presently found himself in better country: better crops, better rainfall, better fences—but still with that feeling of secluded, tucked-away lives lived under rooftops far off the highway.

Halfway to home, he stopped to see how Ken Panten's widow, Tina, was doing. Widowed two weeks ago, she lived alone in a fine old stone farmhouse that showed as a smudge on a hillslope. Widowed not a moment too soon, was the feeling of some of the locals. Ken Panten, an alcoholic of the dreary, mushy kind, had enjoyed cheating at golf, feeling up the daughters of his acquaintances and driving home from the pub in the middle of the road— which, two weeks earlier, he'd done once too often.

Hirsch parked in the shade cast by a cypress hedge and crossed a couch-grass lawn to the front door. The place had the silence of grieving, he thought, stepping onto the veranda, stumbling where some of the cracked old tiles had lifted. Too much of Panten's money had gone on holding up the bar and not enough on upkeep. No doubt Tina had tried her hardest, but Ken had controlled the purse strings. And she was 'new' in the sense that Panten was a fourth-generation farmer and she, a city woman, had only been in the district for fifteen years. No children.

Hirsch knocked, the door seeming to absorb the sound, and waited. No reaction, so he lifted and released the knocker, the impact surely crackling down the hallway beyond it. Still nothing.

He was about to check the car shed at the rear of the house when Tina opened the door. 'Sorry.'

She'd been crying. Knuckling her eyes she added, 'I was just...'

Just what, she didn't say. 'If this is a bad time,' Hirsch said.

She stared past him at the yard, the dusty police Toyota, as if waking to the world carrying on without her. Pulling the door wider, stepping out of the way, she said, 'No, it's fine, glad of the company.'

She was about fifty, attractive still, despite her life with Panten; wearing faded jeans and an Elton John T-shirt. Cardboard moving boxes and plastic storage crates lined the hallway. 'Tea? Let's go to the kitchen.'

The kitchen was a morning-light kind of place but dim now, at this hour of the afternoon. A green-wall-tile and green-Aga-stove kind of place, too, with a huge old fridge, and lace curtains hooked open above a deep French-provincial farmhouse sink. Everything had been costly once. Maybe her late husband's first wife had been a buy-expensive-and-make-it-last woman.

And more moving boxes, one of them loaded with crockery.

She gestured at the table and chairs, and he sat as she

filled the kettle. Her back to him, she said, 'Ordinary black tea, if I remember correctly?'

'Correct,' agreed Hirsch. 'Mrs Panten, Tina, are you selling up and moving?'

The question seemed to drain her spirit. Her shoulders slumped and she placed both hands on the sink for support. 'Tell you in a minute.'

Still with her back to him, she choreographed the tea-making as if she'd fall apart at any deviation: fetching down two mugs, fishing in a tin for teabags, tipping Anzac biscuits onto a side plate. Finally she turned to him, her hands laden, and forced a smile. 'Help yourself. They might be a bit stale.'

He bit into a biscuit. Yes, stale. But he'd been on the road for hours, he was hungry. So he finished the biscuit in three bites and selected another. She approved. She was playing a delaying tactic.

'So, moving out?'

She cocked her head, watching him, and was no longer the Tina Panten who'd been the diffident wife of a not-exactly-popular farmer. Assessing me, Hirsch thought. She has a story to tell and wonders if she can tell it. Wonders if I'm the one she should tell it to.

She said, 'You were good to me after the accident.'

Hirsch had delivered the death knock. Midnight on a Saturday, two weeks ago. He'd stayed with her then, eased her way through the bureaucracy later, phoned her every couple of days. He shrugged now, waiting.

'People say good things about you.'

Not all of them, Hirsch thought. 'I try, Mrs Panten,' he said.

She reached for a biscuit but changed her mind. Settled on a sip of tea instead. 'First, I'm not Mrs Panten. We never married. Tina Callan is my actual name.'

'Okay.' What he meant was, *No big deal* and also *I'm aware how conservative and chin-wagging the place can be.*

She leaned across the table, staring fixedly at his face. 'And do you know why we didn't marry? Because I was a sex worker when we met. I wasn't on the streets, I had a phone and a client list.' She paused. 'Callgirl, if you like.'

'Doesn't matter to me.'

'Mattered to Ken, though,' Tina Callan said.

Hirsch nodded. Shame, or something meaner and more miserable.

'Fifteen years I spent with that man. Looked after him when he went on a bender, cleaned up his messes, always had a meal on the table. A clean house. Full pantry, full fridge. A dutiful wife, if not in name. Let him root me when he wanted to. Well, I mean, I loved him, didn't I? It wasn't rooting, not for me.'

She sat back. 'But it was all a bit off, when I think about it. Ken didn't know how to talk to me, how to treat me. If it wasn't stupid babytalk, it was sarcasm and…and cringing away from me.' She paused. 'He couldn't forget what I'd been, who I'd been.'

'You're moving out to put memories behind you?'

'What?' She looked at him in irritation. 'No.' She took a breath. 'Sorry, I'm in a mood.'

Leaning towards him again she said, 'What I'm trying to get across to you is I spent a good deal of my adult life with a man who was so ashamed of living with a woman who'd been a sex worker, and so ashamed of still feeling desire for her, that he couldn't leave her anything in his will.'

She sat back. Said flatly, 'Everything goes to his only nephew.' She smiled emptily. 'And the nephew's sent me a lawyer's letter asking me to vacate the premises.'

Hirsch tried to tell her that she had legal rights, best get herself her own lawyer, but she pushed away her tea cup and said, 'I'm tired, Paul.'

Hirsch completed his patrol eventually, reaching Tiverton in time to buy frozen fish fillets from the general store, read his emails and check for Facebook posts from the kinds of fuckwits who liked to brag about the cars they'd stolen or the quality of the weed they'd just bought. His heart, though, wasn't really in it.

11

ON WEDNESDAY MORNING he received a message from a Queensland Police senior constable named Duncan Todisco. Did Hirsch really expect him to check all of Noosa's motels, hotels and short-stay properties? In any case, the names Willi Van Sant and Eve Tilling had rung a bell: three months earlier, his colleagues had received a complaint from a local motel manager. The pair had skipped out, owing rent. 'They're long gone.'

Hirsch fired back a thank-you email, then texted Willi's mother: *Noosa police confirm Willi and girlfriend stayed in a motel late June.* Best to be economical with the truth, he thought. At least it would give her a place to start.

He worked through the day, and at 5.30 p.m. was morosely hunting in his fridge for something to thaw when his phone pinged: Dr Van Sant, thanking him for the update. She'd also texted him a photo of a sign nailed to a roadside tree: *Koalas cross here.* Beneath it she'd written, 'I understand this to mean that koalas are placid everywhere else?'

Funny. He texted her a smiley face and wandered through to his bedroom, stripping off his uniform. Ten minutes later, showered, dressed in baggy jeans, and a windcheater over an ancient T-shirt—spring evenings were chilly in the mid-north—he settled on the sofa to call Wendy.

He was interrupted by the buzzer in the hallway: someone at the main door of the police station. Pocketing his phone, he walked through and was unsurprised to see Vikki Bastian on the front step. 'Come in.'

Vikki taught at the primary school across the road. After three months as the acting principal—she was only in her mid-twenties, but her old boss had been arrested for snowdropping—she was back teaching the bubs again. As far as Hirsch was aware, her new boss led a blameless existence.

'Thanks,' she said.

She did this once or twice a month, crossed the highway and knocked on his door after a late session of marking or lesson-planning. Hirsch suspected she had few friends locally, even though she'd grown up on a sheep property near Redruth and had returned to the mid-north after qualifying as a teacher. There was nothing ambiguous about these late afternoon visits. She knew that he was involved with Wendy—everyone did. She was lonely, that's all, and Hirsch had long recognised that listening to the troubled and the lonely was a key aspect of his job.

She worried her hands together. 'You'll tell me if I'm intruding?'

At first sight, Vikki Bastian had the blonde, ice-queen demeanour of a rich grazier's daughter who found things to criticise everywhere, but Hirsch knew her to be shy, a little insecure, and bewildered by ordinary human badness. 'It's fine,' he said, leading the way through to his sitting room.

'You're a good listener,' she'd tell him sometimes. Perhaps her father, a widower, and her friends—whoever they were—didn't listen. The issues Hirsch talked over patiently with her were hardly earth-shattering. Would she get on with the new principal? Had she hurt her dad's feelings when she moved to a rental cottage in Redruth? Was it wrong that she'd taken the soft option at Tiverton Primary instead of a tough inner-city school? But Hirsch had also long recognised that if someone believed their earth was shattering, then he should at the very least hear them out.

He settled her on the lumpy sofa, beneath a print of Wyeth's *Christina's World*, and said, 'Glass of white?'

She shook her head, her scalp-tight ponytail swinging,

and said, too hurriedly, 'Not this time. Thank you, though.'

Distracted and out of sorts about something, Hirsch thought. Rounding the rickety coffee table, he settled opposite her and watched her determinedly draw a laptop out of the hessian bag that went everywhere with her, *Redruth Agricultural Show* stencilled on the front beneath an image of the stone hillside chimney above the old copper mine.

She paused in the act, tense, almost daring him to stop her. 'Something I need to show you.'

'Okay.'

'Don't think badly of me.'

God, what's she done; what's been said about her? 'I won't,' Hirsch said.

She set the laptop on the coffee table and seemed to glance sideways at him, as if wondering whether she'd miscalculated the quality of his friendship. She confirmed it by saying, 'You're my friend.'

To cut across her habit of ceaseless apology, Hirsch gave her an emphatic, 'Yes.' Then: 'What's up?'

She flopped back against the cushions in a counterfeit of composure: he could read her tension. Her cream linen pants were badly wrinkled after a day in the classroom, and the pale-green V-necked shirt had a smudge of red on one sleeve, as if she'd leaned on a kid's drawing. It occurred to Hirsch that he'd never seen her so rumpled; it all jarred with the simple elegance of the silver around her slender neck and wrists. Something to do with her new boss?

But she surprised him. 'I've been going out with

someone,' she said, with no pleasure at all.

Hirsch made a small gesture of encouragement intended to say, variously, 'You're entitled to' and 'He hurt you?'

'His name's Scott Greig.'

'I don't know him,' Hirsch said.

With prim agitation, Bastian said, 'I volunteer at Evergreen one evening a week. I met him there.'

Evergreen, a cross between an aged-care facility and a retirement village, was attached to the little hospital down in Redruth. Hirsch visited sometimes, most recently to inform an elderly woman that her sixty-three-year-old son had been killed when his car hit a tree. 'This is a place of sorrows,' she'd said in response. 'The old duck in the next room kicked the bucket on Monday, the one across from me has dementia, most of the others have suffered strokes, so I go days without a decent conversation, and you come here telling me I've outlived one of my children.'

But Bastian was unlikely to be referring to a resident.

'He works there?'

'Carer,' she said, then blinked. Hirsch guessed she was suddenly unable to fathom her relationship with Scott Greig. He saw her shake it off and take on a little frown of concentration and hard judgment. 'We've been involved since July,' she said. '*Had been* involved.'

Two months. Hirsch knew full well how hard you can fall for someone in two minutes. 'Did he hurt you in some way?'

Bastian drew herself up. Spat it out: 'Not only me. He hurt *humanity*. He and that woman who works for the police.'

Hirsch stiffened. Brandl? Jean Landy? Trying not to show that she'd rattled him, he said, 'He hurt humanity?'

'Actually, could I have that wine after all?'

'Sure.'

He headed through the archway to the kitchen, tugged on the fridge door and took out an Annie's Lane chardonnay and returned, with glasses, to the sitting room, his mind racing. Pausing to check that the Wyeth print was straight—tension always seemed to tip it off-centre—he poured the wine. Vikki Bastian, poised for the moment, took her glass, sipped it, placed it carefully on the floor beside her feet. Then, as if seeing no good alternative, she reached forward, tapped at her laptop keyboard and turned the screen towards Hirsch.

'He was laughing at his phone the other night, so I asked what he was looking at, and he showed me that.'

Hirsch wriggled out of his chair and squatted at the edge of the coffee table for a better view. What her boyfriend had been looking at was video of a woman on the ground, twitching, arcing her back, tight as a drum, her vibrating heels smacking against the front step of a building. After a moment, he recognised the location: just outside the entrance to the Redruth police station. And the woman was Stephanie Ingram. In the throes of her seizure, he realised. Just then the audio crackled and a female voice broke in: *Hey, Scott, look what the garbos dumped outside.*

He watched wordlessly as the hideous little story unfolded, guessing that Petra Osmak had filmed the CCTV feed from the comfort of her nook behind the counter. 'You lousy cow, go out and help her,' he muttered, even as Osmak's voice broke in again: *Acknowledge the traditional custodians? I don't think so.*

'He must've thought I'd find it funny,' Vikki said.

Hirsch heard her as if from a great distance. He blinked and pressed the pause button, then looked at her properly. Gone was the artless young teacher, the cautious seeker of Hirsch's friendship. This Vikki Bastian wanted to spit in her ex-boyfriend's face.

'She sent this to him? Petra? He didn't download it from some website?'

'She sent it. Turns out they were at school together.'

Hirsch trod carefully. 'Girlfriend?'

'Just mates.'

'Can you email me a copy?'

He watched her do it and scanned his inbox to check that it had arrived. 'Did you do or say anything when he showed it to you?'

Looking diminished now, Bastian said, 'Don't judge me.'

'I'm not, Vikki. I'm assuming he's never shown you anything like this before?'

'Never. I thought he was going to show me some dumb YouTube clip.' She rolled her shoulders awkwardly. 'I did ask him to send it to me—but only so I could show you, promise. I didn't tell him that.'

'Have you told him you're breaking up with him?'

'Not yet.'

'Perhaps hold off on that for a few hours. I'll show my boss first thing tomorrow morning. We don't want him to say anything to Petra.'

'That's the thing, he's just as bad,' Bastian said, scooping up her glass from the floor and gulping a hefty mouthful before retrieving the laptop. She tapped a couple of keys and turned the screen to Hirsch again. A frozen image: a small room furnished with a narrow institutional bed fitted with siderails; next to it a very old man in a wheelchair. He was tiny, a slumped arrangement of bones in a badly stained shirt and gabardine trousers. Papery-looking skin; hollow cheeks; errant wisps of white hair. 'That's Mr Heffernan,' Bastian said. 'Press play.'

Hirsch did. A young male hand and forearm entered the foreground, directing a brimming soup spoon towards the old man's lips. The lips opened dutifully but the spoon withdrew. The action was repeated: a taunting pattern of offer and withdrawal. Each time, the old man lifted his feeble mouth, hunted for the soup, and slumped again. A couple of times he bumped the spoon just enough to spill soup on himself.

The camera didn't waver; it's propped up on a cupboard or something, Hirsch thought, trying to visualise the décor of a typical room in the aged-care centre.

'I gather that's not a family member?'

'Not a family member,' Bastian said, hard and deliberate. 'Listen.'

Hirsch had been hearing the soft rustle of clothing, a hint of amused breathing, but now a voice said, *Eat up, that's the way. Oh dear, missed again, what a shame.*

Soup dribbled into the old man's lap. A snigger, and the voice said, *Let's try that again, shall we?*

Hirsch pressed pause. 'I'm assuming that's your boyfriend?'

'*Ex.*'

Hirsch gestured at the laptop. 'What did he say when he showed it to you?'

Bastian flinched a little. 'Actually, I found it on his phone when he went to have a shower. I know I shouldn't have looked, but, you know...'

'Any other videos?'

'I didn't see any.'

That didn't mean anything. And if Scott Greig and Petra Osmak had already uploaded both videos to some hate site...

Hirsch pressed play again. The voice said, *Why do we bother, eh? Why do we bother?*

The spoon stabbed this time. Hirsch imagined more than heard it strike teeth. The old man recoiled weakly as the voice continued, *The money it costs to keep a useless waste of space like you alive. You need culling, you old shit.* A pause. *Gas the elderly, hey, Petra? And all the other human refuse.*

Hirsch shook his head. 'What a prince.'

Vikki Bastian flushed. 'I didn't know!' she insisted. Her voice was layered with unhappiness and a kind of longing, perhaps for the woman she wanted to be, or had once been.

12

ON THURSDAY MORNING Hirsch entered the Redruth police station, walked through to the connecting door with a greeting for Petra Osmak, who was peering at her computer screen, and made his way to the sergeant's office.

Brandl had been expecting him. 'You said it was urgent?'

Hirsch waved a memory stick at her. 'Couple of videos I need you to see.'

'Give me a second,' she said, saving a document on her

laptop. Her hair was shower-damp, her eyes bright after her morning run, and a mug of strong, dense coffee steamed at her elbow. Looking up at him again, she gestured for the memory stick, plugged it in and opened the first clip: Stephanie Ingram.

Hirsch, seated in one of the office chairs, watched Brandl's face. She stiffened. When she recognised Petra's voice twenty seconds later, she smacked the lid down. 'Jesus, Paul.'

Hirsch waited.

'That was just the other day. She'd come here to report the break-in. It had been raining, she said the path was slippery. She fell down and she thinks she hit her head and it brought on a seizure. Where did you get it?'

As Hirsch told her, she frowned intently, as if trying to map the links between the main players. 'Ignoring the fact there *is* a video for the moment, what's Ms Bastian's motive? She thinks her boyfriend's involved with Petra?'

'No. She was genuinely repelled. And as far as she knows, they're just friends from high school.'

'Kids who didn't make it out of the bush,' Brandl muttered. She reached a reluctant hand to the laptop, lifted the screen and watched to the end. 'God, if this gets out…'

Then clapped a hand over her mouth. 'Forget I said that.'

'A minefield, boss,' Hirsch said.

Brandl played the second clip, freezing the action at one point, jabbing a finger at the screen. 'That's assault, hitting him in the mouth like that. Assault, duty-of-care issues...'

Hirsch agreed. 'But what do we charge Petra with? *Do* we charge her?'

'Sack her, certainly. As for charges...Unauthorised distribution or publication of police property, maybe. I'll have to confer.'

Then she looked stricken. 'These aren't online, are they?'

'I honestly don't know. Vikki doesn't think so. She thinks Petra and her mate get a kick out of sending stuff to each other.'

'We need to know. And whether they've uploaded other videos or sent them to friends who might have uploaded them.'

Hirsch shrugged glumly. 'First I think we need to contain the pair of them,' he said. 'Isolate and question Petra—put her in the interview room—and question Greig somewhere else, maybe where he works. Right away. We don't want them erasing anything, or uploading out of spite.'

'Phones, tablets and laptops,' Brandl muttered. 'A warrant nightmare.'

Hirsch was glad he didn't have to do that. 'I'll tackle Greig now.'

'Wait, let me think. There's not a great deal we can or should do. Different police will need to run the main investigation. Let's talk to Petra first.' She groaned, put her head in her hands. 'This had to happen on my watch, didn't it?'

Hirsch counted Hilary Brandl as a friend. She wasn't by nature self-regarding. But her mind was racing, leaping from one ramification to the next. So he wasn't surprised when she said, 'You don't think Tim and Jean…'

'No,' he said flatly, guessing she was thinking that if she reported it to regional command in Port Pirie, they might wonder if a certain culture had developed in the Redruth police station. They might want to cover their arses, whereupon a carload of Internal Investigations suits from Adelaide would come sniffing around. Everyone knew that institutions—schools, the police and the armed forces—were fertile ground for bigotry and bullying. But did they create them? Hirsch was betting that Petra Osmak, not yet a serving police officer and in what was essentially a desk job, had been a bigot long before she arrived, maybe influenced by her family or high school mates like Scott Greig. Not by Tim Medlin or Jean Landy.

'I need to be sure. And they might have seen or heard things,' Brandl said. 'Back in a tick.'

Check how? Ask them outright and expect an honest answer? Hirsch watched her leave the room. He listened intently, eventually hearing a soft rumble of voices from the tearoom further along the corridor. A moment later she was back with Tim and Jean in tow, saying, 'Stand behind me,' as she sat at her desk again. Her hands went to the laptop, but her eyes bored into Hirsch and tilted upwards briefly before she started the first video.

She wanted him to read their reactions.

At that moment, both constables were curious but, as the seconds passed, a hardness, a flattening hinting at disgust, settled in Jean Landy, while Medlin's youth-pastor face showed deep shock. He hadn't seen as much of life as she had. 'That's Mrs Ingram! I can't believe Petra...'

'Wait, please,' Brandl said. 'There's a second video.'

Landy grew colder as it played, Medlin more dismayed. When it was over Brandl told them to sit with Hirsch, taking that opportunity to confer silently with him. He gave her a minuscule smile and headshake.

'Right,' she said, when Landy and Medlin were settled. 'If either of you have seen these videos before, or have any knowledge of them, I expect you to tell me now.'

'Not me, sergeant,' Landy said.

'Tim?'

'Heavens, no.'

'Has Ms Osmak tried sounding you out about anything?'

Jean Landy cocked her head. 'Sounding us out. Do you mean has she tried to see if we think like she does?'

'That is what I mean, yes.'

'The answer's no. And I'd tell her where to go if she did try it.'

'Tim?'

Medlin was bewildered. 'You mean, like, am I a racist or something? No, sergeant. I've hardly ever talked to her.'

'Same here,' Landy said. 'Hello in the morning and goodbye at the end of the day. And it's not as if she's been here that long.'

'Do you know who her friends are?'

Landy gestured at the laptop. 'That second video, it's in the aged-care place, right?'

'Yes.'

'I've seen her at the pub with a guy who works there.'

'Did you form an opinion about their relationship?'

Landy shrugged. 'Just friends, from the look of it. Not, er, intimate or anything.'

Brandl scowled as if she wanted more but knew she wouldn't get it: her two young constables didn't know anything. 'This,' she said, indicating the videos, 'stays in this room for now. Understood?'

'Yes, sergeant.'

'I don't want you telling friends, family, anyone, but there is going to be a stink. You'll probably be interviewed by outside investigators in the next day or two.'

Landy was sour. 'Grilling us to find out if we're all racists. Fucking Petra. Sorry, sergeant.'

A brief, bleak flick of a smile on Brandl's face. 'I won't quibble with you.'

Tim Medlin looked troubled. 'What about Mrs Ingram?'

Brandl slumped. 'I honestly don't know.'

'We need to tell her.'

Jean cocked her head at him, curious. 'But what if no

one but us has seen the video?'

'What are you saying? That what she doesn't know won't hurt her?'

Landy shrugged. 'Just playing devil's advocate, Timbo. She does need us from time to time—same as we need her. Do we want to rock that boat?'

Medlin drew himself up. 'It would be wrong not to tell her.'

Hirsch thought so, too. But who would do the telling? And when? Before or after a case could be mounted against Petra Osmak? Disappointing himself a little, he argued a pragmatic line. 'We need to know what else and who else Petra's filmed, and who she's shared it with. Meanwhile, if she has a reputation for racist abuse, it's possible Mrs Ingram knows about it. So we tell her.'

No one liked any of it. They didn't like themselves very much.

13

SOON AFTER THAT, with Petra Osmak stewing in the interview room and Landy and Medlin called to attend at a prang near the Morgan Road intersection, Brandl placed a *Ring if unattended* sign beside the bell in the reception area: 'Come the apocalypse,' she told Hirsch, 'we're otherwise engaged.'

She wasn't being funny, exactly: he could see the strain in her face. 'To the fray,' she said, and led the way back through the connecting door and along the corridor to the interview room.

Petra Osmak, waiting for them, was jiggling one leg, flexing her jaw. Part obduracy, part fear, thought Hirsch as he swung into a chair on the opposite side of the table. And the room itself, probably—the non-colour walls, grey carpet tiles, plastic chairs and bolted-to-the-floor table. They weren't imbued with the full quota of misery and hate—this was quiet wheat-and-wool country, after all— but they did seem to leach hope from the atmosphere. If you spent time here as a witness or a subject, you were likely to find yourself saying things you didn't want to say.

Right now, though, Petra was still at the bravado stage: 'What's going on? Am I in trouble? Jean was a real bitch just now, like I did something wrong.'

Her tatts and piercings seemed to bristle, fortifying her outrage. Hirsch wondered if she relied on that. If she knew that without them she was just another sidelined small-town kid.

Meanwhile the sergeant was being deliberative. Tapping loose papers together, smoothing the cover of a manila folder, lifting the lid of her laptop, and ignoring Petra. Then finally she looked up. 'Ms Osmak, it is my duty to advise you of the immediate termination of your employment as an auxiliary support officer with the police service.'

Petra blinked. 'What for? I haven't done anything.'

The sergeant ignored her and began tapping laptop keys.

Petra stuck her jaw out. 'I need this job. You told me it would be a good stepping stone for joining the police.'

Brandl turned the laptop towards her. 'We are also investigating the possibility of charging you with misuse of police property, disclosing police information without a reasonable excuse.'

'What?' But understanding was dawning.

Hirsch saw Petra lean back as if the laptop might go for her throat.

Brandl pressed play. 'You made this video by filming the police station's CCTV. One might call it a hate video. Not only that, you shared it with at least one other person. Do you see why we would not want such a person in the police service?'

Petra folded her arms. 'Excuse me, what planet are you on?' She nodded at the laptop screen. 'Look at her, pissed out of her brain. That's what happens when you give them handouts.'

Brandl's voice was quiet, icy. 'Who is "they"?'

Osmak caught herself. Her face shut down.

'Petra? Who is "they"?'

A silence as Osmak wrestled with reserves of resentment and hostility.

'You know, Aboriginals.'

Hirsch saw in the sergeant's face just then a twinge almost of shame for having screwed that admission from a young woman who didn't know any better. But she went on, 'How many of your friends have seen this, Petra?'

Osmak was thinking fiercely. 'Only one, and he wouldn't dob me in. You got it from that bitch he's going out with.'

'Your friend's name?'

'You know his name.'

'Scott Greig?'

'Like I said: you know.'

'Have you sent him other videos of this nature?'

'No.'

'Have you uploaded any videos of this nature to the internet?'

'No. Look, it's just a video. No big deal. You want to look at YouTube if you think this is bad,' Petra said, stabbing a finger at the screen.

'Petra, this isn't a video of a drunk woman—even if it was, that wouldn't excuse what you did. The person in that video is Mrs Ingram, the director of the cultural centre, and she was having an epileptic fit. It was left to a passer-by to call Doctor Pillai.'

'Doctor.' Petra curled her lip. 'Yeah, right. Anyway, I couldn't leave the desk just then, the phone rang. It's not like I ever get any clerical support.'

That's how she's going to play it, Hirsch thought. No hope of saving her job, so go full bore with the grievances.

'I mean,' Petra said, 'what was she even doing here? They hate the police.'

'She had come to report a crime.'

Petra was lost. 'Crime?'

'Someone broke into the cultural centre and threw rotten eggs around.'

Petra almost laughed at that, but she was also struggling with her own lack of imagination, not quite able to comprehend that a woman who wasn't white could be director of anything, have a responsible role or think to report a crime to the police. It baffled her. Offended her, probably.

Hirsch leaned across the table. 'What can you tell us about that break-in, Ms Osmak?'

She recoiled. 'Me? Nothing to do with me.'

Hirsch merely looked at her.

'I know what you're saying and you can just shove it.'

'What am I saying, Petra?'

He felt like a bully, and she dug in again. 'Half of them at the cultural centre don't even look Aboriginal. Got their hands out if there's anything going, though. And you hear stories about where all that grant money ends up.' She pointed at the laptop. 'Be interesting to know what kind of car she drives.'

'Unbelievable,' Brandl said.

We're losing the interview, Hirsch thought. 'Petra, the video: have you made others like it, inside or outside the station?'

'Told you, no. And I can't see how I broke any laws.'

'How many of your friends have seen it?'

'Are you even listening? Only Scott.'

'Does he send you videos?'

142

A shrug.

'What kind of videos, Petra? Ones he's made or just downloads?'

Another shrug.

'Does he post videos anywhere?'

'Not that I know of.'

The to-and-fro was quicker now, with Petra primed to snap and stonewall. Hirsch said, 'Is he a good friend?'

'Who?'

'Mr Greig.'

'Met him in school.'

'Does he care about you?'

'He's a mate.'

'Was it his idea to send each other videos?'

Petra looked lost finally, as if wondering if she'd been used. 'He's a mate.' She paused. 'We like the same things.'

'Petra, we would like to examine your work computer, home computer and mobile phone.'

'That's not fair.' She sounded tired now. 'Don't you need permission?'

Hirsch said, 'Is it that you're trying to protect Scott? We've seen his video from the aged-care home. Are there others?'

She was hunched into her shoulders. 'No. So now you know everything.'

'We need to make sure.'

'I don't have a home computer, just an iPad.' Lifting

her head, clawing back some resistance, she said, 'And I don't give permission. You can just go and get yourselves a warrant.'

After that, Brandl made a few calls and finally told Hirsch: 'The boss says to keep them away from each other—well, we knew that—so I want you to take Tim or Jean with you to charge Greig on summons. Interview him if he's agreeable.'

'Warrants for the phones and computers?'

'The boss is arranging that.' She gave him a sour look. 'Meanwhile I'm to notify Adelaide—and so the arse-covering begins. Meaning we're bound to have a visit.'

'Great.' Hirsch had had his own run-ins with Internal Investigations. He went off in search of Tim Medlin.

Evergreen Aged Care, adjacent to the little hospital on the southern edge of Redruth, was a place of small rooms, low ceilings and jarring notes: muzak, plastic flowers and jolly notices pinned to corkboards, curling in the superheated atmosphere. A rushed-off-their-feet kind of place, too. Masked carers and nursing staff were darting in and out of rooms or fetching back runaway walking frames, so Hirsch and Medlin were able to make their way to the manager's door unchallenged.

Harriet McLean was peering at her computer when Hirsch knocked. 'Oh, thank God, come to save me from the monthly finance figures.' She was small, bulky, middle-aged, with curly silver-threaded hair, and wore diamante glasses that made her look permanently startled. 'Unless it's bad news, in which case I apologise for my levity. But you *are* saving me from plus and minus columns.'

She paused, swivelling back and forth in her chair.

'All right, I can see from your eyes this isn't a good-news call,' she said. 'Have a seat—one of you, at least.'

Hirsch glanced at Tim, who gave a tiny smile of capitulation and leaned against a filing cabinet. Hirsch, removing a scuffed blue manila folder from the only other chair in the room, sat across from McLean. 'Scott Greig.'

She grew very still. Regarded him for a long moment. 'Who goes first, you or me? He's not here, incidentally.'

'Day off?'

'Let's just say that there's been a very recent parting of the ways. Which is also to say that I'm not vastly surprised that he's the reason you're here.'

'How about you go first,' Hirsch said.

She settled back in her chair. 'Complaints, mainly—too many of them. Family members come and go pretty freely here, so there's always a set of eyes passing along a corridor. Young Scott was seen talking to some of our residents rudely, mocking them. Rough handling if they soiled themselves. Impatient. Soon after he started working here a watch went missing—quite valuable, apparently. He was often late getting to work; slapdash about masking. And one day I found him in here looking at residents' files for no good reason. Their financial details? Don't know. He can be charming, but it always seemed a bit fake. Now your turn.'

Hirsch knew McLean. He could trust her. 'A video,' he said, reaching his phone across her spread of paperwork.

He watched as she viewed it, first peering through her glasses, then over them. 'Sorry, not good with small screens.'

Finally she settled and watched, intent, until the end. 'Did he just hit Mr Heffernan in the mouth with the spoon?'

'Yes.'

'The little shit.' She returned the phone. 'That's assault, isn't it? You can charge him?'

'Yes. How is Mr Heffernan?'

'Not good—but he hasn't been good all year. A stroke, heart problems. He's well into his eighties.' She paused. 'His daughter did mention a cut lip the other day.'

Tim Medlin stirred. 'Do you have CCTV?'

'In the corridors.'

'Is Mr Heffernan able to answer some questions?'

'No, dear,' Harriet McLean said, with a smile that implied Medlin had a lot to learn about life in places like hers.

Greig's address, a flat in a blistered, peeling strip of six owned by the hospital, was two side streets away.

'We could've walked,' Medlin said as they got in the car.

Hirsch shrugged. Better to walk a prisoner three metres

146

than three hundred. Prisoners got their nerve back over a longer distance, and he'd had more than his fair share of foot chases over the years.

They parked in front of the flats and walked down a buckled driveway. At Greig's door Hirsch stepped to one side and indicated that Medlin should knock. He didn't want to be glimpsed in those first couple of seconds. Keep the guy on his toes.

Medlin knocked several times. When the door finally opened, Hirsch saw him go tense, then take a step back. Thinking Greig had a weapon, Hirsch stepped in hurriedly, then also recoiled: Greig was an unprepossessing mix of bad breath and bed-hair. He looked about eighteen in his band T-shirt and gaping boxers.

'Yeah?' he said. His eyes switched back and forth.

'Mr Greig? Scott Greig?' said Hirsch.

'Yeah. I'm trying to sleep here, man. I, like, turned the music down hours ago.'

'I'm not here about a noise complaint. Please get dressed. I wish to question you in relation to an incident at Evergreen Aged Care.'

'What incident? I don't work there anymore.'

'Perhaps we can go inside? I do intend to question you and I do not intend to do it out here.'

Greig flinched at the snap in Hirsch's voice. 'Yeah, whatever,' he said, turning, disappearing into his flat.

Hirsch and Medlin followed him down a short hallway, past a poky kitchen and into a small sitting room. None of the empty beer cans and pizza boxes Hirsch had expected. The place was tidy, with newish Ikea furniture and a small TV on top of a bookcase. Fat airport novels, an atlas, a dictionary and film-history texts. Above the TV, a poster of Alfred Hitchcock.

'Let me get some pants on,' Greig said, stepping through a doorway at the end.

They waited. He reappeared in a fresh T-shirt and cargo pants. 'Sit if you want. Anyway, what incident?'

'Assault,' said Hirsch, taking one end of the sofa. 'A video has emerged of you stabbing a spoon against the lips of an elderly resident of Evergreen Aged Care. What can you tell me in regards to that matter?'

'Whoa!' Greig shot out of his chair. 'Assault?'

'Perhaps you could tell us your side of the story?' said Tim Medlin mildly.

'Where'd you get this so-called video? They can be faked, you know.'

'I understand that you were sacked from Evergreen?' said Hirsch.

But Greig was stewing. 'Someone dobbed me in.' He snapped his fingers. 'Fucking Vikki. That explains it.'

Despite himself, Hirsch asked, 'Explains what?'

'How she sounded on the phone last night. Stuck-up bitch.' He walked through to his front door and poked his head out. 'She here?'

Hirsch got to his feet, wondering if Greig intended to run, but Medlin was quicker, following on Greig's heels, herding him back a moment later, Greig jerking away from the hand on his elbow. 'I'm a bloke here in his own house and you're acting like I got no rights.'

'Sit, please, Mr Greig. I haven't finished interviewing you.'

'Got nothing to say. Not answering your police-state questions. No comment.'

'Very well. Scott Greig, you are hereby charged with assault with intent, an indictable offence under Section 270B of the *Criminal Law Consolidation Act*. You will be given notice to appear in the Magistrates Court at a later date, unless you choose to have the offence heard by the District Court. Do you understand this charge, and your rights and obligations?'

'This is bullshit.'

'Do you understand—'

'Yeah, yeah, whatever. Jesus. You got me at a bad time, you know. Lost my job, hardly any sleep, girlfriend's probably going to dump me.'

'Actions have consequences,' Tim Medlin said.

'Fuck would you know?'

'We'll see ourselves out, Mr Greig,' Hirsch said.

As Hirsch and Medlin returned to the car, an unmarked sedan pulled in hurriedly. Two men in suits got out. Detectives: Hirsch knew the look. And they'd got here pretty quickly.

'Gentlemen,' the older one said. He was solid; the spring sun glinted on heavy-framed glasses. 'We have the necessary warrants: phones, tablets, computers.'

'Sir,' Hirsch said, guessing the man was senior in rank. 'Did he kick off?'

'Pretty harmless,' Hirsch said.

The men nodded and walked down to Greig's door. Shrugging, Hirsch and Medlin drove back to the police station, where Sergeant Brandl said she didn't know anything about plainclothes officers serving warrants on Greig. 'Not sticking my nose in, though,' she said.

'Wise, boss.'

'Care to come with me to talk to Steph Ingram?'

'I could murder a coffee,' Hirsch said. 'Then I'm set.'

He went to the tearoom and slotted the strongest coffee pod into the machine. But that look on Greig's face…

He took out his phone, called Vikki Bastian. Told her to move in with her father for a few days.

14

AT THE WURLIE forty minutes later, Stephanie
Ingram said no, she couldn't give them an hour, she was
too busy. 'Plus,' she said, with a glint that wasn't entirely
sarcastic, 'an hour is a whitefella concept. You'll faithfully
stick to that one hour, while blackfella time is no time, or
all time. Too philosophical for you?'

'Or too bullshit,' said Hirsch, wondering immediately
if he'd gone too far. But she flashed him a grin, which
eased the tension he'd seen as soon as they'd knocked on
her office door.

He could see that Sergeant Brandl was on the back foot. Looking earnest, she said, 'How're you holding up, Mrs Ingram?'

'Steph or Auntie Steph, for Christ's sake,' Ingram said. 'Look, I'm fine. It was a mix of things the other day. I've never had many seizures, but stress, lack of sleep, diabetes, missing meals, too much caffeine…Not to mention slipping over and hitting my head.'

'You should have called; we would have come here.'

Ingram shrugged. 'Another time. So, what problem are you talking about?'

'Concerning a—'

Ingram's desk phone rang and she stopped Brandl with her hand as she picked up.

Hirsch tried to follow the call. From the Aboriginal Legal Service in Adelaide, he decided, informing her that no barrister was available to drive up to Redruth on the seventeenth. There was some to and fro. By the time the call was over, a barrister was available.

'Now,' she said, hanging up, 'is there a problem? What are we talking about? I'm the problem? My mob? We get a fair bit of that.' She paused, again with the deadly glint. 'Not giving you the shits, am I?'

'A bit,' Brandl admitted.

'What about you, Sunshine?'

Hirsch had been called Sunshine by legions of senior officers over the years, and his father and grandfather before that—generally because he'd been found wanting in some

152

way. He cut to the chase. 'Auntie Steph, someone videoed you having a fit outside the copshop.'

Her expression was complicated and fleeting. 'Give me the gist...' she began, then said, 'Excuse me a sec: Auntie Rose?'

An elderly woman was hugging the doorframe, waving sheet music. 'Use the copier?'

Stephanie Ingram gestured at the photocopier. 'Go for it.' Turning to Hirsch and Brandl, she explained: 'Women's choir.'

They waited while the woman printed off twenty copies and left the room. 'At the rate we're going,' Ingram said, 'we might need a whole hour after all. So, what's the problem with this video?'

Brandl outlined it, saying, 'Where it gets complicated, she filmed *police* CCTV and sent it to a friend—who might have sent it to others.'

Ingram nodded gloomily. Turning to Hirsch, she said, 'How's Russ Fanning and his eagle?'

Hirsch blinked at the change of subject. She'd make a good cop. 'I...'

'He was telling me about my cultural essence last time I saw him. I know what my cultural essence is and it's not that bloody tourist attraction of his.'

'Anyway,' Sergeant Brandl interrupted, 'we're really, really sorry about the video. Ms Osmak's been sacked and may be charged, and we're investigating her friend. Whether or not he shares her views about First Nations people remains to be seen.'

'Hilary, for fuck's sake—First Nations people.'

'You're not going to make it easy for us, are you?' Brandl retorted.

Ingram grinned, then turned serious. 'Look, don't bust a gut over this. I don't intend to. I trained as a nurse before I did social work, and I didn't just help my own mob. I worked all over, including the prison service, and I dealt with all kinds of stuff: at-risk kids, youth justice, carer abuse, disability, suicide prevention, family violence, you name it. I came into contact with as many whites as blacks. There are hundreds of Petras out there. Thousands. There's nothing special about them. Poor, no education, easily led. Fucked-up family life. Let down by governments since the year dot. Let down by adults who should have known better.'

Her desk phone rang again. 'Stephanie Ingram.'

Hirsch watched her face move from expectation to tiredness. 'Fifteen thousand would have been better,' she said eventually, before listening to the reply. Someone's giving her a heap of weasel words, he thought. Then she said, 'Much appreciated,' and ended the call.

Catching his expression, she said, 'We asked the department for twenty thousand dollars to pay for a maternal and child health nurse one day a week. They're offering ten.'

'Maybe ask the local council,' Brandl said.

'Tried that. Half of them didn't want a cultural centre here in the first place.'

'You could hardly keep operating from your kitchen table,' Hirsch said.

That's how it had started, she'd told him one day. Reaching retirement age, she'd quit work and returned to the mid-north where she'd grown up. Before long some of the local elders had come to her house and, over cups of tea, expressed their concerns: kids and drugs, the youth justice system and suicide; negotiating with Centrelink; Russ Fanning's eagle; Covid and vaccination anxieties. And, simply, their desire to strengthen the Ngadjuri culture.

'You know where that table is now?' she said.

'Not in your kitchen, I take it.'

She jerked her head. 'Down the hall. Tearoom.'

'You should stick a plaque on it.'

She gave him a look: she hadn't made up her mind about him. 'What happens now? I don't want to stand up against some kid in court, no matter how racist she is. Can't you give her a slap over the wrist?'

'We hope so,' Brandl said.

Ingram stared at her. 'You hope so—meaning it's out of your hands now? You sent it upstairs? Why didn't you just send her to me?'

'There are procedures—'

'Procedures,' Stephanie Ingram said, 'that lead to unwanted outcomes.'

15

FIRST THING FRIDAY morning, Jeanette Laurie entered Hirsch's office with her son, Jack, gawky in a Redruth High School blazer. About to catch the school bus, Hirsch guessed. The family lived on a smallholding near the council grader depot and were active members of the tennis club, but that was all he knew about them.

'What can I do for you?'

'It's about a dangerous dog,' Jeanette said.

She was short and round where her son was tall and angular, all wrist bones and ankles. The blazer and gabardine trousers weren't keeping up with his growth spurts. He said: 'It keeps chasing me.'

Jack usually rode his bike to the bus stop, he said, which was outside Ed Tennant's shop. His best route took him past Brenda Maher's cottage, but just lately a rottweiler had been dashing out and nipping at his feet.

Jeanette put an arm around her son. 'He's frightened, Paul,' she said, a hint of relish in her voice. 'What if he gets knocked off his bike and mauled? And I work; I haven't got time to take him to and fro every day.'

'Okay, I know the house you mean. I'll have a word with them.'

'I'd do that myself,' Jeanette said, 'except, you know, the boy who lives there went, you know, went to the toilet on the pub veranda when he was asked to stop doing wheelies in the car park. Not someone I want to get on the wrong side of.'

Jack was fighting a grin. 'What Mum means is he took a dump on the veranda and she doesn't want him doing that at our place.'

'Nice,' Hirsch said. 'I'll have a word.'

But back to his emails first. Mostly junk, except that his presence was required at an interview to be conducted by Internal Investigations officers at the Redruth police station at noon on Tuesday 14 September 2021.

Great. But why him? He wasn't a Redruth cop. And there was no rotten police culture in Redruth anyway. But he found himself thinking of Stephanie Ingram's experience. All of her experiences, all of her life. He phoned her, guile moving through him. Or not guile precisely—he genuinely did want to know how she was, he wanted good relations with her, he hated it when matters went unresolved.

A tinge of guile, though, and she read it in him. 'I'm fine, Paul. And believe it or not, I ran into Ms Osmak getting takeaway last night. Bound to happen sooner or later.'

'And?'

'And she apologised. I'm not sure what for. Not fetching a doctor? For filming me? For her attitude to black people? But it's a start.'

'She saw the human being,' Hirsch said, and immediately regretted it.

'And why wouldn't she?' Steph Ingram said.

'Sorry.'

'Yeah, sorry. Look, Paul, how about one of these days you drop by and talk to some of the kids who come in here?'

'Sure.'

'When I say "one of these days" I mean whitefella time, otherwise it'll never happen.'

'Okay.'

'Joke, Paul.'

Obviously Petra Osmak hadn't been taken into custody, but had Scott Greig been locked up? Moved to another police station? Hirsch called Redruth and was surprised to hear the voice of Ed Pickett, whose retirement had led to Petra's hiring as auxiliary support officer. 'They got you cracking the office whip again, Ed?'

Pickett, a shy, humourless man in awe of anyone in authority, seemed faintly affronted. 'Sergeant Brandl needed someone in a hurry and I was available and I know all the ins and outs.'

'We were all sorry you retired,' Hirsch said breezily. 'Can I speak to the sergeant, please?'

He couldn't, Pickett was afraid—she was addressing students at the high school. 'And Constable Landy is attending at a break-in. Constable Medlin's available.'

'Put me through.'

Medlin came on the line, saying Hirsch had saved him from report-writing. 'What can I do for you?'

'Any updates on our video stars?'

'Sergeant said this morning it's out of our hands now, but as far as we know, Greig'll be done for assault and Petra for misuse of police property. They've been banned from contacting each other and Greig's banned from contacting Ms Bastian.'

'Thanks,' Hirsch said, and called Hedley Bastian, Vikki's sheep-farmer father. He'd helped Bastian a while back: a cancelled outdoor music festival, irate ticket-holders, calming words.

Today he wasn't picking up, so Hirsch stepped outside and peered irresolutely at the primary school on the other side of the highway. Morning recess. Kids swarming, breaking apart, regrouping—like an organism. The only still point was Vikki Bastian, who was not entirely still. Hirsch saw her bend a listening ear to one child, crouch to comfort another. He went back inside, and so the morning passed.

At 11 a.m., Yvonne Muir walked in to inform Hirsch that she'd seen her two-drawer filing cabinet advertised online.

Hirsch, composing an email, lifted his hands from the keyboard, giving himself time to think. 'You were burgled?'

She frowned. 'What? No. I'd put it out for the hard-rubbish collection, remember?'

'That's right.'

'It wasn't good for anything else. One drawer wouldn't close properly and the other one used to stick. I think the runners were bent.'

Where Bob, her husband, was a stolid man who measured his thoughts, words and acts, Yvonne was as twitchy as a bird, her hands flicking ceaselessly about herself, rarely alighting. She was doing it now, worrying the countertop, her cheeks, her breastbone. Not for the first time, Hirsch wanted to lay calming fingers upon her.

'Are you sure it's yours?'

'Positive. Bright red, a bit dented, a long scratch down one side.'

'What did the ad say?'

'Not a lot. Fifty dollars delivered. In repairable

160

condition. Well, it wasn't, really. Bob had a go at it and said it wasn't worth fixing so we bought another one.'

Hirsch stood with his laptop and took it to the counter. 'Show me the ad?'

'That's the thing,' she said, her voice layered with frustration. 'It's been taken down.'

'That means it was probably sold.'

'Maybe, but I sent them a please explain message and the ad disappeared almost immediately.'

'A please explain message…'

'Please explain why they were selling an item that I happened to know was rubbish because I used to own it. Please explain why they had the nerve to charge good money for said item.'

'Did they reply?'

Yvonne shook her head. 'No.'

Hirsch felt bone-tired. 'Not sure what I can do about it, Yvonne.'

'Well, for a start,' she said, now with a bossy tone, 'I think there's something iffy about the whole hard-rubbish collection thing.'

She stood back to dig into the pocket of her faded pink fleece. Removed a folded sheet of paper and smoothed it out on the counter. 'This is the leaflet that came around. You must've got one—or maybe you didn't. It looks legitimate, like it's from the council or a charity or something, but there's actually no contact details. No information at all, really, just some vague stuff about thoughtful recycling

161

and please dispose of hazardous waste elsewhere.'

Hirsch peered. 'There's an apostrophe in tins...and only one *r* in corrosive.'

Yvonne checked. 'There you go,' she said, stepping away with an air of finality. 'It was a scam.'

Turning to leave, she said, 'Dinner tonight? Sevenish?'

'Sure,' Hirsch said, wondering what he was in for. According to Bob, Yvonne was going through a lentil phase.

When she was gone, he checked the town's WTF page. Finding that no one had posted experiences similar to Yvonne's, he scrolled through the local Marketplace, casting a narrow net. Even so, dozens of lawnmowers, evening dresses, planet lamps, tennis racquets and other humble goods cropped up, none of which resembled any he'd seen on the town's nature strips in the lead-up to the hard-rubbish collection.

He returned to the WTF page, uploaded a be-wary post, then called his mother in the Adelaide Hills. 'Happy birthday, Mum.'

'Darling,' she said lightly, and he let her talk for a while. There wasn't much substance to it—what 'your dad' had given her; who she had heard from; the bowls club; the cancellation (again) of their houseboat trip owing to Covid. Except that Hirsch knew it was *all* substance, a soothing confirmation that she was alive, that she was his mother, that she loved him.

16

TIME FOR LUNCH.

Feeling more buoyant than he had for days, Hirsch pinned his mobile number to the front door and walked diagonally across the Barrier Highway, pausing on the footpath for a road train of wool bales. Up onto the general store's warped veranda floorboards and in through the fly-curtain, and Vikki Bastian was there, peering into the dairy cabinet at the flavoured yoghurts.

'Vikki.'

She jumped and turned, and he backpedalled, one

hand raised apologetically. 'Didn't mean to startle you.'

She clenched: 'I thought you'd locked him up!'

She means Scott Greig, Hirsch thought. She wants promises and I can't give her any. 'But he's been charged, Vikki,' he said. 'Summonsed to appear before a magistrate.'

Steadily, helplessly, she said, 'He keeps calling my mobile and last night he rang the house. Dad gave him an earful, but he keeps calling.'

Damn, thought Hirsch. 'What kind of mood's he in?'

She shrugged. 'I didn't actually talk to him, Dad did.'

'What did he want?'

'Dad said he demanded to talk to me. There were things he wanted to say and he'd never call me again. Dad told him to get lost.'

Hirsch's mind raced. Maybe the kid wanted to have the last word before he disappeared? 'He's not allowed to contact you, Vikki. We'll warn him again.'

His good mood vanishing, Hirsch washed down his Cornish pasty with tea and headed out to do some solid police work involving the Lauries' vicious-dog report.

Brenda Maher's run-down cottage sat dispiritedly on its weedy lot under the sun. The VW van was gone, and no one answered his knock, so he walked around to the backyard to find Jacob's girlfriend, Alice McNamara, sitting at a garden table. Her head bent over a book of Sudoku puzzles, she was mouthing numbers, her pen darting in and out.

'Looks like you're good at that,' Hirsch said. 'I'm hopeless.'

She looked up at him, then down again, almost expressionless. It was as if he'd admitted he was unable to walk and talk at the same time.

'Alice, we've had a report of your dog running out into the road.'

She said nothing; merely aimed her pen at the kennel, where the dog watched him, its head on its front paws.

'Is Jacob here?' Hirsch asked. 'Or Brenda?'

'They're out. Don't know when they'll be back.'

'Your sister? At school, I guess.'

'Zoe?' Alice seemed astounded at his ignorance. 'She lives with Gran now, in Port Lincoln.'

'Look, about the dog: please keep it on the leash.'

'It's always on the leash. We're strict about that. It's never out.'

'Well, if you could pass on my concerns.'

'I'll be sure to do that,' she said, turning to a new puzzle, hard intelligence in her.

Hirsch was barely back at the police station when Sergeant Brandl called. She wanted him in Redruth. Pronto.

'I need Tim and Jean to man the fort, and I need you to keep me from doing my block.'

'I spend more time on your beat than my own,' Hirsch said.

'Very funny. If you can get yourself down here in the

165

next little while, that would be great.' The line went dead.

Apparently she'd gone home for lunch after addressing the high school kids on cyberbullying to find *dyke cop* spraypainted on the wall beside her front door. On a hunch, she'd driven to Jean Landy's rental house: the same slogan. Next, Tim Medlin's flat behind the Dugout, a bistro overlooking Redruth Creek, to find that a *poofter cop* lived there.

The same instinctive niggle then took her to the Wurlie. The building was untouched, but *Boong Mobile* and *Abo Auto* had been sprayed onto the cultural centre's old Renault van, parked in a corner of the backyard.

Petra Osmak, out for revenge?

Petra lived out on the road to Morgan, at the north-western edge of town, where the pretty stone houses of Redruth gave way to tin and fibro shacks on patches of undernourished soil. Old cars, starved gardens, hollow-ribbed horses and cats. Petra's house—dusty windows and fibro walls; dead grass in the rusted gutters; a sparkling satellite dish—creaked and cracked in the sun when Hirsch and Brandl hooked their masks on and mounted the veranda.

Brandl rapped her knuckles against the front door. Petra answered, underwhelmed to see them on her doorstep. 'What now?'

'May we come in, Petra?'

'No.'

'It might be more comfortable.'

With a show of dismal obstinacy, Petra said, 'Don't want to be comfortable. Don't want you getting comfortable.'

'Very well,' Brandl said. She was staring at Osmak's hands and clothing. 'I need to know your movements this morning.'

'Why?'

'If you could just answer the question, please, Petra,' Hirsch said, seeing the tic in the sergeant's jawline.

'I got up, went to an appointment, came home again, end of story.'

'What appointment was that?'

'Doctor.'

'Doctor Pillai?' said Brandl. 'She can confirm that?'

Osmak was scornful. 'A proper doctor. Over in Clare.'

'What time was that?'

'Nine o'clock. I left here about quarter past eight.'

'You drove there?'

Petra indicated a sun-faded Fiesta in the driveway. 'It needed a service so I thought, kill two birds with one stone.'

'You don't use Redruth Motors?'

'They rip you off.'

'And what time did you get home?'

'Just now. Ten minutes ago. The car was supposed to be ready but they had to get a part in so I had to sit around in Clare for nearly three hours.'

Hirsch stepped off the veranda and placed a palm on the Fiesta's bonnet. Hot. Engine heat with an overlay of sun heat, he thought.

Petra smirked as he rejoined them. 'Satisfied?'

'What did you do in Clare? Walk around the shops?'

'A bit. Mainly I just sat in the library.'

The service and the doctor's appointment can be readily confirmed, thought Hirsch. And the librarians would remember the studs and tatts.

'Thank you, Petra,' Brandl said, turning to go.

'That's the way it's going to be?' Petra said, her voice curdling. 'I get hassled every time someone does something?'

Laboured footsteps sounded behind her. A greying, heavyset man appeared, walking with the aid of a cane. His features flattened to see cops standing there. 'All right, love?'

'Just police harassment, Grampa,' Petra said.

Hirsch could see that with an audience there, she might work herself up into a state of cataclysmic emotion. To forestall that, he said, 'We'll be on our way, Petra. We're satisfied you had nothing to do with the matter we're investigating.'

'Yeah? We're not stupid. We know you're not finished with her,' the grandfather said. 'It was just thoughtless, that video. She's not a bad person.'

Hirsch and Brandl were backing off the veranda, nodding goodbye. 'It's still being decided,' Brandl said. 'Out of our hands, unfortunately.'

'Yeah? Piss weak.'

The man and his granddaughter shut the door on them. Brandl sighed. 'You ever get sick of the aggro?'

'Every day.'

She unlocked the car. 'Meanwhile I can't get anyone to come out and clean the graffiti until the end of next week. You wouldn't be interested in volunteering your scrubbing arm on the weekend? Sunday? I'm on duty at the football tomorrow.'

Hirsch had made a vague promise to attend Wendy's fortnightly Celtic music jam session on Sunday. He quite enjoyed these sessions if he could lurk unnoticed in the back corner. If anyone noticed him, he was dragged out to sing. 'Sure.'

'Go on home,' his sergeant said now. 'Think who else might have taken up spray-painting lately.'

And so Hirsch returned to Tiverton, his mind working. Dinner at the Muirs' was a relief. A release. Even the lentils weren't bad.

17

SATURDAY.

Hirsch's Law stated that rain never started falling before or after your morning walk. It waited for you to reach the mid-point, minus coat or umbrella. Then it would bucket down. He was twenty minutes from the police station this time, out where the suitcase stiff had been found. Why he'd gone that way he didn't know. Morbid curiosity? He was as susceptible to that as anyone.

No trees; the nearest were around the oval, three hundred metres away, and he ran it, starting with a self-conscious lope. The rain, unimpressed, rode him harder, thrashing him into a punishing sprint back past the culvert, over the deceptive rise and in where fallen twigs and branches thrashed his shins. His feet squelched; his shirt and shorts were pasted to his quivering skin. Rain beat against the leaves above his head, roared in his ears as he sheltered beneath a stand of pines near the goalposts. Then, just as he fished his phone from his sodden back pocket, hoping no moisture had got in, it buzzed in his fingers.

The number came up as belonging to Hedley Bastian, who didn't bother with preliminaries. 'Vikki didn't come home last night.'

Already Hirsch was moving. The effort punctuated his voice and he shouted to be heard. 'She didn't come home after work, or she came home and went out again?'

'I'm assuming she came home and went out again. She called me at five to say she was just leaving work— we've both been super-vigilant after that business with her boyfriend—but I was down in Adelaide and didn't get home until around ten o'clock. Her car wasn't here, but I didn't think anything of it because she said she was having a night out with netball friends. I mean, she's allowed to have a life. Anyway, I went to bed and when I got up just now, I could see she hadn't been home and her car's not here.'

Hirsch, bursting free of the streaming trees, splashed through the gravelly puddles of the clubhouse car park. 'I'll check the school, just in case. Maybe you could call her netball mates.'

'Yeah, well, I don't really know who they are.'

Father and daughter had both been marooned when Mrs Bastian died, thought Hirsch. Did Vikki know more about her father's life than he about hers? Maybe they rode parallel tracks, with the occasional glancing collision at Christmas and birthdays. Like Russ and Noah Fanning.

'Check her desk, wastepaper basket, bedside cupboard,' panted Hirsch. 'There might be a netball roster, a newsletter, anything at all.'

'Will do,' Bastian said, and Hirsch found himself alone in the rain again. Reaching the main road, he turned left, racing along, a madman abroad. The first passing-through motorist of the day grinned ironically as he dashed across the road, then down the side street opposite the police station and into the grounds of the primary school. Around to the rear car park, and there was Vikki Bastian's yellow Beetle, mottled with rain-streaked dust.

In the Redruth hospital ninety minutes later, she was telling Hirsch that her father had drilled into her the importance of checking the VW's rear seats before she got behind the wheel. 'I forgot,' she said. 'Sorry, Dad.'

Hedley Bastian, in a chair on the other side of her bed, gave his daughter's forearm a supportive squeeze. Mostly, though, he was fixed on Hirsch, his jaw tense. *If you'd only done your job*, he seemed to say. *What did you think Greig would do?*

Hirsch returned the glare: he'd been browbeaten by

172

experts. Turning again to Vikki, he asked his next question. 'You're sure he didn't say anything?'

'Not a word. The knife was enough.'

Vikki Bastian had spent the night upright in the driver's seat, unable to shout for help, strapped to the headrest by gaffer tape. Couldn't kick or squirm: more tape around her middle, her ankles strapped to the seat-adjustment lever under the seat. She looked hollowed-out, shadows under her eyes, her lower face and neck patched red by the tape.

'Just one person?'

'Yes.'

'Any distinguishing features? Smell, clothing, height, skin colour...'

Hedley Bastian thrust in. 'We all know what the prick looks like.'

'Mr Bastian...'

'What do you expect her to tell you?' Bastian demanded. 'Something was pulled over her head.'

A ski mask, sent away for forensic testing. Hirsch persisted. 'Anything you heard or smelt or felt or saw or tasted in the first few seconds. Forearm tattoo, aftershave, bitten-down fingernails. Food or drink smells.'

'He was wearing kitchen gloves.'

Hirsch made a mental note to check bins at the school and in the town. 'What colour?'

'Yellow.'

'What kind of knife?'

She tipped her head back unconsciously. A pinprick of

blood under her jaw. 'I didn't see it, I just felt it.'

'Yours was the only car left?'

'Everyone else had gone home.'

'How about out in the street? A car you didn't recognise?'

'I wasn't looking.'

'What kind of car does Mr Greig drive?'

'A Subaru hatch,' Hedley Bastian said. 'Silver.'

'Didn't see one,' his daughter said.

'The school has a couple of CCTV cameras,' Hirsch said.

'They only cover the playground. There's another inside—the main corridor.'

'I didn't see any damage to your car. How do you think he got into the back? Did you give the spare key to anyone? Mr Greig, for example?'

Vikki shook her head. 'Dad's got the spare.' She shifted uncomfortably. 'I don't always lock it at school.'

'Sweetheart,' her father said.

She retorted: 'You never lock yours at home.'

'That's at home. I always lock it when I drive somewhere.'

'School's like being at home. It's just kids.'

'Except that someone—and we all know who—climbed into the back this time and waited for you.'

'How was I supposed to *know*?'

Back and forth, an old pattern of father-daughter quibbling. Again Hirsch was reminded of Russ Fanning and his son. Two baffled widowers, trying to get it right. 'Did Mr

Greig know of your habit of not locking the car when you were at work?'

Vikki shrank further. 'I don't know. I didn't tell him; it never came up. We only went out for a few weeks.'

Hedley Bastian's face wanted to know why she'd ever gone out with him in the first place. Hirsch said, to shift the mood: 'We'll get your car back to you as soon as it's been examined, although that could be a little while.'

She shook her head violently. 'I loved that car but no way am I ever getting in it again.'

Her father stroked the back of her hand. 'Bad memories. But with time you'll—'

Shuddering, she said, 'Dad, I wet myself in it, all right? Twelve hours? I wet myself.'

Jean Landy met Hirsch in the hospital foyer, a little energised by her uphill walk from the police station. Adjusting her mask, she said, 'Sorry I'm late. It's Tim's day off and the sergeant's on duty at the football.'

'That's fine. I'll fill you in.'

He did that on the short drive to Scott Greig's apartment. Leaving the Hilux in steamy shade, blinking against light-fracturing raindrops on the shrubbery around the car park, he said, 'There's no proof it was him, but he did try to call her at her father's house, sounding pretty aggressive. We need to see what he has to say for himself.'

'A two-person job, gotcha,' Landy said, thrusting her chin as she strode beside him.

'Just a chat, Jean.'

'A chat that could kick off,' she said, undeterred.

Hirsch saw the eagerness in her. He'd once liked her without reservation, but he'd come to suspect that she was a purely adaptive person. Right now, Greig was a bad guy and she'd squash him if the situation warranted it. A few days ago, she'd have happily kept Stephanie Ingram in the dark about Petra Osmak's video.

'You helping clean up the graffiti tomorrow?' he asked her.

She shrugged blithely. 'I suppose. Already done mine.'

The world was a practical place to Jean Landy. Hirsch followed her along the path to Greig's door. She knocked. They waited.

The door was jerked inwards, Greig filling the space. 'What now?'

'May we come in, Mr Greig?'

'Legal Aid said not to talk to you without representation.'

'It's not about your case, Scott,' Landy said, 'it's about another matter. Just a quick word.'

'Yeah, I'm not stupid. You're not going to leave me alone, are you?' Greig said, turning away from them, leading the way.

Hirsch couldn't quite read him. He was unshaven and dressed in jeans, a crumpled white linen shirt and black pointy-toed lace-up shoes, looking as if he'd spent the night elsewhere. This was confirmed when they entered his sitting room, where the air was stale, the curtain drawn and an overnight bag rested on the Ikea sofa next to a green Woolworth's shopping bag. Mostly Hirsch was interested in the small foil-wrapped packages, two on the sofa and a third in the shopping bag, nestled in freezer blocks.

Jean Landy said, 'Sir, what's in these little parcels?'

'What? Nothing.'

'Sir, I have reason to believe—'

'Oh for fuck's sake,' Greig said, looking wrung out, 'it's leftovers.' He pointed. 'Birthday cake. Sliced ham. That one's meat loaf. My nana,' he said helplessly.

Hirsch touched Landy's sleeve. 'Mr Greig, a couple of quick questions and we'll be out of your hair. Where were you last night?'

Greig frowned as if Hirsch were stupid. 'Just told you, my grandma's. Her birthday.' He paused. 'I lived with her when I was a kid.'

'And where does she live?'

'Glenelg.'

An Adelaide beachside suburb, and to get there and back, Greig would have taken the Northern Expressway and then South Road and possibly Anzac Highway. Cameras all along the way.

'What time did you get there?'

Greig shrugged his heavy shoulders. 'I dunno. Five? Five-thirty? Six at the latest.'

Meaning he'd have left Redruth about three hours earlier and couldn't have attacked Vikki Bastian, who had climbed into her car at about five-thirty.

'You stayed the night?'

'I wasn't drunk or anything. Just, you know, Nana wanted me to stay and it's a long way.' He gestured, appealing to the world. 'I only just got home and I'm knackered and I need to put all this stuff in the fridge. Whatever it was you're here for, I didn't do it.'

On their way out, Hirsch said, 'Incidentally, I heard that you've been trying to contact Vikki Bastian. You risk a court appearance if you persist in that.'

'Is that why you're here? Something happened to her?'

Hirsch tried to read behind Greig's tired openness. 'No more calls to Ms Bastian, Mr Greig.'

18

THERE WAS A regular pattern to Saturday evenings in the kitchen of the house on Bitter Wash Road. Unless they were dining out, or at Hirsch's place, Hirsch would select the music and set the table, then sit on his usual stool while Wendy deftly flicked between fridge, simmering frypan, sink and cutting board on the business side of the bench. Hirsch's role was definitely conversation, not cooking. If he ventured in to 'help' he found himself gently banished; if he temporarily zoned out, it was the cue for Wendy to prompt: 'This is where you say something in return.'

What he said now was, 'How did the cyberbullying lecture go?'

Wendy paused to look at him. 'Didn't you ask Hilary?'

'I asked. She said, "It went".'

'Close-lipped,' Wendy said. 'Well, she did a great job.'

The kitchen air was fragrant; Hirsch's stomach growled. 'Covering what?'

'Scope and variety—you could tell that some of the kids didn't think being bitchy in a text message was a form of bullying. Possible harm; legal penalties. How to keep yourself safe online.'

Placing the spoon end of the ladle on a side plate, Wendy added: 'I stood at the front of the hall near the stage so I could see the kids' faces. Hilary didn't sugar-coat, and most of them seemed pretty stunned at first. Like they were reassessing things they'd been involved with themselves, that they hadn't even seen as wrong, far less criminal. Or something people could kill themselves over.'

Hirsch had forgotten the placemats. He crossed to the old hardwood dresser against the far wall, selected three and set them on the table, took his seat again.

'Then when Hilary left, the principal had us in small groups,' Wendy continued, test-tasting a sauce ladle with fierce concentration. She added more salt. 'That's what really counted, I think. The lecture was great, don't get me wrong—hard-hitting—but kids switch off after a while. Harder to do that if you're in a small-group situation.'

'How did you think it went?'

Wendy placed a lid on the frypan. 'My group was a bit of a non-starter. The kids didn't have much to add in terms of insights or experiences. But I heard in the staffroom later there were a few tears and a bit of shouting in the other groups.'

Hirsch looked over his shoulder. They were alone, the hallway was empty. 'Kate took part, right?'

'It would have looked odd if she hadn't. I don't know what went on in her group, but there's a Year 9 girl—it's always Year 9—who I think might be one of the little bitches who's been trolling her? She gave me a dirty look in the corridor later on. When I asked Kate what her group talked about, she just said, "Stuff."'

No more forthcoming than Sergeant Brandl. 'It'll take a while,' Hirsch said.

'I know. But she used to tell me everything.'

Hirsch thought. Kate's reserve didn't necessarily relate to the bullying. She might simply be going through an adolescent phase of secrecy, clutching seemingly powerful hopes and fears to herself. 'Did the kids give her a hard time afterwards?'

'I wish I knew.'

Again Hirsch checked the corridor behind him. 'Is she on her laptop?'

'Paul, I have no idea,' Wendy said, swiping at a lank tendril of hair with the back of her wrist. 'I'm not going to go barging in on her. I'm not going to monitor her all the time. Now that she's told us about the bullying and appreciates the wider context, I have to trust that she'll do the right thing.'

'Trust that she'll keep you informed, in other words.'

'Correct.'

Hirsch knew all about shoulder bumps in crowded corridors, tripping feet, smeared dogshit. In his experience, there were consequences if you dobbed someone in. His old CIB colleagues in the city, even some more recent colleagues here in the bush, had given him the death-stares-and-muttered-threats treatment. A bullet in his letterbox. Attempts to compromise him. That kind of thing could consume you. You could almost come to believe you deserved it.

'It's not going to get better overnight,' Wendy said.

Hirsch knew that. And he thought there was nothing sadder than an anxious child.

On Sunday morning he walked around a nearby empty paddock, then read, lingered over coffee and toast and waited for the others to stagger into the sunlight. They were notorious for sleeping the Sunday hours away, and he for waking before 6 a.m. 'Let's never live together,' Wendy liked to say. 'It's our weekend romancing that keeps this thing going.'

'This thing.'

'This whatchamacallit.'

Kate appeared first, in faded yellow tracksuit pants and a plain white T-shirt. Yawning, tousled, she was so hopelessly young-looking that Hirsch flinched from the thought of anyone harming her. 'Pancakes and juice?'

She grunted. The grunts would become syllables, then words, over time. Sentence fragments if he was lucky.

'I'll take that as a yes.'

She wandered out to their usual spot, a sun-drenched corner of the veranda. Hirsch busied himself with milk, flour, butter and eggs as she closed her eyes and tilted her face to the morning sun.

He joined her on the veranda. Touched his juice glass to hers. 'Cheers.'

'Please don't ask me about yesterday.'

'I wasn't going to.' He had been going to do exactly that.

'Everything's all right, now.'

'Okay.'

After a few awkward centuries she blinked, drained her glass and bolted down a pancake drenched in maple syrup. He could see her building herself up again. 'Are you coming to Caldream today?' she said.

Caledonian Dreaming—the Celtic music gig at the Woolpack pub in Redruth. Kate shared with Hirsch a faint, affectionate horror for these Sunday afternoons.

'You're on your own today, sorry. I'll drive you both down there but then I have to help clean graffiti.'

'What graffiti?'

He told her.

'Do you know who did it?'

Hirsch was developing a theory. 'Not yet.'

Kate looked away, troubled. 'There's something going on, a feeling I have. Not just here, everywhere. The world.'

'Okay…'

'Everyone's kind of jittery.'

That was a good word for it. Covid jitters. Moral panic; other kinds of panic. 'Thank God for Celtic music, then,' he said.

Kate gave him a sour look. 'I kind of like it now.'

So did Hirsch. 'Really?'

'You,' she said, pointing, 'go with us because it's important to Mum.'

She likes that, Hirsch thought. 'So long as I'm not expected to sing.'

'You've got a good voice.'

'Nah.' He didn't. A better voice than most of the other men, maybe. Everyone looking at him, that was the problem. And his fear of the odd high note morphing into a squeak.

'You're cleaning graffiti to get out of singing.'

'*Moi?*' He pantomimed outrage, and was rewarded with a tiny grin.

Hirsch dropped Wendy and Kate at the Woolpack, then drove to the sergeant's house. She was there with Medlin and Landy, sleeves rolled. Buckets of cleaning fluid, dripping brushes, splashed gumboots. 'Put your backs into it,' he said.

Sergeant Brandl flicked water at him. 'We've got it under control. Why don't you go and help Auntie Steph?'

Hirsch was expecting to see a working bee at the Wurlie, maybe Uncle Doug and a few kids at work cleaning the slogans off the old Renault van, but the place seemed deserted when he arrived. Just the van, sitting fair and square at the kerb, with stencils of the Aboriginal flag pasted next to the crudely spray-painted *Boong Mobile* and *Abo Auto*.

Okay, he thought. He climbed out, locked up and approached the front door, which was held partly ajar by a green plastic garden chair with a split in the seat. He could hear singing now, a ragged harmony, as he passed the front desk. Along the corridor he came to a large room at the rear of the building and poked his head in.

A dozen grey-haired men and women in a semi-circle, wearing jeans, flannel shirts and fleeces, some comfortably middle-aged, others gnarled by a lifetime of manual work. Uncle Doug was banging at a wonky piano to one side, and Auntie Steph was leading the group in the old Kenny Rogers song, 'Ruby, Don't Take Your Love to Town'. Spotting Hirsch, she waved at a cluster of chairs along the back wall.

Half an hour of country, folk and gospel classics passed, uneven voices singing of broken hearts and faithless lovers until, at 3 p.m., Steph announced a break. The choir wandered to an urn and biscuits on a rickety table at the far end and she joined Hirsch. Her features were drawn but her eyes blazed, as if the singing replenished what the job took away.

'This the over-sixties choir?'

She nodded. 'Getting ready for the Redruth Show.'

'They sound good.'

She saw through that. 'We have quite a way to go before we're ready, Senior Constable Hirschhausen.'

Suitably rebuked, Hirsch said, 'The boss suggested I help clean the van, but I can see that you have other plans for it.'

She gestured; there was irritation in her now. 'Naturally I'm not going to leave it like that. Do you think we like being called those names?'

'No.'

'Do you think we don't experience something like it every day? The gutless wonder who did it probably thought we'd hide in a corner while we repainted the van or something. Well, that's not going to happen. We're driving that heap of shit around until everyone in the district has seen it and maybe even starts thinking and talking. Then we'll clean it. And yeah, you can help.'

'Be glad to.'

She punched him lightly on the upper arm and stood to go, saying, 'I'll let you know when.'

Feeling obscurely that he'd been left far behind, Hirsch stayed listening for another thirty minutes, most of it taken up with a rehearsal of 'Sinnerman', complete with the hand-clapping, in which he took part. Then at 4 p.m. he left to collect Wendy and Kate from the Woolpack.

They were running late, so he sat in his usual spot behind a column in the back corner of the upstairs meeting room, listening to music sparse and simple and hoping he wouldn't be called to test his 'quite passable tenor' on 'Bonnie Was Yon Rosie Briar'.

19

THE MONDAY BRIEFING, and as Hirsch entered the outskirts of Redruth at 7.50, he spotted the Wurlie's van on the back of a breakdown truck. So much for Steph's defiant tour. U-turning, he followed it to Redruth Motors, where he parked against the kerb and walked across to the workshop as the driver hopped down from the cab. Uncle Doug.

Greeting him, Hirsch said, 'Problem?'

Doug regarded him calmly, pulling on heavy-duty gloves. 'Sugar in the tank.'

'Double whammy,' Hirsch said.

Doug was expressionless, as if he'd seen years of luke-warm police responses. Then, apparently satisfied that Hirsch was interested, he turned, yanked open the driver's door and leaned in, emerging with a pair of yellow kitchen gloves.

'Had a hunt around. Found these in the bin outside the bank.'

The old ES&A bank a few doors down from the hall, Hirsch thought. Now an antique shop. But mainly he was thinking of another pair of yellow gloves, found near where Vikki Bastian had been attacked in her car. 'I need to fetch an evidence bag,' he said, trotting back to the Hilux.

The gloves formed part of his briefing report a few minutes later.

'Send them in for testing,' Sergeant Brandl said. 'Are we thinking that one person was responsible for the graffiti and the attack on Ms Bastian?'

She swivelled in her chair to study the photo array on the wall behind her. Head shots of Petra Osmak and Scott Greig. Vikki Bastian's chafed and bruised face and wrists. The ski mask found at the school. The Renault van. 'Presumably a friend of these two,' she said, pointing at the mugshots.

'Maybe if we had their phone records...' Tim Medlin said.

The sergeant shook her head. 'Could be days before we know what's on their various devices or who they've been calling. We need to find out who else they went to school with.'

'Or,' Jean Landy said, 'Petra tied Vikki up and Greig did the graffiti. They trade revenges.'

'*Strangers on a Train*,' Brandl muttered, throwing down her pen.

'Pardon?'

But Hirsch knew: he'd come to the same conclusion but was self-conscious about announcing it, and listened as the sergeant explained. A Hitchcock film about two strangers meeting on a train and trading murders, giving each other perfect alibis.

'Bit far-fetched,' Brandl said. 'But you never know.'

'Scott Greig's a film buff,' Hirsch said. 'And he strikes me as the…the strategist, I suppose. He maybe even suggested the gloves.'

'Or,' cautioned Brandl, 'only one person is responsible. A friend. A relative.' She shrugged. 'Or something else is going on.'

Something in the air, thought Hirsch, musing on the supermarket stormtroopers, Bob Muir's apprentice, the 5G tower, the harassment of Kate and Wendy. Unrelated, but touched off like spot fires by whatever was floating in the atmosphere.

They split up, Brandl and Hirsch to question Petra Osmak, Landy and Medlin to question Scott Greig.

Petra's grandfather answered the knock on the door.

'She's still in bed.'

'Please wake her, Mr Osmak. We would like to interview her further.'

'Is she under arrest?'

'We merely have a few more questions for her.'

That was received stonily, and it occurred to Hirsch that Petra and Scott had another factor in common apart from the videos and high school: both had been raised by a grandparent.

He showed them into the kitchen. 'I'll just go and get her.'

A couple of minutes passed; they could hear murmured voices. Then the sergeant's phone chirped and Hirsch watched her take the call. She listened, looked disgusted, said, 'Ask around,' and put the phone down. 'Greig might've done a runner. A neighbour saw him drive off with a carload of boxes and luggage.'

Be good to have checked for fibres on his watchstrap, Hirsch thought, shaking his head. Paint on the soles of his shoes. The footwell and floormat of his car. Maybe the gloves will give us something.

Before he could say any of this, Petra trailed her grandfather into the kitchen. Her feet were bare, with chipped red toenails, and she wore a washed-out grey shift that Hirsch guessed doubled as a nightie. Her eyes were puffy, her hair kinked by her pillow into tufts and angles. 'What questions? I told you everything. I was in Clare Friday morning. Did you even check? Do your job.'

Sometimes hostility was just hostility. At other times it was a symptom of guilt. 'We're happy to wait if you want to get dressed first,' Hirsch said.

She said, 'No,' and plonked herself at the kitchen table.

'Petra,' her grandfather said waveringly. He propped his cane against the wall, sat opposite her and reached a hand across the table.

She took it in hers. Close to tears, she said, 'They can talk to me here. I got nothing to hide.'

Hirsch had been lingering by the fridge. He hadn't necessarily solved any crimes by examining the items people stuck to their fridges or noticeboards, but he sometimes learned enough to make connections between disparate pieces of information. 'I see you're friends with Cody Morton.'

Curling under an Adelaide Crows insignia magnet was a photograph of Cody, Petra and Petra's grandfather in a beer garden. Pint glasses, cards and wrapping paper on the table. 'A friend from school?'

'My cousin,' Petra said, scowling.

'And therefore another of my grandkids,' her grandfather said apologetically.

'He was an electrician's apprentice last time I saw him,' Hirsch said offhandedly.

Petra looked for the trap, her head tipped to one side consideringly. Her sleep fog was dissipating rapidly. 'It didn't work out.'

'He still in the area?'

'Why? You think he done the graffiti?'

'Just wondered, that's all.'

'Yeah, sure.'

'He's away,' the grandfather said hastily. 'Doing some handyman work out on one of the sheep stations.'

'Maybe I'll run into him again.'

They didn't bite. Sergeant Brandl, also still standing, and looking on with interest, clapped her hands together. 'Right, Petra, I strongly suggest you consider getting dressed. Don't worry about breakfast, we can fill you up on coffee and croissants at the station.'

'Grandpa,' Petra wailed.

He looked up at the sergeant. 'If she's not under arrest, if you're not charging her, why can't you ask your questions here?'

Hirsch saw Brandl wrestle with that. She hated on-site interviews. 'In that case, I must ask you to leave the room, please, sir.'

'Is that necessary?'

'If you stay, you become a witness and may be called to give evidence in the event of a trial.'

Muttering, shaking his head, the old man left the room. Petra, watching him go, turned on Brandl. 'What do you mean, a trial?' she hissed. 'I know about the graffiti. Like I told you, I was in Clare most of Friday. I couldn't've done it.'

'But you were not in Clare at around five o'clock that afternoon. Where were you at five o'clock, Petra?'

She hunched minutely. 'Shopping, probably. I do most of the cooking.'

Hirsch meanwhile was propped against the sink, almost lovingly running a pair of yellow kitchen gloves through his left palm. 'These look brand new,' he said. 'Versatile, too. Do you buy them by the packet, Petra? Share them around?'

She went white. Got to her feet and said, 'Not here. Let me get dressed and I'll come with you.'

That was a mistake. Kicking herself later, Brandl said, 'It's because she looked so pathetic. Still in her nightie, hair all over the place.'

'Fooled me, too, sergeant,' Hirsch said stoutly.

They'd let a couple of minutes pass, Brandl drumming her fingers on the kitchen table, Hirsch ranging around the kitchen restlessly, examining other photos, wall-calendar notes and the bills and receipts in a cane basket on the dresser. Then, in a perfect meeting of uneasy minds, he had turned to Sergeant Brandl and she to him, and they'd each said, '*Fuck,*' and dashed into the corridor leading to the rooms at the back of the house. A sitting room, where Petra's grandfather was bent over a jigsaw puzzle, a spare bedroom, two main bedrooms, one an old man's, the other with a window wide open, drawers ajar and the horrible nightie on the floor.

They had split up then, Hirsch on foot, the sergeant in the patrol car, and had spent a fruitless half hour searching the nearby streets, the main road and Scott Greig's flat. Reconvening at Petra's house again, Brandl said, 'Not a good look.'

'She can't have gone far.'

'Yeah, yeah,' Brandl said, disgusted. 'Let's see what the grandfather has to say for himself.'

In the kitchen a minute later, the old man seemed bewildered. 'Petra did?'

Brandl had already explained that he was merely helping with the police inquiry, but reinforced it by adding, 'You may have a lawyer present.'

'Am I in trouble?'

'Petra is, Mr Osmak.'

'I don't know how I can help you.'

'Do you know her friends?'

'She doesn't really have many. What kind of trouble?'

'What do you know about a young man named Scott Greig?'

The old man looked lost. 'She's friends with him. They were at school together.'

'He seems to have left the area. Do you know where he went? Would Petra go to be with him?'

'I don't know.'

'How about Cody, your grandson? Would she go to him?'

He made an expansive gesture. 'How? Her car's still here.'

'But she knows where he's working? Which sheep station?'

'I suppose so.'

'Do you generally keep tabs on her movements?'

'She's a young woman. I can't tell her what to do.'

'All right. But you sometimes know where she is and what she's doing?'

'Sometimes.'

'How about five o'clock last Friday?'

'I don't remember.'

'Did she go off somewhere in her car?'

'Where?'

Hirsch had been sitting back, watching, listening, trying to read the old man, who still seemed bewildered. But when the sergeant glanced at him he stepped in. 'Is Petra capable of attacking someone?'

'Petra?'

Hirsch didn't want to reveal Vikki Bastian's name or the nature or location of the attack. 'Yes. Especially if she thought this person had harmed her or someone close to her in some way?'

'You're barking up the wrong tree.'

'How well do you know Scott Greig?'

The old man shrugged. 'A bit.'

'Is he the kind to have a hold over your granddaughter?'

'A hold?'

'Is he the kind to make her do things she might otherwise not want to do?'

He could see old man Osmak's eyes darting. Reassessing Greig, he thought.

'I've never really liked him.'

It would have to do. 'So you don't know where she went last Friday, late afternoon?'

'I don't remember.'

Sergeant Brandl indicated the sink. 'Did you buy those gloves, Mr Osmak?'

He grimaced as if acknowledging that he lacked housekeeping skills. 'Petra. I never remember those sorts of things, only milk and bread, things like that.'

'Did the gloves come in a packet of several?'

He gestured helplessly. 'I don't know.'

Hirsch, watching for a flicker in the eyes, said, 'Did you know we can sometimes obtain fingerprints from the inside of a pair of gloves?'

That only served to fluster the old man. 'My prints? Why?'

'What can you tell me about the friendship between Petra and Mr Greig? Did they speak on the phone, send each other messages? Hang out together in her room?'

'They're not boyfriend and girlfriend.'

'What are they, then?'

'They were friends in school and stayed friends. Everyone else left the district, basically, but they stayed and lucked into good jobs.'

'They stayed friends,' Brandl repeated. 'But was Mr Greig a good friend? Or did he boss Petra around? Would she do something illegal just to please him?'

'Like what? It's not fair, you're trying to get me to say something and I don't know what you're on about.'

'How about Mr Greig and Cody, your grandson? Are they friends?'

'I don't know. Not really.'

'But they know each other?'

'Yes.'

'Who's got the stronger personality: Cody or Mr Greig?'

'Is that where you're going with this? If you want me to say Scott's some kind of ringleader, then yes, he is.'

That didn't mean much. The old man was genuinely bewildered. They left, made another sweep of the town. And Greig's flat, just in case.

As they pulled up outside the police station, Sergeant Brandl said, 'Just a reminder, Paul. The team from Internal Investigations is interviewing you tomorrow at noon. Me at nine, Tim at ten, Jean at eleven.'

'Joy.'

'Nothing joyous about it,' Brandl muttered.

20

TUESDAY, DAYBREAK, AND Hirsch, in the jitters about his Internal Investigation interview, found himself counting and punctuating as he stamped around the town: *fuck two three four, shit two three four, shit fuck bugger damn two three four.*

'Are you all right, dear?'

Mrs Lidstrom at 9 Canowie Street, fitting a hose to her front-garden tap. Round, comfortable, white-haired and sharp, she had achieved a kind of commiserative celebrity when it was revealed that several pairs of her 'old woman's bloomers' had been stolen from her clothesline by the former primary school principal.

'Fine thanks, Mrs Lidstrom.'

She eyed him. 'When I was a girl we marched into school chanting, "Left, left, left right left." Correct me if I'm wrong, but did I hear your own personal take on that?'

'You got me,' Hirsch said.

'Rough day yesterday?'

'Rough day coming up.'

'Pull a long face and carry on, as my sainted father used to say.'

Probably good advice, Hirsch thought; he carried on. On past the pub, then down a side street, to check on the lucerne seed business's gates, and finally back along the highway to the police station.

He tried to plan his day. Almost 7 a.m. now, and the interview with the Internals was at noon. He could twiddle his thumbs, or run a short patrol of properties in and around the Tiverton Hills east of the town. A long, low line of blue-grey hills that always seemed to lie in the distance, even when you reached them—because there was always another line of hills beyond them, sombre and mostly treeless. There were old deaths out there, too, unmarked and unremarked. A squabble over a prospecting lease, a woman, the dregs in a bottle of beer or nothing much at all. A shepherd speared for his sheep, or his rapes. A massacre masquerading as an arrest-party skirmish. And, tucked away along the dry creeks and in the clefts and

200

caves, ancient rock carvings and stick-figure narratives.

He'd set out at 7.30, he thought. Patrol for three and a half hours—leave himself time for the drive to Redruth. But at 7.30, just as he locked the front door, his mobile rang. Something about a mad dog.

'Brenda?' Hirsch said. All he heard on the line was scratchy static. Then the noise resolved as ragged panting. Effort. Hysteria. 'Call…ambulance.'

'You did call, or want me to call?'

'Call…ambulance,' she said and the line dropped out.

Calling triple zero and learning that the Redruth ambulance was about to reach the hospital after attending at a tractor roll-over, Hirsch floored it through the town, past the silos and then right, over the railway line to Brenda Maher's cottage.

There was no answer when he knocked, and the grey van was gone. Maybe she'd already left in it.

A growl, a shriek, a thump sounded from the rear of the house. He ran down the side path to the backyard. Little had changed, and everything had changed. The same listing caravan, dying shrubs, dead grass, toys and blanket, dog kennel, sunlounge. No sign of Jacob, Alice or David Hillcock. Only Brenda, sprawled mewling amid the weeds, and the dog on the blanket, gnawing the baby.

It was clearly dead. Anchored by one bloodied paw, it jerked mechanically as the dog tore at it, a growl in its throat. The dog's back was to Hirsch. He loosened the strap on his holster, wrapped his hand around the Glock, took one step and then another just as Brenda moved, rolling onto her stomach and crawling out of the weeds onto the blanket. She swatted at the dog with a useless shredded hand. Her face, forearms, calves and feet were torn open. Little of her was not bleeding.

Now, as Hirsch ran in, she swivelled onto her buttocks and kicked the dog. It snarled, released the baby's forearm and sprang at her. She kicked again and, for a millisecond, the dog was separate, off-balance.

Hirsch stood over it and fired almost straight down, one shot between the thick shoulders. The dog coughed, turned, tried to bite at the wound. Hirsch fired again, into the top of the solid head. The dog didn't flop. It seemed almost to gather itself before, finally, it crumpled.

Brenda, intent on the baby, crawled across the red blanket past the dog's corpse.

Hirsch looked down on the hideous mess at his feet. His breath echoed in his skull over Brenda's small, incoherent noises.

'Brenda?' He tried to collect himself. 'Brenda, where are the others?'

No response.

He peered into the caravan. A fast sweep told him that Alice and Jacob slept there. One of them was a reader. Must be Alice, given the anthology of women poets resting, with an Oxford dictionary and a Jonathan Franzen novel, on the floor beside the bed. Art history, too. That was a surprise—

Fuck's sake get a grip. He jolted back into the moment.

Brenda. And there could be others injured here. He forced himself into action and raced across to the cottage.

Passing blood droplets and smears where Brenda had dragged herself to the kitchen landline phone, he found himself among the mixed odours of sweat, dirty nappies, cheap perfume and old cigarette and weed smoke. A confusion of totemic images in the sitting room: a Confederate flag, a Nazi dagger and a poster of a Sioux warrior in full headdress. Otherwise, a big TV in one corner and a high-end Mac computer with a printer on a card table in another. The card table he'd chucked out for the hard rubbish, he realised. Armchairs and a sofa, a dining table and chairs and, bang in the middle of the table, a big blue-and-yellow bowl heaped with a kind of drug picnic: a bong and matches, a syringe; pills and cannabis in little ziplock bags.

A bipolar kind of main bedroom. Neat and orderly on one side, and a floor tossed with dirty boots, greasy overalls, two syringes and a car magazine spread like a startled plover on the other. Another tiny bedroom containing a single bed and a wardrobe, watched over by a boy-band wall poster. Alice's sister, he thought—now living elsewhere. The bathroom, a blighted scene of bloated chipboard, mould and grime rings.

Finally, the sleepout. Someone long ago had sealed the side veranda from the elements and installed windows, an electric light and a three-ply wardrobe, but no one slept here now; it was a storage space. And if Hirsch had been wondering about the provenance of the computer and the TV, he didn't about the items in the sleepout. That scratched red filing cabinet? Bob and Yvonne Muir's. That little hall table? Nan Washburn's.

All of this took less than two minutes, Hirsch vaguely aware that the strange numbness overlying his actions was advance notice of the horror that would inevitably catch up with him. Darting back to the bathroom, he jerked open cupboard doors. Bandaids, but no bandages. No disinfectant. Aspirin. Cotton buds. Deodorant. A desperate uncapped toothpaste tube. Foam-flecked razor blades.

Grabbing the bandaids, a washcloth, the aspirin and some bottled water from the fridge, Hirsch raced outside again to where Brenda Maher sat, crooning to the broken baby nestled against her chest.

She rode in the back of the Toyota, her neck, shoulders, arms and legs criss-crossed with bandaids and her clothing damp and pinkish red where he'd washed the blood from her torn skin. Six aspirins eating away at her insides. She wouldn't give up the baby but rocked, cried, stroked, the seatbelt turning red. The seat itself.

Time passed. Hirsch, reaching 140 km/h on the broad, straight sections of the Barrier Highway, wishing the ambulance would appear in the distance, wondered if he could take a calming breath now.

But shapes assembled themselves. The baby, the dog, the red blanket swimming up at him. His hands white on the steering wheel. He couldn't think any of these things utterly away. All he had was his job. Job questions. So he asked, 'Brenda, where are the others?'

She didn't reply.

He tried another question. 'Were you alone with Toby when it happened?'

Nothing.

'Has the dog been vicious before?'

Now she spoke. 'Business.'

'Sorry?'

'The others are away on business.'

They're out in the van, Hirsch thought, delivering items scammed from the locals. *All* of them? Maybe to carry the heavier items, like Mrs Reid's bed base. 'Now my husband's gone,' the old woman had told him, the morning he and Ed Tennant helped her haul it onto the nature strip, 'I don't need such a monstrosity.' Hirsch had wondered if she was jettisoning good memories or bad.

'Sorry about the dog, Brenda,' he said now. 'But it was out of control.'

After an age, Brenda said, 'Tobes was just playing on his blankie.'

Hirsch thought that was probably true. It was also likely that Toby had been staring at the dog. Prolonged eye contact—the dog had felt threatened. Cops knew that. Vets. Ambulance officers. Not dog owners, for some reason. This was Hirsch's third dog mauling. In the first, his second week on the streets of Enfield, the result had been minor injuries. In the second, the dog had turned on its probably abusive owner. Hirsch hadn't pulled his gun on either occasion. Now this. Police regulations would protect him in this instance but still, he'd drawn and fired his weapon.

He could see paperwork in his near future, just as he could see flashing lights on the road ahead. 'Here's the ambulance, Brenda,' he said.

For all the good it would do the baby. He felt that he might fracture inside.

21

IT TOOK TIME, waiting for news at the hospital, Sergeant Brandl joining him on one of the scuffed chairs. He was exhausted suddenly: the adrenaline leaking away. And the sergeant seemed rattled from her session with the Internal Investigations officers. And so they sat there with little to say at first, until Brandl said, 'Before I forget: they found Scott Greig's prints in those kitchen gloves.'

'Good. Wherever he is.'

'Wherever he is,' echoed the sergeant. 'Get you a hot drink?'

'Coffee, thanks.' It would come from the hospital vending machine, but what the hell, he needed a pick-me-up.

Brandl returned a couple of minutes later with a flimsy plastic cup in each hand. 'Ouch.' She set the cups on the floor beside the chairs and blew on her fingers.

Hirsch peered at the steaming surfaces. 'What did you get?'

'Hot chocolate.'

'So much to learn.'

They sipped their drinks, the heat defeating the taste for the moment. 'How did it go with the Internals?'

'It went,' Brandl said, and he knew he'd get no more out of her.

But presently he grew aware that she was staring at him.

'You've had a shock.'

'You could say that.'

'If you need help processing it...'

'Sarge,' Hirsch said. He'd rather talk about the things he'd seen inside the house.

Brandl said, with a hard, vivid smile, 'Don't you go vague on me, Paul. I—'

Hirsch was saved by Dr Pillai striding down the corridor from the little surgery, stripping off her bloodied gloves and gown. 'Paul. Hilary.'

'Doc,' Hirsch said.

'Sandali,' the sergeant said.

Pillai turned to Hirsch. There was a smudge of blood

on her mask. 'The baby was already dead—but you knew that.'

'It was dead before I got there.'

'Horrific injuries to the head and neck, as if the dog shook it. Then injuries to the arms and legs more consistent with gnawing.'

Hirsch swallowed. 'Yeah.'

'As for the mother—some nasty bites, with a risk of infection. I stitched the worst of them and I've given her antibiotics and painkillers. She'll need to stay here for a couple of days at least, and she'll need a lot of long-term counselling, I suspect. I actually had to prise the baby away from her.'

'She was talking to it in the car before we met the ambulance, as if she couldn't accept it's dead.'

'Oh, she knew. Her body didn't quite know, though. Like I said, I want her to stay here for a while, and she's going to need a lot of support. Does she have family nearby? Friends?'

'If you could call them that,' Hirsch said.

He supposed it would be up to him to inform Jacob, Alice and Hillcock. A kind of give with one hand and take with the other, since he'd be going in with a search warrant.

'And you might consider counselling, too, Paul,' Pillai said.

Thirty minutes later, Hirsch and Brandl were back in the Redruth police station, Sergeant Brandl struggling to get her head around Hirsch's request for a warrant.

'But has a crime been committed? We're not talking stolen items, are we? The good people of your town put their junk out on their nature strips of their own free will.'

Hirsch shook his head. 'Not entirely. They were deceived, led to believe it was a legitimate hard-rubbish collection. Obtaining property by deception.'

'Bit of a stretch,' the sergeant said.

It wasn't, not to Hirsch, but Brandl was distracted, glancing at her open office door tensely, as if she wanted to march down the corridor to the interview room and rescue Tim Medlin from the clutches of the Internals. Or at least monitor what he was saying.

'Also,' Hirsch said, 'I saw some expensive electronics. Big TV set, computer…'

Gazing at her coffee mug, perhaps hoping it had replenished itself, Sergeant Brandl said, 'That's not enough for a warrant.'

'Cannabis, a bong, pills and syringes.'

'Yeah.' Brandl blinked. 'That might do it.'

'So yes—might be an idea to search the place.'

Looking careworn again, Brandl said, 'All right—but what a mess on top of everything else.' She shook herself back into the shape of an officer in charge. 'Paperwork'll be a nightmare. Be clear that you believe the dog was responsible for the baby's death, that you had no choice but to shoot it and that you suspect criminal activity in the house. CIB will have to be involved anyway, so get someone like

DC Comyn to go with you. But do all that this afternoon, all right? Get your interview out of the way first.'

'No worries,' Hirsch said—which was a lie. He could visualise Hillcock, Jacob and Alice returning to the cottage, seeing the blood, the dog, and panicking. Cleaning up. He needed to secure the place.

He found the local Justice of the Peace, Cathy Duigan, at her vet surgery. Sinewy, lithe, no-nonsense in her flapping white coat, she was in the forecourt of the building, reassuring an elderly woman who was bundling a little dog onto a pet bed in the back of a Corolla. The dog looked dazed. A bandaged back leg; a neck ruff to stop it worrying the injury.

Spotting Hirsch, Duigan gave a little wave and nod as she helped the old woman into the driver's seat, all the while speaking brightly, eyes warm and lively. He joined her. They both waved the little car out onto the Adelaide road.

She turned to Hirsch. 'Senior Constable Hirschhausen. Still in one piece?'

Hirsch grinned. She'd rescued him from a menacing dog last year. She was thirty-four but barely looked twenty-four. He waved the warrant paperwork at her. 'Signature, please.'

'Come in.'

He followed her through a waiting room decorated with manufacturers' displays of collars and packaged food and ripe with odours he couldn't identify. Animal illnesses? Fear? Medications? Faintly unpleasant, anyway.

Nodding hello to the receptionist, edging past the nurse in the corridor behind the front desk, Hirsch followed Duigan to the tearoom at the rear. She went straight to the sink and filled a jug. 'I'm gasping. Tea?'

Hirsch eyed the sink, the little fridge and the bench with its limp teabags on a saucer and its grainy spills of sugar, crumbs and milky water. But there was also a coffee pod machine. 'Coffee, please. Strongest pod.'

Seated at the little table with her a few minutes later, Hirsch outlined why he needed the warrant. He kept his spiel brief, and focused on the drug paraphernalia.

'Why were you there in the first place?'

To shoot a dog. But should he tell her that? She was a vet, after all.

In the end he told her the truth and saw the concern on her face. 'Cathy, it had killed the baby. It was mauling the mother.'

'You poor thing,' she said, reaching across and patting his forearm. 'Its blood was up.'

'Yes.'

'And you saw drugs in the house?'

'Yes.'

'Did these people mistreat the dog?'

'I don't know. I don't think so.'

'Any other animals on the property?'

Hirsch shook his head. 'Not that I saw.'

Now she was fishing a pen from her coat and holding out a hand for the warrant. 'Let me know if you happen to find any Ivermectin.'

'Okay. What is it?'

'An anti-parasitic used to treat horses and cows. It can be taken by humans, but in much weaker concentrations. What I'm getting at is, people are taking it to treat Covid.'

He wondered if she was making leaps and links, as he sometimes did. Was a dysfunctional druggie family more likely to be Covid-deniers or anti-vaxxers? Probably. 'You've been asked for it? You've had thefts?'

'I had a locum here last week while I made a lot of farm calls, and when I checked the drugs cabinet on Friday, I noticed we were almost out of Ivermectin. She told me people had been coming in all week requesting it for their stock. I should have warned her.'

'What can it do to a human?'

'In farm-animal dosages it's very toxic. Seizures, tremors, vomiting and diarrhoea, even death,' Duigan said. She threw up her hands. 'But people will take this stuff instead of a tried and tested vaccine. You have to wonder.'

'Did your locum keep a record of who bought it?'

'She did. I followed them up and they were all legitimate except one—a false name and number.'

'I'll keep an eye out,' Hirsch said.

He realised that Duigan wasn't finished. She was eyeing him, building up to something. He waited.

'Do you know Mia Dryden?' she said. 'She has a

'property in your neck of the woods.'

'Ninety minutes north-east of me, to be exact,' Hirsch said, wondering what was coming.

'I get called out there maybe twice a year,' Duigan said. 'They run a good operation, they're cluey about vet stuff. But when I was there last week, Mrs Dryden asked for more Ivermectin—which she was entitled to do, she runs horses, she's used it before.'

'Okay…'

In a rush Duigan said, 'It's just that she's a rabid anti-vaxxer, in case you hadn't noticed.'

'I'd noticed.'

Duigan shrugged it away now. 'Anyway, what can you do?' she said, clicking her pen and poring over the warrant. Hirsch watched her eyes flick left and right, and when she had reached the end, she asked him to swear to the veracity of the information he'd provided, and signed with a flourish.

Thanking her, Hirsch returned to the Hilux and sat for a moment. The time was 11 a.m. and he felt jittery. He couldn't afford to stay in Redruth until his noon appointment, then spend up to an hour with the Internals. Time was wasting. He needed to head back to Tiverton with the warrant.

Two phone calls increased his agitation. The first was from the charmless Comyn of Port Pirie CIB. 'Heard you shot a dog.'

'I'm fine, thanks for asking,' Hirsch said.

'Oh, did it attack you?' A theatrical sigh. 'You keep causing me grief, my friend.'

'Causing you grief,' Hirsch said. 'My mission in life.' Regulations allowed him to use his weapon to put down a sick or dangerous animal.

Comyn sighed again. 'This fucking job. Takes me all over the joint. Can't you keep the peace over there?'

Silence. Hirsch checked the time. Comyn said, 'Anyway, look, I can't get there to clean up your mess until about three this afternoon.'

'Looking forward to it,' Hirsch said.

Three o'clock? A lot could change by then. Hirsch swept out of the car park and sped back through Redruth, and was pulling up outside the police station when the second call came in. Alice McNamara, sounding hysterical.

'We just got home. There's blood everywhere. I rang triple-oh but they wouldn't tell me anything, so I called the police station and some woman there gave me your number.'

Sergeant Brandl? Hirsch finished parking, switched off, pulled on the brake. 'Alice, I—'

'Did something happen? Cyril looks like he's been *shot*. Where's Brenda? Is she all right? Where's Toby?'

Cyril? That vicious bundle of muscle and fangs? Hirsch gave himself a little shake. He didn't want to sound curt to Alice; equally, he didn't want to tiptoe around the truth. And more than anything, he wanted her and the others out of the house.

'Alice, you're not alone?'

'Now you're really scaring me. Jacob and David are here.'

'I'm really sorry to tell you this, but Brenda's in the Redruth hospital. Cyril attacked her and she's in a bad way.'

There was silence and Hirsch sensed that Alice was edging towards the next logical question. She'd have seen the bloodied blanket on the grass. Then he realised that he could hear scrapes and thuds in the background. Cleaning up? Packing up? 'Alice, how about—'

'Where's Toby?'

'I'm so sorry. Toby was also attacked. Brenda was hurt trying to save him but he, ah, he didn't make it,' Hirsch said. He added, feeling a little—but only a little—like a heel, 'Brenda would really like her family around her right now.'

There was silence again until Alice said, 'They would stare at each other.'

'Sorry?'

'Toby. He used to stare at Cyril,' Alice said, with a constricted sob, as she ended the call.

Ten past eleven now, and Hirsch hurried into the police station, nodding to Mr Pickett behind the front desk, who buzzed him through to the rooms at the rear. A moment later he was hanging on Sergeant Brandl's doorframe. 'Sergeant, I really need to serve that warrant right away.

Alice McNamara just called me. She's at the house and I think they'll get rid of evidence.'

Brandl checked her watch. 'Sometimes I hate this job. What about your interview?'

'I'm happy to talk to them later today, but right now I need to get back.'

'Are they violent?'

Were they? Jacob was aggressive—in a mindless, fuck-the-police way. Alice was surly, but no—she didn't seem violent. As for David Hillcock, her stepfather, Hirsch knew only that he'd been served with a community corrections order for drug offences, and detained for aggravated burglary, charges dropped. But there were weapons in the house: kitchen knives, maybe the odd samurai sword in someone's wardrobe. Saucepans. Cricket bat. And the Nazi dagger.

'I truly don't know. Alice sounded upset.'

'There are three of them, Paul,' Brandl said, 'and being upset can tip over into violence, especially if a policeman's snooping in your cupboard drawers. Take Tim with you. Finish up quickly and get back here. I'll stall the Internals for you—but I'm telling you now, they won't be pleased.'

'Yeah, well, there's police work and there's police work,' Hirsch said.

22

HE FOUND TIM Medlin in the rear yard, hosing dust off the Redruth patrol car with an agitated air, as if trying to wash himself clean. Hirsch knew the feeling. Five minutes with Internal Investigations soiled you to the depths of your soul.

'Got a job for you, Tim,' he said, turning off the tap.

Medlin looked at the spray nozzle as if wondering what had happened to it. 'Like what?'

'I'll tell you on the way.'

A pause as the younger man contemplated the yard,

which was a broad paved path edged by a weed-choked cyclone fence. The station's own Hilux. Jacob Maher's Holden station wagon, still sitting where it had been dumped by the Redruth Motors tow truck last week. 'I'll get my gear.'

'We're serving a search warrant. I need you to be quick.'

'All right, all right,' Medlin said.

A minute later, Hirsch was leading him down the side path to the yard gate keypad, then out onto the street and into the Tiverton Hilux. It, too, needed a good hosing. Then out onto the Barrier Highway, Hirsch trying to think his way into the individual and collective actions of Jacob Maher, Alice McNamara and David Hillcock, now that they knew what had happened at the house. He couldn't imagine that grief, a desire to comfort Brenda and a need to dispose of incriminating evidence would meld seamlessly.

'Searching whose place?' Medlin said at that moment, morose and twitchy in the passenger seat.

Hirsch explained, steering with one hand while passing over his phone. 'Photos I took earlier today.'

Medlin swiped through them, muttering, 'Hello, drugs in plain view. Syringe. Nice.'

'Plus, we check the serial numbers on the TV and the computer, and that furniture you can see in the sleepout was obtained by deception,' Hirsch said, staring at the oncoming cars, half-hoping to spot Hillcock's VW van heading south.

They travelled in silence, until Medlin said, 'What about your interview?'

'I'll do it later.'

Medlin shifted in his seat, checked the time on his watch. 'I hope Sergeant Brandl's okay with this.'

'She is.'

'I don't want any more black marks on my record.'

'What black marks?' Hirsch demanded. He checked the time: 11.25. 'You don't have any, do you?'

Still intent on the sparse oncoming traffic, he sensed Tim Medlin's incredulity. 'Questioned by Internal Investigations? That sort of thing sticks to you.'

Hirsch saw that he should show a bit of pastoral care. 'Tim, answer me this: did you do or say anything that harmed Auntie Steph or the Aboriginal people of the district?'

'Of course not.'

'Did you collude with Petra Osmak or Scott Greig in accessing, sharing or posting racist or hate material?'

'Paul! No.'

'No articles, photos, memes, Tweets…'

'Never.'

'Did you hang out with Petra or Greig after work or on weekends?'

'I've already been asked that. No. I don't even know who her friends are and I barely knew her.'

'So they have nothing on you. You did nothing wrong. No reason to suspect you of doing anything wrong.'

No response, then a muttered, 'Yeah, but still…'

But still, he was right. It didn't matter if Brandl, Hirsch, Medlin and Landy were cleared by the Internals, the fact that they had been the subject of an investigation would linger. A stain, a footprint, in their files. They might apply for a promotion one day, or a new posting, and encounter resistance. The old where-there's-smoke-there's-fire preconception. Even if they advanced in the job, the pace would slow, the postings would be less desirable. Community Liaison, for example. Or somewhere way the other side of Woop Woop.

Hirsch said bracingly, 'You've got nothing to worry about. Meanwhile we go on doing solid police work, like serving this warrant.'

Reclaiming his phone, he clipped it to the dash holder. 'I expect you heard the word "culture" this morning, right? A culture of racism at the Redruth police station.'

'Yes.'

'Yeah, well, what we're about to deal with is a clear example of criminal culture. A household of people whose whole rationale, the way they think and act, is criminal.'

'But they've just lost a baby in the worst possible way.'

That was also troubling him? Hirsch wanted to quit his kindly mentor act and tell him to harden up. Except that he'd said those same words to himself plenty of times. 'We won't trample on their feelings, Tim. Always polite. Firm, but polite.' He turned his head briefly, wanting to read Medlin's face. Medlin was stony.

Then a strained smile as the younger man tried for humour. 'So long as you're first through the door.'

'You bet,' Hirsch said.

Then they were on the outskirts of Tiverton, Hirsch turning left off the highway, the sun sufficiently angled, late morning, to cast them in the bulky shadows of the silos as they bumped over the railway line.

Reaching Brenda Maher's cottage, Hirsch took a moment to assess. As he'd feared, no grey VW van—unless it was in the backyard, loading up. But if it was gone, had anyone stayed behind?

'We check around the back first,' he said, getting out and leading the way onto the driveway and down along the side wall of the house. God, how many times had he done this since the family had turned up in town?

Around the corner and Tim Medlin baulked, hunching his shoulders. He'd seen the blanket, the dog. Flies swarming frenziedly; a menace of crows watching from the back fence. But Hirsch was more interested in the tyre-flattened grass and a chipboard bookcase standing skew-whiff and half-disintegrated where it had been dropped onto the packed dirt of the driveway.

Medlin was pointing, gagging. 'We should—'

Hirsch took his arm, barked, 'Inside,' and bundled him towards the back door. 'Forget that,' he added, guiding Medlin past the blood that was streaked on the kitchen lino and pooled by the landline phone. Into the sitting room. As he'd feared, the blue and yellow bowl was empty of drugs, but the card table was still there, with the printer but not the computer. In their place a receipt sat tauntingly: a Hisense TV, an Epson printer and a Lenovo computer, bought in a single transaction at the Good Guys down in Gepps Cross. You're messing with us, he thought.

Next, the sleepout. The remaining hard-rubbish items had been removed. Returning to the main part of the house, he found Medlin on his hands and knees in the main bedroom. 'No syringes.'

'Keep looking,' Hirsch told him. 'The underside of drawers, the freezer, you know the drill.'

That left the caravan. A couple of drawers were open, empty, and most of the clothing was missing. No books or paperwork anywhere apart from a part-completed booklet of Sudoku puzzles.

Hirsch returned to the sitting room. Poked about desultorily and noticed that a warning light was blinking on the printer. Out of paper? A jam?

He poked and prodded, realising that the back panel was removable. A concertina of ink-smeared A4 paper was caught in the machine. He took it out and smoothed it, staining his fingers black. 'Dear bitchface,' it read, 'you put out your piece of shit filing cabinet to be collected, remember? No one twisted your arm. Finders keepers, bitch. Remember we know where you live. Fucking slag.'

Hirsch was glad Yvonne Muir hadn't received the note. But had she received abusive calls? A criminal culture, he thought. There seemed to be no disconnect between a Brenda Maher who was wretchedly grieving the death of her baby boy and a Brenda Maher who wrote foul-mouthed abuse to strangers.

Although…maybe Brenda hadn't typed the note. He sent Wendy a quick text—*Did you ever teach an Alice McNamara?*—then called Sergeant Brandl. 'They're not here. But they could be visiting Brenda in hospital by now. Driving a grey VW van. I'll send you the details.'

'Would they be that stupid?'

'Who knows? I haven't found anything very incriminating. Maybe they feel confident.'

'I'll check myself,' the sergeant said, completing the call.

Hirsch returned to the cottage and found Medlin unscrewing the side panel of the bathtub. He looked up and said, 'Wish we had a sniffer dog.'

Hirsch grunted, 'I've gone off dogs a bit,' as Medlin tugged at the panel. Cobwebs, a whiff of moisture, but otherwise the cavity was empty.

Next, Hirsch went to look for paperwork. Bank statements, passports, personal letters, bills, receipts for storage rental or property titles.

He found nothing, and then Sergeant Brandl called. 'They were here, trying to get Brenda to go with them. But even she knew she wasn't up to it. Quite aggressive, according to one of the nurses.'

'Long gone, I suppose?'

'Long gone. I've put out an alert on the van.'

Then Comyn arrived from Port Pirie, an hour earlier than he'd said. After he'd taken Hirsch's statement, he joined in the search. Hirsch thought he knew all of the old hiding places, but Comyn went straight to the sitting-room curtains, felt the fabric, slipped his hand inside the UV coating and pulled out a sheaf of bills and receipts. A storage locker in Gawler. And a recent electricity bill in Brenda Maher's name—for 6 Bundaleer Street in Muncowie, half an hour north. It rang a bell. Her previous residence?

As Hirsch was pondering that and photographing the invoice with his phone, he heard voices and turned to see his old nemesis, Inspector Gaddis, in the doorway.

'Carry on, Senior Constable Hirschhausen,' he said. 'And as soon as you're done, you need to make yourself available for an interview.'

23

HIRSCH OFTEN ASKED himself: who am I here? What role am I playing? It seemed that sometimes a place determined who he was or was meant to be, and at other times he determined its nature and purpose. He was always being made and unmade.

Take the little room that was the police station. When he was in there, everything about it said that he was a cop, with a cop's authority. He answered work emails, his uniform cap hung from a hook, there was a wanted poster on the wall and the public walked in off the street expecting him to be a cop. Yet sometimes there were breaches that transformed him into a different version of himself. Like yesterday, when he'd tossed out a kitschy postcard from his mother. At that moment he was no longer a policeman but an ungrateful son.

To further complicate matters, he didn't exactly leave home to travel to his work space. He simply walked through the connecting door from his three cramped rooms at the back of the building. And when he was in those rooms, he was not necessarily a man in repose—feet up, removed from work.

Certainly not at this very moment, with the Internal Investigations duo in his sitting room. Inspector Gaddis and his offsider—introduced to Hirsch as Sergeant Denise Nikitin—had looked with such distaste upon the pokiness of the front room, with its fly-specked posters and solitary visitor's chair, that Hirsch had shown them through the connecting door and along the little corridor—past his messy bedroom—to the sitting room with its attached kitchen. Here he gestured them onto the lumpy sofa beneath his print of *Christina's World*—hanging crooked again—while he offered cups of tea, then took the armchair across from them.

Not a cop now, or a bloke at home but a nervy guy: on the back foot, embarrassed by the state of his living quarters. Yet there were times when he was a cop here, seated in that same armchair. When he questioned nervous teenagers, for example. They didn't clam up, as they might in the formal confines of an interview room.

Hirsch was thinking these things, waiting for the questioning to start, when his mobile buzzed: a text from Wendy. Now he was three things at once, in this close, shabby room: cop, lover and less than satisfactory public servant, if the frown on Inspector Gaddis's face was anything to go by.

'Sorry, sir.'

Wendy had simply written: *Didn't teach Alice, taught her sister Zoe.* He switched the phone to silent, slid it into his pocket. That was uncomfortable, so he placed it on the coffee table—dusty, he noticed. But, sitting there, the phone resembled a recording device, so he got to his feet and took the phone through to the kitchen, feeling like an idiot.

Gaddis evidently thought he was. 'Stop fussing, Senior Constable Hirschhausen. For a man who can call someone a Covid moron, you're being a bit of an old woman,' he said, allowing himself a little chortle.

'Well put, sir,' Hirsch said, going along with it.

The place was stuffy. Shut up all day when Hirsch was at work. Poor airflow even with windows open. Stale old op-shop furniture. The lies and false promises of the past inhabitants. Gaddis's aftershave. Sergeant Nikitin's damp underarms. Hirsch knew Gaddis; didn't know her. She stared at him, unsmiling, her glum, doughy features saying he must be guilty of something if he was sitting across from her.

Hirsch returned his attention to Gaddis, who had grilled him twice before, the first time during the corruption inquiry into his old CIB squad, the second concerning reports that he'd sought favours from civilians—to wit, a bucketload of ratepayers' asphalt to patch the Tiverton police station's potholed driveway. Gaddis had treated Hirsch dismissively on both occasions and Hirsch was expecting more of the same. He wasn't disarmed by the relaxed, blokey manner. The Covid moron remark was intended to remind Hirsch that Gaddis had his ear to the ground; was maybe even keeping an eye on Hirsch. It was all of a piece with the guy's appearance: thin, ferrety, clean. And a vision in blue today—suit, shirt, tie; even a tinge to his skin.

'Moving right along,' Gaddis said now. 'First, though, do you feel up to talking to us today? You've had quite a shock: the dog, the baby.'

'I'll see how I go, sir,' Hirsch said, thinking that the day had gone by so rapidly, he didn't know how he felt.

'You might have changed out of your uniform,' Gaddis said, staring at the blood on Hirsch's chest and sleeves.

'Wanted to get this over and done with, sir, so you can get back to the city in good time.'

Gaddis snorted. 'If you need a break at any time, please say so. And I strongly suggest you contact the police service's welfare section, Senior Constable Hirschhausen— do you think you can do that?'

'Sir.'

'Right. You do know why Sergeant Nikitin and I are here today, I take it?'

'Yes, sir.'

Gaddis tapped a long, bony finger on the file in his lap. 'To ascertain whether or not a certain culture exists in this police district.'

Hirsch said nothing. He glanced at Nikitin, who stared back at him evenly and slightly too eagerly. She didn't seem fatigued by the long drive up from Adelaide and the hours interviewing the Redruth crew. Gaddis has briefed her about me, he thought.

'Do you understand what I mean by "culture" in this context, Senior Constable Hirschhausen?'

'Yes, sir.'

'I expect you do, after your stint at Paradise Gardens. Corrupt conduct all round, I think?'

'Sir, I was not found to be corrupt.'

Gaddis was waspish. 'You weren't found to be clean either.'

Hirsch waited him out. Gaddis was tense, with a quality of stillness in him indicative of fury poised to blow. And the long seconds passed, until Sergeant Nikitin said, her voice a mild rumble, 'In particular, Senior Constable Hirschhausen, we need to know if a *racist* culture exists in the Redruth police district. Was Ms Osmak acting alone, or did she have support or approval from you or your colleagues?'

'I'm based here, not Redruth.'

'You attend weekly briefings in Redruth. Your sergeant is based there. You step in if they're short-staffed.'

'I do, but the briefings aren't long and I have very little to do with the day to day running of Redruth. I spend most of my time here'—he pointed down the little hallway—'or out on patrol. I barely know Petra Osmak.'

'But the others do,' Gaddis said, sounding stilted, perhaps miffed that Nikitin had stepped in. 'Tell us what you know about their interactions with Ms Osmak.'

'I don't—' Hirsch paused. Was that his phone buzzing on the kitchen bench?

'Pay attention,' Gaddis snapped.

'Sorry, sir.'

'The Redruth officers' interactions with Ms Osmak...?'

'I can't add anything, sir. I didn't witness it, or hear them talk about her.'

'Very well. Were you ever shown written or visual material of a racist nature by the Redruth officers?'

'Never. They're decent and professional; they wouldn't do anything like that.'

Gaddis gave him a stop-stonewalling look. 'Police officers drift sometimes, over time; we all know that.'

'Do they, sir?'

'You know full well they do. They lose perspective. Feel unappreciated by the public. Grievances fester, real or imagined.'

Hirsch didn't know what he was expected to say to that. Had some admission been made by the others that morning? Had Gaddis, the ferret, ferreted something out of one of them?

'I'm not aware of any grievances or complaints or whingeing or prejudices or anything other than total professionalism, sir.'

Gaddis folded his arms; grunted.

Hirsch went on: 'And as far as we've been able to discover, Ms Osmak and the kid she sent the video to were acting alone. They're friends, without other friends. Young and stupid. Thoughtless. They egg each other on.'

There was enough finality in Hirsch's words and tone for Gaddis to throw down his pen. Sergeant Nikitin, still stony-faced, gave him a hint of a nod.

When they were gone, he checked his phone. A follow-up text from Wendy: *PS Zoe was expelled.*

24

MID-AFTERNOON NOW and Hirsch was alone. He felt grimy: the Internals, and his bloodied uniform soaking in the laundry sink.

He washed down a sandwich with strong black tea, booked an appointment—for next Monday—with a police-service-recommended psych in Gawler, climbed behind the wheel again.

First entering into his GPS the Muncowie address on the electricity bill found hidden in Brenda Maher's curtains, he headed north, wondering if he'd find Alice, Jacob and

Hillcock there. Or another branch of Brenda's family. Or no one at all. It was a loose end, however, and it was nagging at him. Not that loose ends could always be tied off neatly, in his experience.

Muncowie was in his patrol district, and he called in once a week if he could, even though the place rarely mustered up the energy for bad behaviour. Bad thoughts, maybe. Too small, too forgotten, too purposeless for anything else. A shop, a pub and a handful of houses on a crosshatch of six streets; two running north–south and four running east–west. Crouching little fibro and weatherboard places defeated by time and the sun. Blinds drawn to hide the inhabitants from intruders, and vice versa.

And 6 Bundaleer Street fitted right in, a paint-peeling, buckled-veranda house behind a massive oleander. Every second property in the district seemed to boast an oleander—if not a cypress hedge or peppertrees. Toxic despite their beauty, oleanders, which he sometimes thought was fitting.

He pulled into the kerb and got out. The street was short, wide and apparently dead. Over on the highway, a road train rumbled past. Somewhere on the struggling grassland surrounding the town a tractor sputtered. And something—a quality of stillness—told Hirsch that 6 Bundaleer was vacant.

Recently vacated? As he stepped through a small bent gate in a collapsing, knee-high brick fence and glanced along the side wall, he spotted the corner of a battered blue dump bin in the backyard. Rather than knock on the front door, he walked to the rear of the property, into a yard like many he'd seen over the years: a Hills hoist, a rusty wheelbarrow, dead and dying plants, a garden tap on a lean beside a tumbledown garden shed. As for the bin, it hadn't been there for long; grass was trapped around the base. He photographed the words *Mid-North Bin Hire* and contact phone number stencilled on the side, then, hunting around for something to stand on, upended a rusty mop-bucket and looked in.

Empty. He knocked on both doors to the house. They were locked and no one answered. Curtains drawn over every window.

He called Mid-North Bin Hire, identified himself as a police officer to the man who answered and learned that the bin had been hired for one week by a Martina Golos.

Golos. Another penny dropped. Jake Maher had bought the station wagon from her.

Then the bin-hire man was saying, 'Can I ask why?' A note of apprehension in his voice.

'Nothing to do with your company,' Hirsch said smoothly. 'But I do need to talk to the householder. Unfortunately, the place looks to have been vacated. Would you have contact details for Ms Golos?'

'You sure you're police?'

'If you call the Redruth police station and ask to speak to Sergeant Brandl...'

'That's all right,' the man said, rattling off a mobile

number. 'She told us her nephew lived there. He died recently and she's cleaning up—to sell it, I suppose. She lives in Adelaide somewhere.'

Hirsch tried the number: no reply. He tried a handful of motels and hotels in his contacts list. No Martina Golos in residence. He googled Golos, finding LinkedIn and Facebook accounts, but he had no way of knowing if they referred to the woman who had hired the bin.

Next, he set out to knock on every door in the street. Two people were at home and three houses were vacant. A young woman jiggling a baby on her hip said, 'Druggies live there,' but couldn't tell Hirsch anything more, or identify photographs of Brenda, Jacob, Alice or Hillcock.

A short, furry man with bushy white eyebrows at 3 Bundaleer said pre-emptively, 'I mind my own business.'

Hirsch swiped through the photos again. 'Could be,' the old man said vaguely.

'When's the last time you saw someone there?'

'Yesterday, just before the bin was delivered. A lady. Said she was cleaning up, her nephew died. First I knew of it.'

Hirsch showed Brenda's photo again. 'Her?'

'No.'

This mysterious Golos, Hirsch thought. 'I checked the bin: it's still empty.'

'She's coming back tomorrow morning.'

'You had quite a chat.'

'I don't know about that. But she said she's coming

236

back to pack everything up and good riddance, I say. The smell sometimes.'

Cooking meth? 'Was it a chemical smell?'

'Just, you know, a bad smell,' the man said, uttering a phlegmy cough as confirmation.

'Can you do me a favour?'

'Depends.'

Hirsch didn't ask on what; just handed him a card. 'When the lady arrives tomorrow, please call me.'

The man held the card as if it would incriminate him. 'I mind my own business.'

'It's just that she and I keep missing each other,' Hirsch said offhandedly.

The old man actually touched the side of his nose and winked. 'Got you.'

Hirsch called Sergeant Brandl before setting out for the drive back to Tiverton. 'I thought it'd be worth coming up here to see if Alice and the others were hiding out.'

'Jesus, Paul. I could have sent one of the children with you.' She sighed. 'Do we know of other family?'

'Maybe this Martina Golos is related to them,' Hirsch said. 'Brenda's sister or cousin,' he added, 'or Alice's mother? Hillcock's ex-wife or sister or cousin?'

'Something to be said for the traditional nuclear family structure,' Brandl muttered. 'The nephew who died—have you got a name?'

'Not yet. Anything from Brenda?'

'Still sedated. Maybe tomorrow.'

They finished the call and Hirsch headed south. He was drawing into the outskirts of Tiverton when his phone pinged with a text from Janne Van Sant:

You were economical with the truth. I investigated further and found the motel manager who advised the police that my son and his girlfriend did not pay for their room. This man served in Afghanistan with Sam Dryden. A coincidence? I think not. A man who would assist a fellow soldier in a cover-up is a more likely story. Such a man would fake a postcard, too. I shall return at once.

Hirsch texted back: *Stop in and see me first.*
She didn't reply.

Hirsch, Kate and Wendy rarely saw each other during the week—homework, writing lesson plans, marking, Hirsch always on call. But after the day he'd had, Wendy said, he should come for dinner. Curries from the bain maries at the Caltex in Redruth this time, bought when Wendy left school at 4.30, reheated at 6.30. The three of them liked a bit of spiciness, but that's not what you got from the Sikh family who ran the servo: they had the palates of the mid-north pegged.

'Tasty, though,' Hirsch said.

Kate, mopping up with naan bread, agreed. 'Not to mention that we've been saved from your spaghetti bolognese.'

He stared at her. She stared back.

'Cut it out, you two,' Wendy said.

They ignored her and kept it up until Hirsch cracked, and Kate mimed her triumph.

Good sign, he thought. A bit of shared stupidity as an antidote to her sadness—and his own, for that matter. The images were creeping up on him.

As if reading his mind, Wendy reached a hand to his across the table. 'Did you see Alice today?'

'Just Brenda, the others were out. Alice came home and saw what had happened, and she called me.'

'A shock for her…'

'Of course,' said Hirsch carefully.

'As I said, I didn't teach her, I taught Zoe, her sister.'

Hirsch happened to glance at Kate. The keen intelligence in her eyes. She knows we're tiptoeing around something crucial, he thought, just as she said, 'Zoe was expelled.'

'Yes,' Wendy said.

'Because of you.'

'Indirectly.'

Hirsch broke in. 'Tell me about that.'

'I caught her stealing from my bag one day. As soon as I confronted her, she turned on me. Kicking, screaming, she went right off. So I called it in—it takes a lot for me to report a kid—and she attacked the principal. Scratched her face, threw a laptop across the room…'

Kate was bursting in her chair. 'That explains all the online stuff. She's been getting back at you. Us.' She smiled without much warmth in it. 'Yep, all down to you, Mum.'

'Thanks for that, sweetheart,' Wendy said. 'But Zoe didn't strike me as much of a strategist.'

'And she's been living with her grandmother for the past couple of months,' Hirsch said.

Kate was rocking in her chair. 'It was *Alice* who wanted to get back at us, then.'

'Possibly.'

'Of course it was. Is she smart?'

'I'd say so,' Hirsch said, thinking of the Sudoku puzzles, the books beside her bed. Her steady, indifferent gaze the day he'd called in about the dog. He could see her vengeful, creative fingers on a keyboard: the house for rent, the hard-rubbish scam, the toxic texts and messages.

'Vicious little cow,' Wendy muttered. She helped herself to mango chutney and added, 'Got to remember she's had a terrible shock, I suppose.'

'Yeah, I know,' Hirsch sighed. The messiness of life, nothing cut and dried. 'But where she is now, no one knows. I doubt it'll be me who has to deal with her.'

At nine o'clock on Wednesday morning, Hirsch received a call from Muncowie. 'That lady's here,' the old man said. A hoarse whisper, as if he might be overheard.

Hirsch pinned his mobile number to the front door and headed north, overtaking the Broken Hill bus, tucking back into his lane again as an oncoming farm ute flashed its lights. The poor guy at the wheel looked embarrassed when he realised he'd hassled a cop. Hirsch tried an embarrassed smile and wave as the guy passed, thinking, *shit, shit, shit.*

Half an hour later he was pulling up outside 6 Bundaleer Street. A silver Camry was parked there, a Port Adelaide Power sticker on the rear window. With a wave to the old man on the other side of the street, he entered the yard. Didn't knock: hearing a thump and the tinkle of glass breaking, he reckoned that rubbish was being tossed into the dump bin at the rear of the property.

He found a heavyset middle-aged woman there, reaching down to grab a bulky garbage bag. Threadbare jeans, a baggy black T-shirt and grubby tennis shoes. Her hair, in a messy ponytail, swung wildly as she lifted the garbage and swung it over the lip of the bin. She paused to wipe her hands on her shirt. Saw Hirsch.

She scowled, glanced uneasily at the bin, at the bags at her feet, at Hirsch again.

'Ms Golos? My name's Paul Hirschhausen, from the police station down in Tiverton. I tried calling you yesterday.'

She said defensively, 'I had my phone off. The reception up here's terrible.'

'Sure is,' he agreed.

He glanced at the remaining rubbish bags. Glimpsed a short section of glass tubing and the base of a beaker. Golos winced. Took a step to block his view and yawned, as if she wasn't cleaning up her late nephew's meth operation.

'Wondered if I could ask a few questions.'

'Help you if I can,' Golos said shortly. 'Maybe we could sit on the veranda?'

A futile distraction, but Hirsch smiled and said, 'Sure, why not.'

When they were seated—on a deckchair and a plastic recliner—Hirsch said, 'I understand that your nephew owned this house? He died?'

'That's right.'

'Did he live alone?'

She shifted uncomfortably. 'Far as I know.'

'Do you know someone called Brenda Maher?'

'No.'

'Her name is on an electricity bill for this address,' Hirsch said.

He saw Golos try for different expressions and finally settle on resignation. 'Look, okay, maybe he did have people living with him. He was always a bit, you know, pathetic. Surrounded by no-hopers leaching off him.'

'How about these names: David Hillcock, Jacob Maher, Alice McNamara?'

'Never heard of them. He was my late brother Keith's boy and I been looking out for him a bit, the past year. Let him use an old car I had, things like that.'

Hirsch tingled. 'An old Holden station wagon?'

'Yes.'

'Your name and this address were on the registration papers.'

She frowned. How did he know? 'It was so the renewal

242

papers came here but it stayed in my name.'

'So you were close to him.'

'No, I wasn't close to him. Just looked out for him a bit. He was the kind of person everyone takes advantage of, you know? That's why my brother bought him this place, get him away from his druggie mates in the city. But I'm thinking they found him. Wanted the house and his money.'

'What money?'

'Damien inherited a bit of money when Keith died, not much, ten grand maybe? And here he is, in a house way out in the bush, perfect for making drugs. That's what you're here for, isn't it?' Golos asked, gesturing at the bin. 'I didn't find much equipment, just some glass tubing under the sink. I suppose his mates cleaned everything out after they killed him.'

Hirsch was tingling again. 'Killed him. Was his last name Pierce?'

Martina Golos looked at Hirsch askance, as if he was a bit dim. 'Yeah, Damien Pierce. You know, the body they found in the suitcase.'

25

'AND SHE DIDN'T think to get in touch with us?' Comyn said later.

To get a mobile signal, Hirsch was standing at wobbly attention on top of the dump bin. If not for that, he might have theorised at length about the world being full of dull, incurious people like Martina Golos. Either over-respectful of authority or chronically suspicious of it. But Comyn knew all that.

'It just didn't occur to her,' Hirsch said. 'She barely knew her nephew. She wasn't even close to her brother. He dies, a few months later the nephew dies, leaving her to pick up the pieces.'

'Incredible.'

'So if you could inform Homicide?'

'Sure.'

'And a crime-scene unit.'

'Yeah, yeah,' muttered Comyn. 'You think he was killed in the house?'

'Maybe. Plus there's some lab glassware that should yield prints.'

'Where's the aunt now? We need to eliminate her prints.'

'Staying at the motel in Peterborough. I took her statement.'

'Or she's involved. Done a runner.'

'I didn't get that feeling,' Hirsch said.

'Famous last words,' Comyn said, ending the call.

Hirsch climbed down, strung crime-scene tape across the front of the property and sat in the Hilux to wait.

But waiting meant inactivity. An unwelcome opportunity to connect with his thoughts. He saw a tremor in his right hand, his gun hand. He was holding himself tensely. Images of the mauled baby came roaring up in him. The dog. The baby...

His breath came short and fast as he walked around and up and down the little street until the flashbacks eased and it was just a spring day again.

He waited. It wasn't until late morning that Inspector Alwin arrived with Comyn and a crime-scene unit. 'Homicide can't spare anyone until tomorrow morning,' Alwin said, on the footpath outside the house, 'meaning we start canvassing the neighbours and hope forensics get their skates on to rule this in or out as the murder site.'

He cast a disparaging look at the house. 'Did you go in, Senior Constable Hirschhausen?'

'No, sir.'

Alwin watched a crime-scene officer kneel at the front door and dust the knob for prints. 'I'm assuming the aunt did?'

'Yes, sir.'

At that moment Hirsch's elderly witness edged out of his front gate with three fold-up chairs, tottered across the street and plonked them on the footpath. 'Gentlemen.'

'Great minds, sir,' Alwin said.

For a moment, Hirsch wondered if the neighbour was hoping for a quid pro quo, but the old man bobbed his head, said, 'I'll leave you to it,' and limped back the way he'd come.

Alwin repositioned the chairs in the shade of next door's front-yard gum tree. Dropping his mask briefly to rub the bridge of his nose, he said, 'Let's work out what we've got before we start knocking on doors. You first,' he said, nodding at Hirsch. 'What led you here, for a start.'

Hirsch told him about the dog attack, the search warrant

246

and finding the electricity bill in Brenda Maher's name.

'It's good you acted straight away,' Alwin said. 'Yes, this woman has suffered a terrible personal tragedy, and she's in hospital, but the show must go on.'

'Sir.'

'You're saying she pays the electricity for this place,' Alwin said, indicating the house behind him, 'yet it's owned by our man in the suitcase? How does that work?'

'Some of this is conjecture, sir,' Hirsch said, going on to tell the story of Damien Pierce, a weak man, an addict with minor drug convictions running with a harder crowd in the city—to the despair of his father, who bought him a rundown house in a country town. 'If he wanted to turn his life around, it didn't work. The grifters found him and moved in. Well, not *in*. They couldn't live here with him—too small, especially once they put the lab in as well. I'm assuming Pierce was the main cook. And they put Brenda Maher's name on the paperwork because she was a cleanskin.'

'Why did they kill him?'

'I don't know, sir. Maybe he ripped them off, or got cold feet, or wanted a bigger slice.'

'How many of them are there? Are they up to anything else?'

'Leaving out the baby and a teenage girl who went to live with her grandmother, there are four of them. I'd say Brenda is the controlling influence. Hard, cunning. Her son's in the picture, too, Jacob. Car thief. Not very bright. There's a boyfriend called David Hillcock, father of the baby. He's known to police. And there's his stepdaughter, Alice McNamara, who happens to be Jacob's girlfriend. She's smart. They've all come to my attention a few times—shoplifting, dumping rubbish, letting the dog chase a kid on his bike...'

'God save us,' Comyn cut in. 'They don't sound very organised.'

'Organised enough,' Hirsch said, going on to describe the hard-rubbish and house-rental scams. 'Plus a bit of online bullying. They've been careful, actually. I haven't heard a whisper about their drug activities.'

'And they've done a runner,' muttered Alwin.

'Brenda's in hospital and not getting out any time soon,' Hirsch said. 'She might have other ideas, of course. Or the others might come for her.'

'Be a good idea to monitor the hospital. But if they do show up, all we can do is question them. Even if we can prove this place was a meth lab and there's a big pool of blood in the middle of the kitchen floor, do we have enough to charge them with murder? Might be others involved; might get this Maher woman claiming she was paying the bills out of the goodness of her heart.'

Comyn broke in again. 'The thing is, why dump a body down in Tiverton, where they live? Not only that, draw attention to it by trying to burn it?'

They were both looking at Hirsch, as if expecting him to shoot down their misgivings. He almost shrugged and nodded, but then the picture came into his head of Jacob Maher at the wheel of the station wagon, coming over the rise beside the town paddock, spotting him and hightailing it out of there.

'Mr Hirschhausen?' the inspector said. 'Are you with us?'

'Sorry, sir. Just remembered we have one of their vehicles.'

Comyn and a crime-scene officer were instructed to follow Hirsch in the Port Pirie CIB sedan. Thirty minutes to Tiverton, another thirty to the Redruth police station; it was afternoon before he'd collected the key to Jacob Maher's station wagon from Sergeant Brandl, who looked on curiously as he unlocked it. Then they stood around in the backyard, watching and waiting as the crime-scene officer made a preliminary search for blood.

'No immediate signs,' she said at last, backing out of the rear compartment. 'And no indications that anyone's tried to clean the interior—it's filthy.'

Hirsch was philosophical. 'He was found inside a suitcase.'

'Then I suggest testing the suitcase for fibres from this car. Meanwhile, you might want to check the dashcam footage.'

She pointed. A little morsel of anomalous hi-tech, mounted to the front windscreen of Jacob's shitbox.

Not a top of the range model, though. It operated with

the motor running, she said; recorded only about three or four hours of video to a 16GB micro-SD card before the oldest files were overwritten. 'Still,' she removed the card and handed it to Hirsch, 'you might get lucky.'

'Let's watch this in the briefing room,' Brandl said.

They trooped in behind her, crowding around as she inserted the card into a reader and played the footage through the large wall-mounted screen. The first file showed a flat stretch of farm fences and highway signs streaming by, the camera juddering: Jacob redlining the shitbox, Hirsch thought. A wonder it didn't blow a gasket. Then the outskirts of Tiverton and the speed dwindled. Past the police station, the shop, the Catholic church, the silos, and over the railway line and around to the cottage. The second file showed the same trip in reverse, ending at the house in Muncowie. Then back to Tiverton, more sedately this time.

Now the fourth file. Dusk, the station wagon's head-lights illuminating a backyard and a caravan. 'We're still at their house in Tiverton,' Hirsch murmured to the others.

'What's that in the foreground?'

'Looks like a tarp.'

Comyn grunted. 'Wrapped around Pierce?'

They continued to watch as a slight figure moved into the top of the frame.

'Who's that?'

'David Hillcock,' Hirsch said. 'With a suitcase.'

'Looking good,' Comyn said with satisfaction.

Another figure stepped into the foreground, bulky, dressed in a hoody.

'Brenda Maher,' Hirsch said.

They saw her lean over, her backside looming in tights, and grab the tarp. Drag it towards the suitcase. Then Hillcock was helping her unfold the tarp and tumble the contents into the case. Probably a body, probably Damien Pierce's; either before or after rigor mortis, Hirsch thought, judging by the way they tucked it, prodded it, bent it at the joints. Then Maher and Hillcock disappeared from view, hauling the suitcase with them. A motion of the car; a tiny, up-and-down swoop of the headlights on the back fence.

'Just loaded it,' Comyn muttered. 'And if they've got any sense, they'll now take it out to the middle of nowhere...'

But that hadn't happened. They continued watching to understand why.

The car rocked again—someone's getting in, Hirsch thought. He continued watching the footage as the car began to reverse, darkness swallowing the yard and the driveway in the process. Then a ninety-degree sweep of the headlights as the car backed onto the road and headed out over the railway crossing, before turning left onto the highway. Down through Tiverton.

Where, at that very moment, Hirsch happened to be standing in the street outside the police station. The camera caught him locking the Hilux and looking up at the approaching vehicle. Cop curiosity, that's all. 'I have no memory of that,' he told the others now. Day's end, he thought. About to put my feet up.

'All down to you, Paul,' Sergeant Brandl said a moment later, when the headlights didn't continue through the town but swung off the highway, around past the oval and along to the culvert on the service road. 'You panicked them.'

Probably, thought Hirsch, as they watched the head-lights stop moving. But they were not switched off. They were used to illuminate what happened next: Hillcock and Brenda dragging the suitcase to the culvert and tumbling it in.

They made no attempt to burn it. Just got back in the car and drove the long way back to the cottage—around behind the pub, avoiding the police station.

There was one final file. Broad daylight this time, the car tracing the same route to the town paddock. Flying over the gentle rise, then braking, twitching in the gravel, because there was Hirsch again, shaking his head this time, as if rolling his eyes at the antics of the driver. A panicked U-turn. Back to the railway cottage and the patch of grass where he'd found Jacob tinkering with the car later that same day.

'Yep, all down to you, buddy,' Comyn said, slapping Hirsch on the back.

'Get stuffed,' said Hirsch—absentmindedly, thinking that if there was no dashcam footage of the suitcase being set alight, then another vehicle had been used—presumably the van. Be useful to understand that part of this chaotic story.

'We're dealing with idiots,' Comyn said, as if reading his thoughts.

Sergeant Brandl said, 'Idiots can be dangerous.' Also reading Hirsch's thoughts.

26

THURSDAY, 6.30 A.M., the sun setting off sparks in the dewy cobwebs that trembled on fence wires, garden shrubs, veranda posts. But Hirsch had slept badly: no bounce in his step this morning. Bad dreams when he was asleep; images of the baby and the dog when he was awake, which seemed to be most of the night.

He came upon Bob Muir again, stowing gear into his new work van.

'Been waiting months for this,' Muir said, gesturing with a roll of coaxial cable. 'Covid's held everything up.'

He looked at it with distaste, then at his free hand. 'And when it arrives, you find yourself wondering where it's been, so you slap on the sanitiser.'

'A permanent condition,' agreed Hirsch.

A ripple of emotion passed through Muir's stolid frame. 'Heard about the dog and the baby, Paul. Terrible thing.'

Hirsch blinked back the sudden dampness in his eyes as Muir coughed, turned away and stowed the cable into a gap between a toolbox and a plastic crate. He fished a set of keys from his overalls pocket. 'Better get on with it before rain sets in.'

'Rain?'

Muir pointed; Hirsch turned his head. Tiverton was drenched in dawn sunlight but clouds were massing over the distant, dry-country hills. They looked benign to Hirsch, but what did he know? Bob Muir had lived in this place all his life and knew its rhythms.

'Before you go, Bob,' he said, 'is Yvonne on Facebook?'

Muir cocked his head, his mind working. 'She was until recently. Is this about our old filing cabinet?'

Hirsch nodded. 'The hard-rubbish drive was a scam.'

'Not a genius one,' Muir said.

'They were counting on everyone thinking it was a charity.'

Muir nodded, thinking it through. 'As soon as Von sent her email, she wished she hadn't, scared she might have antagonised them, especially because she'd mentioned informing the police. She closed her Facebook account in case they tried to get at her that way.'

Hirsch didn't tell his friend that Brenda's crowd *had* felt antagonised. Had set out to retaliate, in fact—because that reflex, he was beginning to think, was one of their defining attributes. Along with greed and a few other choice traits. One of them, sharper than the others, must have remembered where they'd collected the filing cabinet. Unable to get back at Yvonne on Facebook, they'd pivoted to traditional methods of harassment, thwarted by a printer jam.

'Let me know if any suspicious letters arrive,' he said. 'Try not to handle them too much, we'll need to run tests.'

'Are we talking that mob over by the silos?'

Hirsch went very still. 'What makes you say that?'

'I saw them Tuesday morning in that grey van of theirs, pulling a trailer with Bert Cromer's old veranda fridge on the back.'

Everyone knows everything in this town, Hirsch thought. He'd be hard-pressed to identify his own fridge if he saw it anywhere other than where it normally stood in his kitchen.

'Where?'

'Heading south.'

'What time?'

'Late morning. Hillcock with Brenda's boy and his girlfriend.'

Hirsch contemplated that gloomily. They must have been heading south at about the time he was heading north, with Tim Medlin, to search the railway cottage. Maybe they'd turned off towards Clare. From Clare it was two hours to the second-hand dealers of Adelaide.

By 7.30 Hirsch was checking emails and making catch-up calls. No answer from Janne Van Sant. According to Sergeant Brandl, Brenda Maher had been moved under police guard to a hospital in Adelaide. According to Comyn, efforts to find Hillcock, Jacob and Alice through extended family tracing were proving fruitless.

'I heard this morning they're towing a trailer,' Hirsch said.

'Yesterday's news,' Comyn said. 'A second-hand dealer in Peterborough told me about it, so I asked around: they rented it from Redruth Motors on Monday.'

'I doubt they'll get it back,' Hirsch muttered. 'What about Alice McNamara's sister?'

'Nothing there. Claims neither she nor her grand-mother have seen Alice or the others for weeks, and I'm inclined to believe them. Not that it's my concern anymore.'

Over to Homicide, thought Hirsch.

'Meanwhile,' Comyn added, 'your former auxiliary support and her boyfriend? We had follow-up questions.'

'About?'

'We found their names on a membership list.'

Boy, did I misread that pair, Hirsch thought later. Antipodean Storm, same as Bob's ex-apprentice, Cody.

Had Petra been placed in the Redruth police station as a spy? He had pressed for more information, but Comyn had shut down. *Need to know, pal.*

The day passed and Hirsch attended to the low-key issues that were his bread and butter. He witnessed signatures, settled a fence-line dispute, investigated the theft of a ride-on mower—suggesting that the owner lock his shed in future—and ran a fruitless half-hour RBT north of the town. One motorist who'd had a drink: right on .05.

But all the while he was bothered by not knowing which member of Brenda's clan had returned to the suitcase stiff with a can of diesel and a match. In the grand scheme of things, it wasn't a major gap in police knowledge but it'd be helpful to know.

Back to basics. He'd talked to Laura Cobb on the day of the fire, but not her brother Daryl.

From habit he walked around to the Cobbs' backyard, a green, cultivated space compared to the front, which collected weeds, cigarette butts, drifts of cellophane and hopelessness. Marie Cobb was out there, unexpectedly watering flowers. A nervy, bony woman ravaged by her bipolar meds and her bad luck, and a lost soul if not for the guardianship of her children. Looked like she was on an upswing today, striding from one garden bed to another, jerking at the hose like it was a dawdling child. The spray nozzle was on full and she was allocating each plant ten seconds of water, counting them under her breath: 'One and two and three and four and...'

She spotted Hirsch. Eyes blazing, she said, 'Too busy to talk.'

Hirsch smiled, nodded, knocked on the back door. Daryl opened it. Now in his late teens, he was still a big, drowsy, downy-faced lump. Baggy T-shirt, baggier track pants, bare feet. Smell of stale sweat.

'Laura's at Mrs Washburn's,' he said, glancing worriedly past Hirsch to his mother. He went to close the door again.

'Actually, Daryl, maybe you can help me.'

Daryl was a mouth breather. It grew pronounced. 'I didn't do nothing.'

'You're not in any trouble. I just need a word.'

Daryl thought laboriously. Glanced at his mother again and said, 'Mum's a bit...you know. We're on top of it but.'

'I'm not here about your mum, I just need your help with something. Maybe inside?'

Shoulders slumped, Daryl turned and trudged towards the kitchen, finally coming to a halt beside the old laminex table as if waiting for further orders. Hirsch pulled out a chrome and vinyl chair and gestured at a similar chair on the other side of the table. 'Take a seat. I won't take up much of your time.'

Daryl sat, his face empty of expression. Waiting for whatever was about to fall on his head to get on with it.

Hirsch placed his uniform hat on the table. 'It's about the day you and Laura flew the drone.'

'Yesterday?'

Seeing that he'd have to be very precise, Hirsch said, 'Last week. The day you saw the smoke coming from the town paddock road.'

'Wasn't us who lit it.'

'I know that. I'm trying to find out who did.'

'Didn't see who.'

'Did you see a car or a person in the general area, though? Before you reached the oval?'

'We didn't know where else to go.'

'I'm happy for you to fly the drone on the oval, Daryl,' Hirsch said patiently. 'Not a problem. Just avoid flying over people's houses, that's all. You know, safety reasons.'

Daryl gave that a lot of thought. Apparently seeing no traps, his face lit up. 'Okay.'

'Did you see anyone?'

'What did Laura say?'

'She couldn't remember seeing anyone, but I wasn't able to check with you when I called in because you were reading to your mum.'

'It calms her.'

'So, if there's anything you remember? A vehicle, a person…'

'The man who, you know, second-hand furniture and that.'

That was about as clear as Daryl could get. 'Mr Hillcock?' Hirsch asked.

Daryl nodded, adding, with an oddly proud air: 'I done some work for him once. Loading and that. You know…chairs,' he said, as if unable to remember any other furniture item.

'What was he doing when you saw him?'

'When?'

Hirsch closed and opened his eyes. 'The day of the fire.'

'Driving past.'

'Past where?'

'We just got to the oval.'

'He was driving past on the street?'

'Yeah.'

'In an old station wagon?'

'No.' Daryl gave him a scornful look. 'His *van*.'

'What was he doing?'

Daryl looked lost again. 'Just driving.'

Hirsch tried to work it out. He could understand why Brenda and Hillcock had dumped the body in the culvert that Wednesday evening—they'd spotted him standing outside the police station. Too spooked to go back and pick it up, they'd left it overnight. Too spooked to pick it up in broad daylight, too. Quicker and easier just to set a match to it. Then, rather than retrace his route home, Hillcock probably drove on past the culvert, looped around to join the highway north of town, and, on his way back through Tiverton, spotted the kids with their drone. Watched for a while. Went home, fretted, sent Jacob to investigate.

'Not dealing with geniuses,' Hirsch muttered.

'Pardon?' Daryl sounded hurt.

Hirsch patted the boy's forearm. 'Not you, don't worry,' he said, getting to his feet. 'I'm really grateful, Daz. You've given me just the information I was after.'

Daryl looked as if he was casting his mind back on everything he'd said. 'Okay.'

'Whenever you helped Mr Hillcock, did you go with him anywhere? A house, a storage place, another town in the area?'

That defeated Daryl, so Hirsch left. Marie was weeding this time—yanking, trowelling—and didn't look up. Late afternoon now, and he was just sliding his key in the front door of the police station when the first fat raindrops fell.

27

FRIDAY, AND HIRSCH was out on patrol, the farmland west of town this time, and was barely halfway through his regular route when a call came in from Rod Brewster, who managed the little airstrip a few kilometres outside Redruth. Crop-dusters used it. Weekend pilots. Wool-buyers and stud managers flying in from New South Wales sheep stations.

Pulling over near the summit of Munduney Hill, Hirsch said, 'Rod. What can I do for you?'

Brewster's voice betrayed unease. 'Not sure who to

contact. I think Pete Aronson's overdue.'

'I don't know the name,' Hirsch said.

'Lives near Spalding and flies an ultralight. Aerial photography, stuff like that. Postcards, calendars…'

'Okay.'

'His car was still here when I locked up yesterday and it was still here first thing this morning. I decided to give it a few hours, in case he spent the night somewhere—not that he's ever done that before. Anyway, look, it doesn't feel right so I thought I should report it.'

'You didn't worry when he was late last night?'

'It hasn't been a problem in the past. He's a regular, hangar access, in case he gets in after I've gone home for the day.'

'Family?'

'Lives alone, far as I know.'

'Where was he flying yesterday?'

'Russ Fanning wanted new snaps of the eagle. Surrounded by wildflowers at the moment, apparently.'

'Have you called him?'

'Yep. Said he was up in the city yesterday. He assumed Pete had been and gone.'

Advising Brewster to notify the Transport Safety Bureau, Hirsch U-turned and headed back across to Tiverton and then deep into the hilly regions east of the town. He knew from experience that a spring rain out in that country could give you a gritty red paste centimetres deep, trenches scored across the roads; fences washed away by the trees and dead sheep that rode the flash floods. And so he was tense, relieved, by the time he finally pulled into Russ Fanning's yard and parked alongside a little mud-splattered Mazda 2.

His arrival alerted Fanning, who emerged from the house. Shaking Hirsch by the hand, he said, 'Looks like you had a hairy trip.'

'I was in four-wheel drive most of the time,' Hirsch admitted.

Together they surveyed the damage. The Toyota was barely white anymore; it looked like it had been unevenly dipped in mud, with great gouts of it clinging to the flanks, the windows, the mudflaps. Hirsch was fucked if he wanted to clean it. Pay Daryl thirty bucks to wash it, he thought. You never knew when the area commander might pop in for an inspection and start spinning bullshit about the public image of SA Police.

He looked around the yard. The trees, garden beds, house and sheds looked washed clean but there were no little ponds drying, no tyre-churned tracks. 'Looks like most of the rain missed you.'

'Very patchy,' Fanning agreed. 'You're here about Pete?'

'Until the air transport people get here—which could take a while.'

Fanning shot an edgy look at his house, then swung back to Hirsch again, his features tense. 'There's not much

I can tell you. I wasn't home yesterday—but I wouldn't have seen him anyway, he flies out here, takes his photos, flies back again. Then he emails me the photos and I let him know the ones I want.'

'Was Noah here? Or your overseer?' Hirsch asked, stepping up to the Toyota and booting the nearest mudflap. He was grimly satisfied to note the special adhesive quality of the region's mud.

'They both were—but the eagle's a few kilometres away. Neither of them saw anything.' Twitchy again, Fanning added, 'All I wanted was one or two good snaps. For a new range of postcards.' He paused. 'Not the wisest decision of my life.'

'In what way? What's bothering you, Russ?'

Fanning toed the dirt, as if to find the words he wanted. Then he sighed, looked at Hirsch and said, 'It seems I keep rubbing people up the wrong way.' Glancing up at the clouds, he muttered, 'A grey day all round.'

'What people?'

'You'll see. Come and have a cuppa,' Fanning said, striding towards the house.

'You're being pretty mysterious.'

'Am I?' Fanning said, and Hirsch, following close behind, saw him shrug. 'Let's say there's more to this than meets the eye.'

They entered the house, stepping through to the calm, spacious main room. The paintings. The refectory table gleaming. Three scattered islands of club chairs around thick floor rugs. And Stephanie Ingram, sitting tense but graceful on the edge of a stiff chair.

She rose when she saw Hirsch. 'Paul.'

He shook her hand. 'Mrs Ingram.'

'I've told you before, call me Steph.'

Russ Fanning clapped his hands together, buoyant, trying too hard. 'Cup of tea, Paul? Coffee? Mrs Ingram brought homemade oatmeal slices.'

Hirsch looked from one to the other—and they steadfastly looked only at him. Talk about cutting the tension with a knife. But he hadn't had lunch. 'Strong coffee and a couple of oatmeal slices, please.'

That all took a while, no one speaking, and then they were seated around a coffee table and Hirsch, brushing oat flakes from his fingers, was thinking it was time someone started the ball rolling, so he turned to Russ Fanning's visitor and said, 'How's the choir coming along, Steph?'

'Fine,' she said, partly amused, partly impatient.

Fanning's turn. Hirsch eyed him, his head on one side. 'Russ?'

Fanning shifted in his chair. Stared across at his late wife's paintings as if for inspiration and stalled with a bit of throat-clearing. Finally said, 'Mrs Ingram's here because she—'

The interruption was cool and clear. 'I've said, Russ, call me Steph.'

'Steph,' Fanning said, and then his words came in a rush. 'Steph drove out here to talk about the eagle and clearly we don't see eye to eye and now it seems my son doesn't see eye to eye with me either, with the result that he's gone off in a huff and now you're here and I have to think about a fucking ultralight aeroplane—excuse the language, Mrs Ingram. Steph.'

He stopped in his tracks, uncertain how to move on. He rubbed his palms against his thighs. Hirsch glanced at Steph Ingram. 'The eagle?'

'Yes, the eagle,' she said, her voice ringing out, holding the room.

Fanning slumped, possibly relieved. He waved a careless hand. 'You tell it.'

Steph turned to Hirsch. 'I came here to ask Russ to get rid of it. Plough it over.'

'All that work,' Fanning muttered. He looked beseechingly at Stephanie Ingram and Hirsch understood that an old refrain was about to play. 'It's a marvel, viewed from above,' Fanning continued. 'It's unique. It's respectful of Aboriginal culture and dreaming. It celebrates it. It's not tacky, it's…elegant.'

'That's not how we see it.'

'How *you* see it,' muttered Fanning. He turned to Hirsch. 'She's even got Noah onside. He called it cultural appropriation and said I was in it for the money.'

'Careful, Russ—*I* didn't say you were in it for the money,' Ingram said. 'And I didn't put words in your son's mouth.'

Hurt, bewildered, possibly angry, Fanning said, 'Sorry,

I know—but all that stuff about cultural appropriation and disrespect…'

'Well, Russ, there was never any real consultation.'

'It's not as if I put the eagle there. I just restored it.'

'But without proper consultation,' Steph Ingram said. She turned to Hirsch. 'Clearly you walked in on something, but I should point out that Russ has actually been the perfect host. He let me pitch my argument—and when I say *my* argument, I mean the local Aboriginal community. But Noah was here, too, and got upset—which was never my intention.'

'Got upset and tore off out of here on one of the mustering bikes,' Fanning said.

'You're worried he might have an accident?' Hirsch asked.

Now Ingram let some harshness in. 'Mr Fanning is obfuscating a bit.' She turned to Hirsch. 'Noah got the bobcat out, initially. I think he might've been planning to grade over the eagle. But Russ intercepted him—grabbed the keys out of his hand, in fact.'

Fanning squirmed in his seat. 'Look, that's between me and him. A bobcat's a piece of heavy machinery. It's not a toy.'

This is more about generational estrangement than anything, Hirsch thought. Father doesn't know how to show love; son wants love, isn't getting it, and decides to punish the old man by adopting someone else's cause.

He got to his feet. 'Look, I'm sorry you find yourselves

in a bind, but I've got more pressing things to do, like knocking on doors to see if anyone saw Mr Aronson or his plane, and that's going to take me the rest of the day out here.' He paused; looked at them one by one. 'You might consider getting a mediator in?'

Fanning and Ingram glanced at each other, then away. Hirsch shrugged, began to cross the room and heard the oncoming howl of a motorbike. Then Noah Fanning was charging into the house, yelling something that took a minute or two to become clear.

He'd found the plane, it seemed. And so had some people with guns.

28

HIRSCH WAS PATIENT with him, trying to elicit some clarity. 'How many people?'

'Two,' Noah said. 'Man and a woman.'

He'd moved tensely to the windows looking on to the roses. Disconcerted to find a policeman in the house, and reminding himself that he was supposed to be angry with his father. And so Hirsch took it slowly. 'They got out of a Land Rover with rifles and stood looking at the wreckage?'

'That's what I said.'

'Did they see you?'

'I told you, I don't know. I don't think so.'

'Where, exactly, son?' said Fanning.

'Don't you listen? At the eagle.'

'Yes, but where exactly? The eagle's three or four kilo-metres wide.'

'At the tip of the wing, all right? The right wing as you face towards it.'

Noah was heated: his father, the situation, his inability to tell the story in one smooth, coherent flow. And then Stephanie Ingram walked up to him, gave him a brisk hug and said, 'Must have been pretty full-on.'

Hirsch smiled at her gratefully. And the boy seemed to loosen. Closing and opening his eyes, he announced: 'Western Australia.'

Hirsch understood. 'The numberplates?'

'Yes.'

Hirsch recalled seeing a Land Rover with WA plates the day he'd driven Dr Van Sant to talk to the Drydens. 'What did they do after looking at the wreckage?'

'Drove away again.'

'What direction?'

Noah waved vaguely to the north-west.

'What did you do then?'

'Went to look at what they were looking at.'

Hirsch was trying to work out who went where, and when. Noah, watching Hirsch's face, tried to clarify. 'When I saw the Land Rover, I was bush-bashing the bike,' he said, with a guilty look at his father, 'you know, up on that high bit where it's all up and down like sand dunes. It didn't seem right, you know, on our property and everything, so I got off and watched them. Then when they drove away, I rode down to have a look.'

Now Noah faltered. He looked stricken, and Hirsch guessed that images of the wreckage had begun to chase off his earlier certainty. 'What did you do then?'

'I, you know, came home.'

'And the plane was completely burnt out?'

Noah looked at his hands. 'Yes,' he said in a small voice.

'The people in the Land Rover didn't set fire to it?'

'No. The fire was already out.'

'And the pilot was still in the cockpit? He couldn't have crawled out before it caught fire?'

Noah hunched his shoulders—seeing it, smelling it. 'No. You could tell.'

Hirsch glanced at Russ Fanning. 'Can you take me there?'

'Yes.'

'Noah, you stay here with Mrs Ingram, all right?' Hirsch said, with a quick glance at Stephanie, who nodded.

'We won't be long, I hope.'

'Take as long as you like,' she said.

Russ Fanning's smile was strained. 'Don't brainwash him too much.'

The moment teetered. Then Steph Ingram smiled and said, 'I'll just plant a few more seeds.'

Fanning clapped his hands together. 'Excellent.'

—

They took the Hilux through the cultivated surrounds of the homestead, into rougher terrain. Pitching and rolling up steep gradients and along barely discernible tracks over a surface of arid-country grasses clinging gamely to hard dirt and stone reefs. Splashes of wildflowers here and there.

'Don't you love it?' Fanning said.

Just then, Hirsch didn't. His hands were tense and aching on the fractious steering wheel, his eyes on the faint tyre impressions immediately ahead. They were on the gibber plain now, a great shallow bowl, and all around them were low, blue-grey hills struck with ochre lights wherever and whenever the sun burned a path through the clouds. And there were powerful winds up there, driving the clouds, their manes streaming, reminding Hirsch of the old Johnny Cash song, 'Ghost Riders in the Sky'.

He couldn't match Fanning's emotion—hadn't chosen to live here, didn't own anything here, hadn't raised a family or buried a wife here. He was an interloper. But so were the Fannings, the Drydens and everyone else who'd staked out their place. The land hadn't been ceded to them.

He didn't say any of this. All he said was, 'I am getting used to the place.'

'You have eyes,' Fanning said contentedly, 'and a soul.'

They passed the ruins of a shepherd's hut: tumbled stone walls and half a chimney. Hirsch did a double-take. 'Your wife painted that.'

'She did.'

They fell silent and the Toyota lurched along in first gear, sometimes second and third. After a time Fanning touched Hirsch's forearm, as if to stall their progress. 'Paul, what should I do?'

Hirsch understood what he meant. 'I think Steph and her mob have a point.'

Fanning looked away.

'And be patient with Noah.'

Fanning said nothing. Then: 'He got really worked up.' Pause. 'Pissed off with me, but also, you know, engaged about the whole cultural identity issue. Or whatever it is.'

'Well, that's a good thing, isn't it? Maybe encourage that.'

What Hirsch couldn't say was, let Noah and Steph dismantle the eagle together. With any luck, Fanning would work it out.

They rolled on over the rough terrain until Fanning pointed and said, 'See that gap? It'll take you up onto the wing.'

Hirsch slowed, ground his way up the slope, and found himself on graded soil. The going was smoother now, and a kilometre later he sensed a narrowing as they neared the eagle's wingtip. And, in the still air, with the side window down, he caught an acrid whiff in his nostrils. He didn't want to smell it. Burnt plastics, fuel, rubber; cooked flesh. He knew the ingredients.

'Poor Noah,' Fanning said, as if imagining the things

his son had seen and felt. Then he stiffened, pointed. 'There.'

It was the tail assembly, sticking up at almost ninety degrees.

They parked, walked to the stone rim and looked down into a shallow depression. The wreckage looked puny to Hirsch. You think 'plane', you think large, even if it's an ultralight, but this was just a small mess of bent struts, oily, blackened fabrics…

And the pilot. Slumped over the controls, badly charred and clenched in a rictus familiar to Hirsch from other fire victims.

'Poor bastard,' Fanning said. 'Wonder what happened?'

Hirsch pointed at the dirt leading up to the stone border. 'See here? Tried to land.'

Fanning looked. 'Okay. Overshot and skidded over the edge.'

Nose-first into the depression, whereupon the engine—part of a pod suspended under the wings that also housed the cockpit—had presumably burst into flames. Poor bastard indeed. 'And here's where the Land Rover parked,' Hirsch said, indicating tread marks in the dirt. Footprints, too, he noticed.

Fanning nodded glumly. 'Still doesn't tell us why Pete needed to land, though. Ran out of fuel, maybe? And who were those people? Why didn't they come and tell us?'

Hirsch needed to know more before he'd speculate. He took photos and video of the tyre and shoe impressions, then stepped over the rim of stones and down into the depression. Took photos and video of the wreckage: the pilot, the engine, the tilted, melted wings and tyres, the tail assembly above. Then he edged closer, careful not to tread in the ash.

The construction was a mix of tubular metal, slab metal—the engine—and sheet metal—the engine cowling. He spotted what he'd been looking for, one in the cowling, the second in the back of the pilot's seat.

'I've got bullet holes here.'

29

FANNING DUCKED AS if he could feel snipers making a bead on him. Glanced around at the nearby hills and elevations. 'He was shot down?'

'Possibly,' Hirsch said, scrambling up to join him. 'Probably. Sometime yesterday. The fire's been out for a while.'

'Was Pete hit or just the plane?'

'An autopsy will tell us.'

'He might have been able to glide a fair distance before he crashed.'

Hirsch nodded. 'Why the shooters didn't find him yesterday.'

'But were they taking pot shots?' Fanning said. He gave his mouth a humourless twist: 'Mistook Pete for one of my rams?'

Or Pete saw something he shouldn't have, Hirsch thought. He examined his clodhopping shoes, the mess of tracks in the surrounding dirt. 'I need to preserve everything, Russ. Maybe if you could hop in the car for now?'

'Sure,' Fanning said, turning to go. 'There's a camera over there, by the way.'

He pointed, just as the sun flashed off the broken lens of a camera lying in a tussock of grass.

Hirsch rummaged for a paper evidence bag, then thought better of it. Leave the camera to the forensics team. 'It looks like a regular digital. I assume he used a special camera bolted under the fuselage?'

Fanning shook his head. 'There is one, but it's not special, just a little GoPro for video and general backup.' He looked gloomily at the wreckage. 'Destroyed, probably. But the Nikon'—he pointed—'was his pride and joy. It's a DSLR with good zoom and vibration reduction and he usually had it set on continuous shooting mode. Saved everything to a memory card.'

Hirsch's eyes glazed over a little. 'Okay.'

With Fanning now inside the Hilux, he opened the Toyota's storage cabinet and took out a large poly tarpaulin. Sliced it up into four ragged rectangles, placing the first over the Land Rover's tyre tracks, the edges weighed down by stones, the second over a set of boot prints, the third over a smaller set, possibly trainers, and the fourth over the Nikon camera.

He rejoined Fanning, who said, 'Looks like he tossed the camera into the bushes? Must've known he was a goner.'

Hirsch had already guessed that. 'Possibly.'

'I'll go out on a limb and say probably,' Fanning said. 'It's just as well the shooters didn't spot it.'

Hirsch nodded absently. Unclipping the radio handset, he made the first of several calls. As he'd predicted, he was told to secure the scene and wait for investigators to arrive. But wait for several hours? No thanks.

He didn't say that, however. Hoping his silence would indicate assent, he signed off and turned the ignition key. 'I'd better get you home. And I should warn you, you'll have a flood of visitors over the next few days, some of whom might treat you as if you're a suspect.'

'Fuck 'em,' Fanning said. 'And where are you going? To have a word with Mia Dryden?'

Hirsch said nothing. Merely put the Toyota into reverse.

'Paul...' Fanning said, more agitated now.

'Russ, I'm not going to speculate about anything, or explain my next moves. I still have to check if anyone saw the plane yesterday.'

'She could put a bullet in you.'

Hirsch made a sharp half-circle, his eyes on the side

280

mirror, then centred the wheel. 'Like I said, police business. But let's say for argument's sake Noah saw Sam and Mia Dryden earlier. Wouldn't he recognise them?'

'No. I've only met them a couple of times myself.'

Hirsch accelerated gently along the wing of the eagle, found the gap between the stones, and bumped down onto the track of stone reefs, sand drifts and washaways. He was trying to put himself in the shoes of the pilot and the shooters when Fanning asked a question he'd already been asking himself: 'Be good to know what direction he came from.'

'It would. Let's hope I find someone who saw him yesterday.'

'And it would be good to know what *time* he was shot at.'

'Maybe late afternoon?' Hirsch said. 'So they stopped looking for him when they ran out of daylight, and resumed searching today.'

'Or it was raining heavily where they were,' Fanning said. He paused. 'What if they come back with earth-moving equipment and bury the lot?'

Hirsch hadn't thought of that. His next stage would need to be quick.

The day had been hectic and chaotic. It wasn't until Hirsch was alone, rolling along the Manna Soak Highway, that the images came back into his head again. The baby ripped apart, the dog dropping like a sack of grain, Brenda's injuries, Damien Pierce folded, leaking, into a suitcase. His breath shortened, he felt the twitches of panic. Slowed; stopped. Got out to walk around and try to slow and deepen his breathing. He wasn't right inside. The urge to weep was strong.

He drove on eventually and finally found himself on the Dryden Downs entry road. The surface was blessedly smooth, a counterpoint to his inner agitation. He tried his breathing technique again and forced himself to reassess what he intended to do once he reached the station homestead.

He knew he was being impetuous. Investigators more senior, more experienced, would be coming along behind him, and wouldn't thank him for muddying the waters— let alone alerting Mia Dryden. In any case, all she needed to do was deny everything. There was no proof she was the shooter, or indeed that she was the armed woman Noah had seen.

The best Hirsch could hope for was to rattle her or find an inconsistency in her story. Otherwise, hunt around the sheds for the Land Rover with Western Australian plates. If he was challenged, he'd say the driver would need to register the vehicle in South Australia if he—or she—intended to stay. Meanwhile photograph its tyres. Collect soil samples from the treads. And do what with that evidence? Expect the forensics lab to drop everything and test them? He didn't even have a case number.

Meanwhile, as he knew full well from her Facebook

and Instagram posts, Mia Dryden liked to blast living things with a rifle.

Hirsch found himself clenching again. Ducking, as Russ Fanning had done at the crash site. He pulled over and got out again until his breathing eased and realised, from the state of the road, how localised the rains had been. Just here, nearer the homestead, the surface was spongy, and there were shallow pools in the paddocks, with matted clumps of twigs, bark and dirt blocking the ditches on either side. He drove the last half kilometre very slowly, not wanting to bog the Toyota, not wanting to spoil the driveway. Not wanting to get worked up again, in fact. He would be bland, pleasant Senior Constable Hirschhausen from Tiverton, calling in at Dryden Downs on the off chance they'd seen an ultralight aeroplane. A cup of tea would be great, thanks. You must be delighted about the rain.

He paused at the top of the rise. Nothing moved—not a horse, dog, ute or station hand. Instead, the homestead seemed to slumber in the sunlight that was breaking through the fraying clouds of mid-afternoon. Pressing gently on the accelerator again, he followed the road down and around to the stand of trees beside the main house. Got out. Looked over at the dressage ring: Mia's horse looked back at him.

Hooking his mask on, he stepped up onto the veranda and knocked. The door rattled and the sound of his knuckles was hollow, seeming to lose itself along the hallway dimly visible through the flyscreen. When there was no answer, he opened the screen door and this time sent a hard crack of the main door's brass knocker down the hallway. A sound that meant business, but again there was no reply. Yet the house felt occupied.

Undecided, he turned, stepped off the veranda and began scouting around each of the sheds on the property. There was a big black Porsche Cayenne and a silver Mercedes sedan in the garage next to the house, and four other vehicles scattered around the property: a ute, two Jeeps and a small Isuzu truck. No Land Rover.

He was halfway back to the house, trying to scrape reddish mud from the soles of his shoes, when the cook, Barry McGain, emerged from a fenced-off area of garden beds—flowers, herbs, vegetables—swinging an enamel kitchen pail by the handle, a mask around his chin. He stopped when he spotted Hirsch. Covered his nose and mouth again and carried on, wearing an apron over a T-shirt and jeans, running his other hand over his military-style flattop as if to reassure himself he still had hair on his head.

He stopped when he reached Hirsch. His voice muffled by the mask, he said, 'Help you?'

Wondering about the mask—the absence of masks had seemed to be a point of honour on Dryden Downs—Hirsch said, 'Where is everyone?'

'Out mustering. We start shearing on Monday.'

'Everyone?'

There was a pause. McGain shook his head. 'Mrs Dryden's having a sleep. She was up all night with Mr Dryden. The flying doctor came for him this morning.'

Hirsch had sensed that the house wasn't empty. 'What's wrong with him?'

'Seizures, vomiting, diarrhoea.'

Hirsch twigged: the Ivermectin. 'Barry, if he's got Covid, and if Mia's been treating him with horse medicine, he could be in big trouble.'

McGain shrugged. 'I'm no doctor.'

'Nor is Mrs Dryden. Is she also sick?'

McGain didn't want to answer. 'Is this any of your business?'

'I'm thinking of my own safety, for a start,' Hirsch lied. 'I find myself in close contact with you. I touched the front door. And I know some of the station hands like to drink at the Tiverton pub.'

McGain screwed up his face. 'All I know is, she seems fine, just a bit wrung out looking after Mr Dryden.'

'Including this morning?'

'Including this morning.'

If that was true, she hadn't been out searching for Pete Aronson's ultralight, Hirsch thought. 'Did you see Doctor Van Sant the other day?'

It was a cheap trick, swerving to put people off balance, but it often produced results. McGain frowned unconvincingly. 'Who?'

'You remember, Willi's mother?'

'Oh. Yeah. Haven't seen her.'

Hirsch switched topics again. Glancing at McGain's hand, he asked, 'What was in the bucket?'

McGain stared at him evenly. 'Compost.'

'I guess there'd be plenty of food scraps on a place this size.'

'Plenty of food scraps,' McGain agreed.

'What are Mrs Dryden's symptoms?'

Another look. It seemed to say, 'I know your game.' Then McGain shrugged and began to edge around Hirsch, saying, 'Exhaustion, all right?'

Hirsch fell into step with him. 'Let's hope *you* don't catch Covid.'

'Yeah.'

'Is there good hunting around here? Wild goats, kangaroos? Mrs Dryden likes to hunt, so I'm told.'

McGain pulled his mask down and his voice was clear: 'What do you want?'

'I was just wondering if sometimes Mrs Dryden brings you a wild goat to butcher and cook. Maybe a sheep. Is that where the fresh meat on the place comes from? Shot? Trapped? It's not something I'm very familiar with. City boy,' Hirsch said.

If Hirsch was inviting contempt, he got it. McGain curled his lip. 'If it makes you happy, sometimes Mrs Dryden shoots a feral pig, sometimes Mr Dryden shoots one, sometimes one of the shedhands. Or we kill a ewe. I do the butchering.'

'Do you like to hunt?'

'I hunt recipes on the internet,' McGain said.

They were near the house now. McGain veered right, taking a path along the side wall to the big cookhouse at the rear, his footsteps crushing the gravel. The sounds must have alerted Mia Dryden: her voice came, clear but shaky, from an open window: 'Who is it?'

'Me, Mrs Dryden,' McGain said.

'Could you do me another cup of tea, please?'

'Sure thing,' McGain said, going on his way again.

Hirsch followed him into the cookhouse, which smelt of heated oils, and here McGain plonked the enamel pail on a bench beside the sink and said, 'Look, I'm busy, all right? And no, I'm not going to let you question her.'

'Fair enough. Quick question before I go,' Hirsch said. 'I was wondering if you noticed an ultralight plane flying over here yesterday.'

This stopped McGain. He stared at Hirsch and said flatly, 'No. What about it?'

'It's overdue.'

'Can't help you.'

'But you know the one I mean? It's flown overhead before?'

'Nup, not that I know of.'

'Would the Drydens or one of the station hands have seen it?'

McGain was fed up. 'No one has. The station hands have been out bush all week, and Mr and Mrs Dryden have been here with me.'

'Where are the hands mustering? Maybe I can talk to them.'

'Forget about it. They're half a day away from here,' McGain said, indicating, with a wave of his arm, the back country. 'They camp out there. Tents and swags. Now if you don't mind, I need to get on with it.'

'It *is* Covid, Mr Dryden's illness? He and his wife aren't calling it a bad cold?'

With a flicker of emotion, McGain turned away. His voice was muffled when it came: 'Like I said, I'm busy.'

Hirsch returned to the Hilux. His radio was crackling: a voice snarling, where did he think he was? Police and air safety officials were waiting for him.

Already? Shit, bugger, damn.

30

LATE AFTERNOON NOW, long shadows striping the land. Hirsch's doppelgänger Hilux running bulkily beside him as he entered Russ Fanning's driveway. The sun was not quite smearing the horizon yet but the air was cooler and this was the end of a long day and he didn't really want some prick on his case, barely before he'd turned the engine off.

'Senior Constable Hirschhausen?'

'That's me,' Hirsch said, shutting his door, turning to face the newcomer—and he realised, looking beyond the man's facemask, that he'd seen him before, with another man, outside Scott Greig's flat, about to serve a warrant.

'My name is Cottrell, I'm an inspector with the Australian Federal Police. Is there a reason why you failed to safeguard the crash site as requested?'

Federal? Hirsch took a moment. A police helicopter was parked between Russ's house and his array of solar panels. It was empty, but he doubted that Cottrell had arrived alone. He glanced at the house, half-expecting Russ to come out. Steph's muddy Mazda was gone.

The helicopter explains the quick arrival, he told himself glumly. It also says this is not just another murder.

He swung his gaze back to Cottrell. Mid-forties, solid build, with a neat part in thick, greying hair. A suit jacket and pants, white shirt, no tie. Glasses with heavy dark rims, and already a patina of back-country dust on his toecaps. But he didn't look incongruous. He had that scowling look of competence and authority sometimes found in people who take command of places and situations.

'I apologise, sir. I assumed—'

'Yeah, well, don't—ever.'

'Yes, sir,' Hirsch said.

'So? Where were you?'

'I was following up a lead, thinking it could be hours before anyone got here.'

'What lead?'

'Have you spoken to Mr Fanning and his son, sir?'

'I have. What lead?'

290

'Then you know that Noah Fanning saw two armed strangers at the crash site, a man and a woman, driving a Land Rover with WA plates.'

'You are not writing the preface to a detailed report, Senior Constable Hirschhausen. Cut to the chase.'

'Sir.' Hirsch pointed in the general direction of Dryden Downs. 'A local woman named Mia Dryden owns several high-powered hunting rifles. She likes to post on Instagram, posing with her guns and the animals she's just bagged.'

A faint tension in Cottrell as Hirsch named her. But it was there and gone again and all he said was, 'That's it? A bit on the slim side.'

'Yes, sir. But I don't know of anyone else out this way who's so keen on shooting things. Also, someone shot one of Mr Fanning's stud rams earlier in the year, and I saw a Land Rover with WA plates a few days ago, coming from the direction of Mrs Dryden's property. It seemed like a worthwhile avenue to follow.'

'And?'

'I'm afraid it didn't pan out. Mr Dryden's been in bed with Covid all week, and Mrs Dryden's been nursing him. No sign of the Land Rover.'

'So, a waste of time and meanwhile you left the crash site unattended. I'm thinking wind, rain, wild animals...'

'Sir.'

'The others are already at the scene. I waited for you. Come on.'

Cottrell tugged on the Toyota's passenger door handle

and climbed in. Hirsch, shrugging philosophically, slid behind the steering wheel. A long day, getting longer. Harder.

When he turned the ignition key, Johnny Cash came on, 'The Man Comes Around.' He turned off the sound hastily. The words were apt, though: a man going round taking names.

Cottrell rode silently, looking out at the late afternoon shadows and the patches of dirt, scrub and low hillsides that blazed when touched by a ray of the sinking sun. Not a restful silence. Cottrell was chewing on heavy thoughts, it seemed to Hirsch. And why had a federal policeman been sent here? Why an inspector? Why a helicopter? Why the urgency, in other words.

He tried for conversation. 'Where are you based, sir? Adelaide?'

Cottrell said, 'Tell me more about Mia Dryden.'

'Only met her once, sir, and like I said, she's been nursing her sick husband.'

'Don't be obtuse—who is she? What does she do? What do you know about her?'

Hirsch had the odd feeling that Cottrell already knew the answers. He's interested in what I think and know, he thought. Humble beat cop that I am. 'Well, sir, it's ironical that her husband has Covid—she's an anti-vaxxer and possibly a Covid denier.'

'Go on.'

'Hunting animals is a kind of noble imperative for her. Somehow tied up with notions of individual freedom and sovereign rights. She uses the words "sovereign rights" quite a bit in her Instagram posts.'

If Hirsch was expecting Cottrell to be frustrated or impatient with this abridged account, he was mistaken. The federal policeman merely grunted and the Hilux continued to complain and pitch about on the heaving track.

Cottrell said, 'What about the husband?'

Again, he seemed only half-interested. Hirsch said, 'Polite. Undemonstrative.'

'He shares her beliefs?'

'I only met him once, and he doesn't have much of an online presence, so I couldn't say.'

Cottrell grunted again. 'Polite, undemonstrative.'

'And ex-army,' added Hirsch, 'with political ambitions.'

'Interesting that you did research into both of them, Senior Constable Hirschhausen. Would you care to speak to that?'

Hirsch was distracted briefly by a kink in the road: 'Kink in the Road', his theme song. He wrestled with the steering wheel until they reached a relatively smooth stretch and said, 'I like to know who my constituents are, so to speak.'

'Don't bullshit a bullshitter.'

So Hirsch rolled his shoulders and said, 'I met them for the first time a couple of weeks ago in the company of a woman from Belgium named Janne Van Sant, who's out here looking for her son, Willi.' He filled Cottrell in briefly, concluding: '…the Drydens told us Willi had left the property several weeks earlier to drive to Queensland with his girlfriend.'

Cottrell gave another of his signature grunts and Hirsch, rather than speculate about the Noosa motel manager's connection to Sam Dryden, merely added: 'They intrigued me.'

'Intrigued you.'

Judging by Cottrell's tone, Hirsch might have been downloading porn.

Two utes awaited them at the crash site, both stencilled with the words *Wildu Station Merino Stud*. It was clear why two vehicles were needed—apart from Russ Fanning, who had presumably led the way, there was an Australian Transport Safety Bureau officer and four investigators. Cottrell didn't introduce them but told Hirsch to wait with Russ Fanning, who was leaning against the ute, a dark expression on his face.

'Been railroaded?'

'You could say that,' Hirsch replied, also leaning his rump against the ute. Heat rose from the engine. 'Sorry I wasn't around when they arrived.'

'No problem.' He shrugged. 'Our input's surplus to requirements anyway. They ignored me when I floated our theories about what might have happened.'

Another of my theme songs, thought Hirsch. He

watched Cottrell step over the stones marking the tip of the eagle's wing and join the men gathered at the wreckage, photographing, videoing, collecting samples. Another was wider afield, strolling head down in a grid pattern.

'How's Noah?'

Russ Fanning unfolded his arms and said, 'Interesting you should ask. He's gone off with Mrs Ingram. I mean, she invited him, after checking with me first. I said it was okay.'

'Gone off where?'

'Back to Redruth. I think she could see how upset he was about this'—he gestured at the mangled plane—'and wanted to distract him. Show him the kinds of things she does there. Pastoral care, I don't know, whatever.'

Fanning looked dazed, the world slipping past too quickly. 'Just till Monday.'

'Steph's okay,' Hirsch said, conscious of sounding trite.

'You know what he said? I live on unceded sovereign land.'

Sovereign—everyone's go-to word, thought Hirsch. 'Give him time. It's good that he's interested in things.'

'Maybe.'

A disturbance of the air: the crash investigator patrolling on the fringes had shot his hand up and shouted, 'Got a camera here.'

Fanning muttered, 'Clever boy. Just as well it wasn't hidden under a bit of bright blue tarp.'

Hirsch grinned along with him. They saw Cottrell

wander over to check the camera. Kneel. Reach out a gloved hand. Then he was upright again, coming back, scrambling up onto the flat ground and striding determinedly towards them.

Stopping short, he gave a jerk of his head and said, 'Which one of you geniuses went around placing bits of plastic over everything?'

'Me, sir,' Hirsch said. 'Protection against the elements.'

'And did you also remove the memory card from the camera?'

Hirsch went still. 'No, sir. Didn't even touch it.'

'You, Mr Fanning?'

'Not me, not my son.'

'Jesus Christ.'

'As I mentioned, sir,' Hirsch said, 'two strangers were here before us. They could have taken it.'

'Yeah, yeah,' Cottrell said in disgust.

'If it's any use,' Fanning cut in, 'I know the pilot had a little GoPro mounted underneath, near the front wheel. For backup mainly, and video. A kind of record of where he'd been.'

Cottrell looked further disgusted and returned to the crash site. He conferred with the other investigators and they bent to peer under the fuselage pod. Time passed and the sun sank further and then Cottrell was calling to them: 'Yeah, it's here, but it's wrecked.'

As if they were to blame. With a look at Hirsch—and muttering, 'Against my better judgment'—Fanning stalked across the dirt to the edge and looked down at Cottrell. 'Another thing you could try, look for Pete's phone. He had an app for the GoPro, set to automatically transfer and save whatever he filmed.'

Cottrell turned away again to confer. Fanning, left adrift, wandered back to join Hirsch. He shivered. 'Should've brought a coat with me.'

Finally, Cottrell called to them again: 'His leather jacket withstood a lot of the flames. There's no phone, as far as we can tell.'

Hirsch stepped away from the ute. 'If he tossed the camera away, maybe he tossed the phone, too.'

And already he was moving. If Pete Aronson had tossed the Nikon in one direction, odds were he'd tossed the phone the other way. He stepped down into the hollow and found the phone within minutes, a big Samsung with a smashed screen. A rectangle of glass and metal encased in thick plastic and lying amid dust and pebbles as silent and old as the centuries. Another interloper, like the ultralight plane.

He didn't shout, 'Found it,' but pressed the power button and saw the screen light up. As expected, it was password protected. And then Cottrell was removing it from his grasp deftly, saying, 'If you don't mind...'

31

HIRSCH WAS LATE home that Thursday evening. The shop was shut and the pickings in his freezer were slim. A pub meal was out of the question since the publican had taken over the cooking now that his wife had run off— apparently with the craft-beer rep for the mid-north. Also, the locals would act as though they only had to stare avidly enough and he'd spontaneously cough up the details of the railway-cottage horrors.

And it seemed that he'd forgotten the tennis club's annual general meeting. He'd been secretary and treasurer in the past, the outsider trying to make a good impression, not realising until too late that their smiles of appreciation were actually relief: a kind of 'more fool you'. Nowadays he was just another committee member, but, even so, he should have been at this meeting. He'd probably been punished in his absence, signed up for court upkeep, net repairs and keeping the urn filled.

He rummaged in the freezer again. Found a kind of stir-fry he'd whipped up—months ago?—from leftover roast chicken and vegetables. He defrosted it. Frypan-tossed it in butter for a couple of minutes and ate it in front of the last quarter-hour of *7.30*. The prime minister was on, saying he understood the needs of women because he had a wife and daughters.

And all the while, he was in motion. Legs jiggling, fingers tapping. Couldn't keep still, couldn't get comfortable. He finished eating and prowled his miserable quarters for a while, room to room, trying to take in enough air to survive, feeling that his lungs had been reduced to a tiny bellows at the top of his chest. He wanted to strip off his clothing as if that would let more air in. He felt the need to cry, and couldn't.

He was saved by his phone.

Wendy's voice. 'Just calling to see how you are.' Affectionate, heartfelt. Alive.

He sat, the bands loosening fractionally. 'Not all that good, actually.'

'No wonder. Look, since Kate and I are going away

this weekend, why don't you come here again tonight? Sleep in tomorrow. Call in sick.'

Hirsch uttered a snuffling laugh. 'You have no idea how appealing that sounds.'

But if he thought he'd be love-bombed and that would be it, he was mistaken. Sure, there were kisses, a three-way hug, shampoo-scented heads tucked under his chin, concerned eyes. And dessert was pancakes with ice-cream and maple syrup, and the kitchen was warm and Kate had some of her old spirit back.

Then she wandered away to finish her homework and the mood changed subtly; some of Wendy's warmth had ebbed. Hirsch, drying the dishes, tried deflection. 'How's Kate doing?'

There was a pause. 'Better. She's had two sessions with the school counsellor.'

'Does she like her?'

'Yes.' No elaboration.

They finished the washing-up in silence and then Wendy grabbed his elbow and led him to the table. 'Sit.'

He did. She sat opposite him, took his hands in hers and kneaded the backs of his fingers with her strong thumbs. 'Okay, tell me what the matter is.'

He described his symptoms.

She said, 'Sounds like a panic attack.' She gave his hands a determined shake and smacked them down on the table. 'Again. Tell me what the matter is.'

'Isn't that—' Hirsch stopped.

He saw his mother with his father. It was 2008, in the old house in Tonsley before his parents moved to the Adelaide Hills, and he'd called in with a load of dirty washing one day, to discover them holding hands across the kitchen table, his father weeping. He'd been retrenched: the Mitsubishi plant was closing down.

'Let it out, darling, let it out,' his mother was saying, having given Hirsch a quick little frowning glance that said not only was it time he grew up and did his own laundry, but she also didn't have time for her son just then, as she returned her attention to the distressed man seated across from her.

The memory was powerful. His father, in tears. And Hirsch blinked his own tears away. 'It's all getting to me.'

'Of course.'

'I need a tissue,' Hirsch said, with a watery cough as he slipped his hands from Wendy's and stood abruptly, ejecting his chair with a scrape across the old linoleum floor.

The tissues were on the bench beside the landline handset. He plucked one. Behind him, Wendy said, 'Bring the box back with you.'

When he was seated again, eyes mopped, his hands in hers again, he said, 'Phew.'

She wasn't impressed. 'You said everything's getting to you. What is?'

Hirsch could feel within himself the urge to dodge

and parry. It was what he did. He began to cast the first evasive sentence in his head.

And Wendy saw him doing it. She should have been a cop. 'Aitch,' she said warningly. Adding: 'We're in a relationship, remember?'

She'd said it once before. And now, as if for the first time, he saw what that entailed.

He took a breath. 'It's been happening off and on since Tuesday, feeling panicky. Worse tonight.'

She looked at him. 'And?'

'I keep...re-seeing things. I could be just driving along the highway and images will pop into my head.'

'Like...?'

'The baby, mostly. All torn up, all that blood. Would it have known what was happening, before, you know...?'

Her fingers kneaded his. 'Did the department offer counselling?'

'Yes.'

'Take it,' Wendy said, removing her hands, folding her arms.

Was this what normal people did as a matter of course? Clarified a problem, then dealt with it? Accepted that you felt like shit sometimes, but you could also call on someone to help you *not* feel like shit?

'I made an appointment,' he said.

A flicker in her eyes. Why hadn't he told her?

She took his hands again. The kitchen light was harsh and under it the woman he loved was tired, her face lived in, a map of her own heartaches. A beautiful face, giving him just then a measure of tough love.

Her phone pinged at her elbow. She glanced at it, still holding tight to him. Frowning, she released one of his hands and lifted the screen to her face. 'Weird.'

'What is?'

She nudged the phone across the table. Hirsch looked. A text; unknown number. Three words: *Sorry for everything*.

'Mum?' Kate came into the room, staring at her own phone.

32

LOVE HAD REACHED out to him, albeit sternly, and Hirsch did sleep in on Friday. Which meant that he was late setting out for the long-range patrol he'd had to curtail the previous day.

It was uneventful. He checked on a couple of licensed guns, helped clear a fallen tree, spoke to a couple of Pandowie kids he saw skateboarding when they should have been at school, sat down in too many kitchens and got back to Tiverton with a leaden stomach: all that black tea, all those Anzac biscuits.

In the evening he called Wendy. Background noise: she and Kate were in the Golf, heading up to the Murray River to stay two nights with her brother. She wanted to know if he'd had news of Alice McNamara.

'No. No sightings, and I check the house regularly. No one's come back.'

They'd speculated about it last night, Wendy wanting to believe that Alice had sent the sorry messages. 'We'll be back Sunday night,' she said now. 'Love you.'

'Love you, too.'

Then he phoned Russ Fanning, who said, 'Noah called. Or Steph made him call me.'

'Okay...'

'He hopes he can work something out with his school. Some kind of internship with her.'

Hirsch couldn't quite read the man's voice. Oddly proud with a tinge of doubt? He said, 'You'd see him more often.'

'That's if he wants to see me. And what if he gets tired of it? He's a bit impetuous—like his mother.'

'Give him a chance.'

'I told Steph I'd help,' Fanning said gruffly.

He'll throw himself into it, thought Hirsch. Get in everyone's way, say the wrong thing. Keep trying.

Saturday, 6.45 a.m. Hirsch was taking his morning walk and thinking about the meaning of his morning walks. Meanings, rather. In his early days here, he walked, as he

305

always had, for exercise. Then the city boy in him started to feel the strangeness of this place, and he'd walked in order to map the town, learn it, make it his. Later still, understanding the town's vulnerabilities, moments when threats encroached, he'd made sentry walks, a lone guard keeping the place safe—not in so many words, he chided himself. Not in such heightened language.

And now he was mainly walking for exercise again—of a more holistic kind. Sure, the town still seemed a little alien, and it would never be entirely peaceful, but it was more that if he didn't walk every morning, the day would seem incomplete.

The dawn walks marked him out, though. There were always plenty of people around at that hour—Bob Muir stowing gear in his work van; Mrs Lidstrom watering her roses—but he knew of only two other people who walked each morning simply to walk: widows of the vigorous gardening and community activity kind, who would smile, nod and stride by, elbows pumping, whenever he encountered them.

This morning he walked to the far end of Tiverton, beyond the silos and back down Wirrabara Street and its little railway cottages. There had been a shower overnight, the sun flashing like diamond lights on the raindrops again—and, in the dirt at the side of Brenda's house, a fresh set of tyre tracks. That's what his life had become, crime scenes and fresh tyre tracks. He walked to the rear: nothing had altered. He checked the back door and the door to the caravan. Both were locked.

Maybe the visitor was a stickybeak, a ghoul...or a reporter? He'd have to monitor the place more conscientiously now. On top of all the other stuff piling up in his life.

It hit him again: the plump, mangled little forearm, the blood...He hurried back to the road. Paused to breathe in and out, to slow his heart, expunge those pictures.

He checked his watch: no way he'd get back to his poky quarters in time for the 7 a.m. news and so, with no point in hurrying, he ambled on down Wirrabara Street, planning a long, slow loop that would bring him in behind the primary school, opposite the police station.

But he was barely a hundred metres past Brenda Maher's cottage when a car came creeping in beside him. He moved further off the road, stepping over the ditch and crowding against the fence wires before gesturing with his right hand, waving the driver on.

Instead, the car slowed to keep pace with him. A dark blue BMW M3 with tinted windows, utterly out of place here in the land of dusty farm utes and Japanese sedans. Hirsch halted, his heart racing. Mapped out his next few seconds: three or four running steps to the closest fence post, right hand on top of it for leverage, a clean vault over into the paddock and then a racing zigzag across it to a distant farmhouse, the roof showing as a patch of faded red iron above a hedgerow of cypresses.

The rear window slid down and Inspector Cottrell's face appeared. 'Get in.'

—

Hirsch was enveloped in soft leather, subtle aftershave and whisper-quiet engine noise as the BMW moved on again. That, and the 'abduction', were unnerving enough, but in the front passenger seat was Barry McGain, the Dryden Downs cook, dressed as before in jeans and a T-shirt. The driver looked like a younger, chunkier, more unimpressed version of Cottrell, in wraparound sunglasses.

Hirsch rubbed his hands on his thighs, conscious that he hadn't showered or shaved and had dragged on the jeans, shirt and hoodie he'd been wearing, morning and evening, since Monday. His mind worked furiously, trying to connect every weird fact and impression that had touched him for the past two or three weeks.

'I've stepped into something,' he said finally.

'You could say that.' Cottrell's face was smooth, his shirt crisp. He might have been a bank manager.

'I'm guessing you found something on Pete Aronson's iPhone.'

'Unfortunately, no. Or rather, only material from earlier flights.'

Showing a bit of hostility to cover his nerves, Hirsch said, 'You going to tell me why you snatched me off the street?'

'A bit melodramatic,' said McGain from the front seat.

'So is sneaking up on me like a kerb-crawler.'

McGain half-turned his head. 'We snatched you off the street, as you put it, because we want you to back off.'

'Back off from what?'

'Poking your nose in where you shouldn't. This is a need-to-know situation, and you don't need to know.'

It was like being in a bad spy film. Hirsch turned to Cottrell and said, 'Who is he?'

'Federal police, that's all you need to know. Undercover, needless to say.'

'Federal,' Hirsch said, unimpressed. 'I've seen you in three contexts now: serving a warrant on Scott Greig— who has disappeared, as you probably know—appearing at the scene of a shot-down plane and now this bit of amateur cloak and dagger. Care to join the dots?'

'Paul,' Cottrell said, using Hirsch's first name like a weapon, 'we are currently engaged in a sensitive long-term operation and if you make further unannounced police visits to the Drydens' property, you risk jeopardising that operation.'

Pompous arsehole. 'What are the Drydens up to?' Hirsch said.

'We're asking you, on a matter of grave importance,' McGain said, 'to pull your fucking head in, okay?'

Hirsch ignored him. 'I'm guessing someone from the property *did* shoot down Mr Aronson?'

This time the driver spoke. 'What don't you understand about "pull your head in"?'

Hirsch ignored him, too. 'Are there international ramifications? The missing backpacker?'

Cottrell was weary with him now. 'Please leave it with

us, Senior Constable Hirschhausen. Be patient. We hope to have the answers you need in a matter of weeks.'

'I'm not sure Willi Van Sant's mother will wait a few weeks. I think she thinks something happened to her son on the Dryden place.'

Cottrell seemed to fight himself for an answer that would suit Hirsch. 'We hope to have an answer to that matter, too. Meanwhile we need—'

'Has she contacted you?'

'Not directly. To the best of my knowledge, she contacted Foreign Affairs some weeks ago, and they referred the matter to us. That's all I'm willing to say at this stage.'

'I'm talking about more recently, the last couple of days,' Hirsch said.

The general store slid by on the other side of the tinted glass next to Cottrell's head. 'I'm not aware,' he said, 'of any recent contact.'

Now the driver made a right turn and took them past the side-street lucerne seed business, then left towards the oval. So much for cloak and dagger. Half the town would be wondering who they were and what they were up to. 'She texted me during the week to say she was coming back to the area,' Hirsch said.

Cottrell sharpened. He didn't seem to like this development. 'What was the gist of her text, if you don't mind?'

'I need to put it into context,' Hirsch said. 'When she and I met the Drydens we were shown a postcard, ostensibly from Willi's girlfriend, saying they were both

310

holidaying in Noosa. I made an inquiry on Doctor Van Sant's behalf and learned from local police that the kids had been staying in a motel in the area but had skipped, owing rent.'

Cottrell was giving him a get-on-with-it look. 'And?'

'Doctor Van Sant did some of her own investigating and discovered that the manager had served in the army with Sam Dryden.'

Cottrell gave a little wince. He rallied. 'Coincidence.'

'Like hell. I'm betting Willi and his girlfriend never stayed there. Never left Dryden Downs.'

'Supposition.'

'Intuition. Doctor Van Sant said she was coming back here and I'm thinking she intends to challenge the Drydens—if she hasn't already done so. I texted her to contact me first, but she didn't respond. So, I'm asking again, did she show up?' He leaned into the gap between the seats. 'Perhaps the Drydens' cook can answer that.'

'Fuck off,' said McGain.

'That's enough, sergeant,' Cottrell said.

The driver grinned. He was heading around the oval now and down along the town paddock's access track, then right at the intersection with the highway and back to Tiverton. They reached the outskirts and there was one of the vigorous widows, swinging her arms. She narrowed her eyes in concentration as the BMW crept into town again. Hirsch waved, knowing she would only see panes of darkened glass, not him, not his abductors.

He turned back to Cottrell. 'You serve a warrant on Scott Greig and then he disappears. Any coincidence that he and Petra Osmak belong to a gang of nutcases calling themselves Antipodean Storm?'

'Just keep out of it, Hirschhausen,' McGain said. 'That's all we want from you. Just go about your business.'

'Go back to investigating haystack fires and sheep-shaggers,' the driver said.

No one admonished him. No one laughed, either. After a moment, he pulled his head into his shoulders.

'Before I go, Bazza,' Hirsch said, 'before you *let* me go, how's Sam Dryden doing?'

McGain said nothing. He looked straight ahead. Then: 'Boss?'

Cottrell said, 'It can't hurt.' Turning to Hirsch, he said, 'He took a turn for the worse. He's on a ventilator.'

Hirsch took a chance. 'Does that mean you're bringing your operation forward? Cranking it up a notch?'

No reaction. He shrugged. 'Has Mia gone to be with her husband?'

Again no one answered. The driver glided the BMW to the kerb outside the police station. 'This do you, cobber?'

Prick.

Hirsch got out. But so did McGain, who gave him a tight smile and an unexpected handshake before climbing into the back with Cottrell. They knew my morning routine, thought Hirsch, as he fished out the key to the front door. Just then he heard a motor start, a touch of warm-up revs, and looked across the highway. A Pajero was peeling away, punching through the gears.

Hirsch checked the numberplate later that morning. Cody Morton.

33

SUNDAY, HIRSCH WAKING in his own bed again. A day of rest, not that that meant anything to a country copper. He rolled out, slipped on his jeans, windcheater and runners and walked the town. No action at the railway cottage.

And as he walked, he realised that he was not feeling so jittery. He'd slept fairly well. The bloodied blanket, the other images of his day- and nightmares were not so vivid. He wasn't fooled; he knew he hadn't really returned to himself. But he did feel less contingent, more certain.

Wendy's stern talking-to had helped. The promise of a psych appointment next week. The general busyness of his life. (Note to self: don't forget to notify Sergeant Brandl and lodge the paperwork.)

By 7.09, muesli and coffee inside him and the ABC weather update burbling on the radio—scattered showers expected again in the mid-north—he was planning his day. Call in on people as an acquaintance, if not a friend. He was allowed a life, after all, even though his phone might drag him away. The Muirs, for example. Nan Washburn. Phone his parents, unless they called him first. Maybe start painting the sitting room.

Or not. Hirsch stood up from the garden table where he breakfasted when the weather was mild, went inside, stared at the walls and ceilings for a while. Took a shower. Then, dressed in jeans, T-shirt, windcheater and runners again, he stepped outside to gauge the state of his police Toyota. He'd parked it on the street overnight: big mistake. There was a new message written in the dust and mud: *Pride of the fleet.*

Eight-thirty now, the town dead quiet, no one up, only one lonely vehicle passing through the town—possibly headed for mass in Redruth. He doubted Daryl Cobb would be awake. He doubted Daryl would be interested in washing the Hilux—or not for thirty bucks. Maybe forty?

Couldn't hurt to slip a note under the Cobbs' back door. Not the front door, which was never used, or the mail slot in the front fence, since there were no mail deliveries in Tiverton—everyone had a keyed mailbox in a bank of boxes set into the front wall of Ed Tennant's shop.

With a scrap of paper in his pocket bearing a scribbled request and an offer of forty dollars, Hirsch wandered on down to the Cobbs' mute, stunned little house. As usual, it seemed to be shut against the world. He stood for a moment in the driveway, listening. No voices; no sounds of backyard watering or weeding, hyper or otherwise.

He walked along the side wall to the yard at the rear and then up a step to the back door. Slipped his note under it and returned the way he'd come. Out onto the footpath, where his attention was drawn to the narrow mail slot in the front fence. A tatty brown A4 envelope, half hanging out. Hand-delivered, obviously. Torn up by being shoved into a too-small aperture. A flap of brown paper ruffling in the breeze that had sprung up since his dawn walk.

Hirsch leaned over, intending to push the envelope the rest of the way, but it caught. He stepped through the gateway and checked from behind: stuffed with junk mail, some of it very old, some of it rain-stained. What the fuck did he think he was doing, solving the Cobbs' stupid mailbox problem? Tamping down the junk mail to make more room, he returned to the footpath and removed the tattered envelope, intending to fold it along the middle so it would fit—and saw through the tear that there was a magazine inside with a note paperclipped to it.

He read the note. It said: *Daz, here's that magazine I was talking about. Be good if you could come along next time.*

Sink a few coldies, watch a few videos, workshop some ideas.
Like I said, we need to be ready. It's coming dude, race war
and societal collapse. When, not if. Blood and honour. We do
not kneel and die, we stand and fight and live. Stay in touch,
use Telegram or Element. Mort.

Cody Morton?

Staying in touch with his good mate Daryl via encrypted messenger services.

Better not to get caught standing there reading someone else's mail. Hirsch returned to the police station with the envelope. Sat at his desk and, as his computer fired up, flicked through the magazine. It was titled *Red Ensign* and he'd been expecting cheap paper and a jumble of fonts, but it was professionally designed and printed.

And poisonous. The cover was simple: the title and a stylised Celtic cross. The inside cover listed the contents and stated that *Red Ensign* was the mouthpiece of Antipodean Storm. Hirsch flicked through the pages. Apart from a handful of graphics and photographs, it was mainly full of articles: the looming race war, the deep state plot against Donald Trump, global banking and other conspiracies, the illegitimacy of Australia's political and legal systems, Covid and vaccination lies, bomb-making. The by-lines included Proud Boy 18, The Lad, Single Beating Heart, Truth-Viking, Klansmen Fetch my Rope, Azov Volunteer, Serniki Supremo and This White Life Matters, Yo.

Hirsch switched to his desktop PC. 'Azov' referred to the Azov Battalion, neo-Nazi, currently operating in

Ukraine. 'Serniki' referred to the Ukraine village of the same name where 850 Jews were massacred in 1942. One of the perpetrators settled in Australia after the war, living and working under the radar until his arrest in 1990. Tried for crimes against humanity in 1993 and acquitted.

Hirsch was troubled. His first impulse was to tackle Daryl—or, better still, his sister. Find out what was going on, who he'd been talking to, what his intentions were. *Protect* him. The kid would have been a soft target for Cody Morton and whoever Cody hung around with. Poor, not much schooling, drifting through life, he'd have responded to strong authority figures who might explain exactly how he'd been marginalised by wealthy elites, immigrants, Muslims, Aborigines, homosexuals, feminists, Jews, banks, government regulations and a multicultural society. By matters that affected him directly, too, such as Covid regulations, the bureaucratic nightmare that was Centrelink, the lack of local jobs. They'd have encouraged any nascent anger he showed.

Daryl, angry? It was hard to picture—but he was idle and bored. He'd respond well if someone took charge of his life. The love of his mother or his sister—tired and distracted as they were—would never be enough.

The unease grew in Hirsch. He'd been picking up rustles and whispers for weeks now. At first, he'd put it down to conspiracy theories flourishing in a time of crisis, and people—like Petra Osmak, Scott Greig and Cody Morton—giving themselves permission to act out their prejudices. But something more concerted was also occurring. A recruitment drive. Deranged plans for the future. And a secret federal police operation.

Which leaves me, Hirsch thought, a dutiful bush constable ordered to butt out, not rock the boat. Do as you're told and don't expect any crumbs from the table.

So he started looking for Cottrell's name in his contacts list, only to put it on hold because just then there was a sharp knuckle tattoo on the street door and Stephanie Ingram walked in, trailed by Noah Fanning.

Hirsch took them through to his backyard, where the morning sun splashed warmly on the paving stones he'd laid, then brought out three coffees and a side plate loaded with Tim Tams. Old towels on the rickety chairs, absorbing the remaining dew.

'Noah has something to tell you—something to *show* you,' Ingram said.

She was comfortable in jeans dragging one unravelling cuff, black sandshoes and an old-style windcheater over a white T-shirt. She looked alert, as if she'd already handled a day's worth of emergencies. Noah, on the other hand, looked slightly dazed, a kid who'd partied all night and had just stumbled out of bed. He looked...hunted, somehow, too. As if expecting the world to fall on him in the next few minutes.

Hirsch smiled, trying for encouragement, then remembered that a prisoner had once told him she'd seen warmer smiles on a snowman. 'Ready when you are.'

Noah stared without focus at the top of his coffee. 'I took this,' he said, tilting to reach into the right-hand pocket of his jeans.

He froze, his hand probing, and reached into his other jeans pocket. Patted his hoodie pocket, and the other, increasingly alarmed. He heaved to his feet, bumping the table, causing seismic trembles in the coffees, and reached both hands behind him into the patch pockets on his rear. His face cleared. Pitifully relieved, he brought out a small black tab and handed it to Hirsch.

'The missing memory card?'

Noah rolled his shoulders. Tears threatened to consume him. 'I didn't mean to.'

Stephanie Ingram said warningly, 'Noah…'

'I mean, I…I don't know what I mean.'

Hirsch tried to help him. 'You thought you'd find photos of the eagle on it?'

Noah looked grateful. 'Yes. Like Auntie Steph told Dad, it doesn't reinforce her connection to Country, it repudiates it.'

Hirsch glanced at Ingram. She looked faintly embarrassed, not denying what she'd said but certainly wishing Noah Fanning would rein it in a little.

He didn't. 'Me and Dad have been living on unceded sovereign land!'

Stephanie reached across and clasped the boy's forearm. 'We need to stay on track, Noah. No point trying to do everything at once. Right now, Paul needs to know what to do about this. Now, you told me you removed the memory card from the camera because you thought it contained photos of the eagle and you were worried your dad would use them in some way.'

Seeing the kid shrink into his chair, Hirsch said, 'You won't get into trouble, Noah, I'll make sure of that.'

Noah sat straighter again, his expression grateful. 'I just thought, you know, he'd paid to have photos taken and he'd turn them into tourist crap again. Too bad if meanwhile someone gets killed.'

'Noah,' Steph Ingram said. 'He's not a monster. He was upset about Mr Aronson.'

Noah went through some contortions as if his clothes didn't fit; as if nothing felt quite right. 'Maybe. I wish he'd just, you know, let me be sometimes.' He looked up wretchedly. 'Coming home...it's just...He doesn't know what to do with me. What to say. I wish I had somewhere else to go.'

The words were not quite straight, and Hirsch saw Steph Ingram's eyes flare a little as if she wanted to say she wasn't his mother. Had the boy become a burden to her? He must be overreaching, surely, in his plan to become an intern at the Wurlie? It would involve a fair amount of negotiation with Steph and her mob. Not to mention his school, his father.

Sipping his coffee, chasing a crumb with a damp forefinger, Hirsch asked, 'Why didn't you just take the camera?'

Noah looked at him in astonishment. 'It was broken. And, you know, it was Mr Aronson's.'

The way people's minds work. 'When exactly did you remove the card from it?'

Noah frowned. 'The day, you know, the day I found the plane.'

'You weren't at the crash site the previous day?'

'No! Swear!'

'Could it be that you found the crash before you saw the people in the Land Rover?'

'No,' the boy said sulkily.

'So the camera was on the ground? You didn't move it or remove it from the plane?'

'On the ground. It would've burnt in the plane.'

Hirsch stared at the kid and waited a while. Noah's foot began to tap. Hirsch built on it: 'Strange that the people in the Land Rover didn't find it and take it with them...'

And Steph Ingram said, on a stern note: 'Noah, you promised.'

'Okay. All right. I got there before them. I found the camera and took the card out.' He shrugged. 'It was on the ground. Promise. Then I saw them coming—you can see a long way, it's so flat out there—so I hid and watched them.'

'Did they look at the camera?'

'Yeah. Fiddled with it and left it there.' He'd been looking down glumly. He glanced at Hirsch and, as if pleased that Hirsch or the police might be thwarted, added:

'They were wearing gloves.'

Hirsch stared back levelly. 'Have you looked at what's on the card?'

'We both have,' Stephanie Ingram said. 'Noah first, then he showed me because he couldn't make sense of what was on it.'

'I was expecting the eagle,' Noah said. 'Instead, it showed other stuff. Buildings.'

'Do you know where?'

'No.'

'Steph?'

'It's not an area I go walkabout in search of witchetty grubs, if that's what you're getting at.'

Hirsch was about to sigh when he saw the amusement in her eyes. 'Okay, let's have a look,' he said.

Plugging the Nikon's memory card into his laptop, he opened the contents. No video, but several distinct sequences composed of rapid-fire photographs that formed virtual movie clips. And they told a story. Pete Aronson had happened upon a broad, natural hollow surrounded by stony hillocks. Why, though? He was hired to photograph the eagle in the wildflower season. Perhaps he saw a vehicle? Interest piqued, he'd followed it? Or he saw an out-of-place sun flash? For whatever reason, he'd spotted an area of stone ruins and more modern accommodation.

Hirsch saw a roofless old farmhouse, tumbledown outbuildings, a couple of newish metal garden sheds and a motley collection of military-style tents, various sizes.

Another—a big marquee with open sides—appeared to be a mess tent: tables, chairs and bench seats could be glimpsed in one of Aronson's low passes over the camp. A small collection of vehicles, too—four-wheel drives, utes, a sedan, two station wagons.

He went back to the image of a dusty white 4WD and enlarged it: a Pajero. Too pixelated to tell if it was Cody Morton's or the one he'd seen at the defaced 5G tower in Redruth. He then enlarged each of the other vehicles. Nondescript. He took a second look at a rectangular shape next to the vehicles. A camouflage net. Hiding another vehicle?

Aronson made four sweeps, not getting too close at first. In addition to the buildings and vehicles, Hirsch saw fuel and chemical drums, a pallet piled with wooden boxes, heaped firewood, a barbecue pit, two portaloos, a tower bristling with antennas and a narrow stretch of flat ground about three hundred metres long. He couldn't work out what it was: clear of obstructions at one end, but with haybales at regular, staggered stages at the other end, starting at about one-third of the way along. Aronson had been curious, too. He veered around, coming in low, shooting at a shallow angle with his Nikon.

It was a firing range. Haybale targets at 100, 200 and 300 metres, Hirsch guessed, each one propping up a big red bullseye on a white background.

But no figures in view yet; no one with a rifle. Aronson—perhaps nervous by now—started to veer away.

And suddenly the Nikon was photographing the fuselage, the landing gear, the propellor and the open sky. Reacting to the first bullet, Hirsch thought, the one that hit the engine cowling. And then, when a succession of blurred shots completed the sequence, he guessed that the second bullet had found its target and Aronson was filming the knees of his pants.

34

TEN MINUTES LATER, Cottrell's voice rasped in Hirsch's landline handset like gravel sliding off a shovel. 'Do you know where the pictures were taken?'

'No, sir.'

'Are you intending to visit the campground in question?'

A curious inflexion; a curious choice of words, thought Hirsch. Cottrell knows where it is and he's warning me off? 'No, sir.'

'Good.'

'Shall I email the photos, sir?' Hirsch said, before thinking that would take forever, given the state of Tiverton's internet.

'I need the memory card itself. I'll send a courier straight away.'

From Adelaide, Hirsch thought. I'll be twiddling my thumbs here for three hours at least. 'Sir.'

'Getting back to your bit of fiction, Mr Hirschhausen.'

'Sir?' said Hirsch, thinking yeah, the story he'd told the inspector was a complete and utter bit of fiction.

'You say you weren't satisfied that the shooters had removed the memory card from Mr Aronson's camera?'

'Yes, sir.'

'So you went back for another look.'

'Sir.'

'And there it was, simply lying on the ground.'

'Quite hard to spot, sir. I don't blame your team for not finding it. I only saw it myself because I'd squatted down and glimpsed it under a bit of grass.'

Cottrell was silent, perhaps hoping Hirsch would keep talking and dig a hole for himself. Then he said, 'And why would Mr Aronson do that, in his dying moments? Take the trouble to remove the card and toss it in addition to tossing the camera?'

'He'd stumbled on something fishy, and knew they'd come looking when he didn't crash nearby or straight away. Perhaps he hoped they'd find the camera without the card and assume that either others got there first, or it was in

327

one of his pockets and got burnt up.'

'And you went out there, acting on that hunch.'

'Yes, sir.'

'A nice line of bullshit. Has anyone else seen what's on the card?'

'No, sir.'

'Hypothetically speaking, if any hypothetical person of your acquaintance did happen to view the contents, that hypothetical person should keep his or her hypothetical mouth firmly fucking shut.'

'Sir.'

In the end, he didn't wait for three hours: a rider on a powerful black Kawasaki came by less than an hour later. From where? The guy merely grunted at Hirsch, pocketed the card, which Hirsch had tucked into a small envelope, and snarled away again. This all happened on the front step of the police station, at a time—mid-Sunday morning—when the town was beginning to go mildly about its business. Old folks in their front gardens, kids kicking a footy around on the school oval, a couple of young mothers with toddlers in pushers. Word would spread again.

Hirsch had held on to the *Red Ensign* magazine, figuring that Cottrell had access to his own copies. Rolling it into a tube, he walked with it around to the Cobbs' house, where he found Laura sitting on the back step, in the sun, her thin bare legs at a slant and her head bowed. She was painting her toenails.

'Good colour,' he said. A shade of red that struck him as elegant. She shot him an unsurprised look, then leaned into her task again. Her voice muffled behind a curtain of shiny straight hair, she said, 'Almost finished.'

'Delicate stage?'

She didn't answer. Hirsch hunted around, saw a big old wooden cable spool, and dragged it closer. Perched his backside on it. Watched her.

'Finished,' she said, leaning in effortlessly to blow on her toes.

Laura Cobb was young and trapped and struggling, that hadn't changed. But right now Hirsch saw that she was more than a shy, small-town kid without prospects saddled with a family that relied on her. She was young and pretty, and she was waking up. Expanding. He hated to think of all of that being worn down; worn out.

Spotting the magazine in Hirsch's hands, she said, 'I saw that in the mailbox when I went to feed Nan's horses this morning. When I came back, it wasn't there.'

Her response told him two things: there had been prior issues of the magazine, and she didn't want Daryl reading them. That was encouraging, but there was also the possibility that *she* was an avid reader of the magazine and didn't want Hirsch, a policeman—and a kind of friend—to know that.

'I had a quick read,' he said casually. 'Quite an eye-opener.'

She gave him disgusted look. 'Yep.'

Disgusted with the contents, Hirsch thought; disgusted with me trying to catch her out. She hooked a strand of hair behind her ears, releasing a wisp of perfumed air. Not a cheap shampoo. Wendy used the same one.

'Are you here to talk to me or to Daryl?'

'Daryl, eventually.'

'He's still in bed.'

'I thought he might be. Is it something we could discuss with your mum?'

'You must be joking. She's manic at the moment. I don't want anything to set her off.'

'Okay,' Hirsch said, looking away. The garden beds were damp; water droplets trembled.

Laura brought him back. 'I can tell you what I know.'

Hirsch rubbed his hands on his thighs. 'There was a note attached. A kid called Cody Morton wrote it. What can you tell me about him? How he knows Daryl, what influence he has over him, if any? That kind of thing.'

Laura blushed, winced, glanced away. Eventually she said, 'He was my boyfriend for about five minutes.'

Tread carefully, thought Hirsch. 'You've stayed in touch?'

She looked fully at him, worrying her bottom lip with her teeth. 'No. He's stayed in touch with Daryl, though.'

'How did you meet?'

She looked away again, concentrating furiously. 'I'm not the greatest catch in the world.'

Hirsch shook his head. 'You're—'

'*Don't,*' she said sharply. 'I'm stuck here looking after my mother. No proper job. No car. Never been anywhere, done anything. But I got talking with Cody at the pub karaoke a few weeks ago and we hit it off.'

The pub karaoke? The first Hirsch had heard of it. Not that he'd have gone. Wild horses, et cetera. 'Okay,' he said feebly, not wanting to lead her.

'It was good at first. Fun.'

'Until it wasn't?'

She gave him a sharp look. 'He didn't hit me. Didn't cheat on me, if that's what you think.'

'Okay.'

'He paid attention; he was nice. He made me feel good, and I think he was keen on me, and that counts for a lot.'

Hirsch knew it did. 'What happened? You broke it off?'

'He had this other agenda.'

Hirsch had placed the magazine on the ground. He toed it with his shoe. 'This?'

She looked down. Nodded. 'In the long term, yes.'

'And in the short term?'

'Little things at first, like asking me my views on immigration and that. Black people, Muslims, did I know they were taking our jobs, a burden on the economy.'

'What did you say?'

She blushed and looked away. 'I don't get time to read the papers or watch the news.'

'You got great marks in Year 12. You've got a good brain.'

'Wish I could use it,' she muttered.

'What else did he say?'

'He wanted to know my thoughts on Covid and vaccines, and it turned out he thinks Covid's a myth and the vaccines are dangerous, but he could get us fake certificates, plus this phone app to bypass Covid and QR check-ins.' She paused. 'And this is where I did use my brain. Mum and Daryl's health isn't that great so I made sure all of us got triple vaxxed.'

'Did he ever try to get you to join Antipodean whatever it is?'

'Not really. Not directly or straight away.'

'In a roundabout way?'

She gave him an incredulous laugh. 'He wanted us to get married! I mean, Jesus, I haven't even been out of South Australia yet.'

'Sounds like he was pretty keen.'

'Yeah, but it was also part of his agenda. He said childless couples are evil. No family values. We need families with children—you know, keep the white race vital and alive.'

'Forget about love, eh?'

Laura gave him a hard look. She had felt love, and she had been loved. He was taking that lightly. 'I thought he was being overly romantic, if you must know,' she said. She shrugged. 'But I liked being in a relationship.'

Hirsch didn't risk smiling, but gave her a nod.

She was searching his face furiously. Apparently

332

satisfied, she said, 'As for joining the cause, it was a kind of slow burn, asking what I thought about things and saying how it enriched his life, networking with like-minded people around the world, joining organisations.'

'Such as?'

She concentrated. Said, eventually: 'One was called Combat 18. Another was Proud Boys.' She snorted. 'Boys is right.'

She stuck out a leg, examined her painted toes. 'They're not boys, though. One of his mates was ex-army and had a licence to own a gun. Worked as a bouncer at a club in the city. Another was a skinhead and been in prison.'

'I can see why you might want to break it off.'

She gestured dismissively. 'I never took any of it too seriously. What tipped me over the edge was, he showed me a video of the Christchurch massacre.' She looked up, wide-eyed. 'As though I'd be impressed.'

'Horrible, I bet. I've never seen it.'

'So I broke it off and now he's hanging around Daryl.'

'How did he take it?'

'He was actually quite upset. I think he really liked me, so he tries to stay close by getting tight with Daryl, I think. I won't let him in the house, and I told Daryl to wake up to himself. But I think they see each other when I'm not home.'

'What does Daryl make of everything?'

Laura gave it thought. 'He's easily led, you know that. And he just spouts stuff without knowing what any of it means. Like, the Holocaust was a myth and we need a race war so that when society collapses, he and Cody and the others can step in.'

'There have been a few incidents lately,' Hirsch said carefully. 'I can't go into it, but does Daryl ever go off with Cody, do things with him?'

'Actually, you nearly caught them once. Something about the phone tower in Redruth.'

Hirsch nodded.

'Don't arrest him, please. He wouldn't last five seconds in jail.'

Hirsch, seeing that the sun was in her eyes, scooted around to her other side. 'I'll do my best. Does he listen to you?'

'Sometimes. Not really, not anymore.' She paused. 'The other day he told me he'd sworn an oath.'

'An oath? What kind?'

Laura kept her eyes half-lidded as she called up the memory. 'How it was his duty to be a warrior and defend his people and speak the truth, and how his blood would live on if he got killed. I mean, crazy stuff.'

'I can't see him following through, Laura.'

'I know, nor can I, but he's got these attitudes now. Like he says he hates gays and trans people, even though he doesn't know any. And after we took Mum to Doctor Pillai on Friday, he called her a coconut. I mean, Doctor Pillai! She's our guardian angel. And you know how soft he is—I mean physically. Flabby. The other day he said he's going to get a haircut and go for runs to get fit. Take up mixed martial arts, stuff like that. Still spends hours in front of his computer, though, *not* getting fit.'

'Gaming?'

'Always. Since he was little. But also chatrooms, forums, videos, memes.' She looked pained. 'He calls himself People's Warrior.'

Hirsch gave her a small, sad smile, thinking that kids like Daryl were legion. Without the ordinary circuit breakers of family, work, school and other social contact, they were wide open.

She went on: 'But you know Daryl, he's easily distracted. Give him a Coke and a bag of chips and he's happy. He doesn't understand half of what he reads and his room's full of books and magazines from Cody that he's never even looked at.'

'But going out with Cody and damaging property is something else, Laura,' Hirsch said. 'That's more than just being a keyboard warrior.'

She shrank. Hirsch knew there was more, and waited patiently. The sun was higher now, angling into the yard.

Beginning slowly, quietly, she said, 'Cody took him to a lockdown protest in Adelaide.'

Where he was probably filmed. 'Anything else?'

She said in a rush, 'A training camp somewhere out east, okay?'

Hirsch felt cold. 'What kind of training?'

'You know how he is, half what you say goes in one ear

and out the other. He said there were lots of speeches and lectures, like being at school.'

'Just him, him and Cody? Others?'

'About a dozen.'

'What about military training?'

'There was a bit of that,' Laura said, in a low voice. 'Marching around, you know, hup two three four. Singing Waltzing Matilda.'

'What about weapons?'

'I knew you were going to ask that. It was the first thing I asked. He said there were some guns but he didn't shoot any. The others did. I sort of believe him.'

Hirsch wriggled; his backside was numb. After a while, he said, 'You could have come to me, you know.'

'Don't think I didn't consider it,' she shot back at him. 'But I didn't want him to get into trouble, and he's just not that motivated. He'd rather fly his drone. I'm hoping Nan will give him some regular work at the stables, and maybe Mr Tennant can get him stocking shelves at the shop, things like that. Keep him occupied.'

She paused, looked away, and he barely heard her: 'They want him to go on another camp soon.'

'Don't let him go, Laura. It's too dangerous. He could get arrested.'

She was shocked. 'You'd arrest him? You know what he's like.'

'Not me,' Hirsch said. 'The federal police. They know what's going on and I think they mean to act pretty soon.

We don't want Daryl getting caught up in a raid. But I have to tell you, his name's probably on a list somewhere. There could be a knock on your door one day.'

She started rocking. Teary, a kid again, with too much to bear. Hirsch patted her shoulder and said, 'If that happens, ask for me.'

35

THAT WAS SUNDAY. On Monday, early, Sergeant
Brandl called. 'Good luck today.'

'Good luck?'

'You know what I mean,' she said. 'Hope it goes well
with the shrink, therapist, whatever. Don't hold back. Get
better soon, et cetera.'

Brandl at her gruff, awkward best. 'Thanks, sergeant,'
Hirsch said.

Seven-thirty. He finished his calls and emails, showered, changed, had a second coffee, made a cheese and

salad sandwich for later in the day. If he left at 8.30, he'd have plenty of time to reach Gawler and find the psychologist's office, and so his walk across to the general store to buy the *Advertiser* was an amble, dragging a morning shadow after him. Half a dozen town and farm kids were mingling on the shop veranda, waiting for the school bus, the boys mostly shoving and insulting each other and the girls mostly on their phones. The Redruth High uniform was dark brown over grey: everyone hated it.

He nodded and smiled, thinking: *running the gauntlet.* As a group they were terrifying. Individually they were shy, uncomplicated kids.

The girls, apparently absorbed in gossip or social media, were nevertheless the first to spot him. 'Hello, Mr Policeman,' one of them said in a sing-song voice. Another, bolder, called, 'Paul. Hey, Paul.'

Hirsch nodded and smiled again genially, finding a path through daypacks, gym bags and uniformed torsos. They all knew he was involved with Wendy Street, head of maths at their school. Did they know she'd been getting online abuse? Kate, too? Surely they did. But what did they think about that? They'd have attended Sergeant Brandl's warning lecture, but if they weren't victims or perpetrators, would anything she'd said have sunk in?

Good kids, he told himself. Liked to tease, but basically good natured.

The youngest and shyest was Jack Laurie, who'd been chased by Brenda Maher's dog. He followed Hirsch into the shop and said, stumblingly, 'Sir? Mr Hirschhausen?' Then, finally, 'Paul,' on a hesitant, downward note, as though aware, too late, that he might have breached protocol.

Hirsch turned. 'Yes, Jack?'

The kid had changed his appearance, going for what passed for sophistication around here. His head was shaved above his ears, his product-laden hair arranged strangely on the crown. Two angry-looking pimples. 'I can ride my bike here again because you, you know, shot the dog.'

Hirsch nodded encouragingly.

In a rush: 'I saw someone at that house just now, on the way here.'

Hirsch went still. 'Who?'

'At first all I saw was a car.'

'Can you describe it?'

'A white Hyundai.'

'In the driveway?'

'In the street.'

'And then you saw someone?'

'That girl—her sister used to go to my school? I had her in maths.'

Alice. 'What was she doing?'

Another shrug. 'Going around the back, you know, like she'd just loaded something in the car.'

'I'll check it out right away. Have you got a phone?'

Puzzlement. 'Yes.'

'If you see any more activity there, this afternoon or in the next few days, see if you can get a shot of a face or a numberplate? But be careful about it.'

'Okay. Should've thought of that. But I can tell you it had a barcode in the back window,' Jack Laurie said. 'They do that on rental cars.'

Hirsch raced around there. No car in the street, only cellophane tossed by a bit of dismal wind. Was there ever a bright, lively wind in that street? He checked the front and rear doors of the cottage. Both locked. But Alice had been to the caravan: the door was ajar; more clothes and bedside books were missing.

He called Sergeant Brandl, who said she'd inform the Homicide Squad. Who called Hirsch before he'd barely made it back to the police station to collect bottled water and his packed lunch. He didn't catch the man's name, only his attitude: Hirsch must have been asleep on the job to let a suspect come and go from his town.

'There's only me,' Hirsch said, 'policing an area the size of Belgium.'

'Yeah, well, that house should be your priority.' Pause. 'Anything else?'

'According to the witness, she was driving a white Hyundai, probably rented,' Hirsch said—glad it wasn't going to be him who stuck a phone against his ear and started calling Europcar, Hertz, Budget…

By now it was 8.45 and he couldn't afford to waste more time in Tiverton, so he set off at a fast clip down the Barrier

Highway. Ten minutes later, as he was slowing for the little wheatbelt town of Penhale, his mobile rang. A woman's voice, sounding hysterical.

'This is Elly. Elly Kline?'

Hirsch remembered: Ed 'n' Elly; Wendy's screen door. 'What's the problem?'

People were fighting outside her caravan in the backyard of the pub, she said, and Ed would've been there to sort it out except she didn't know where he was and could Hirsch come right away?

Fate, thought Hirsch as he sped back to Tiverton. He was fated never to have this counselling session.

On the other hand, maybe his real problem was self-delusion. Was it overweening, this sense of responsibility to his job, his town and patrol area? Would everything actually fall in a heap if he were ever to say, 'Can't, sorry, busy today on a personal matter, maybe Redruth or one of the other local stations can help you.'

Another, related question: was he using Elly Kline's call to put off this psych visit?

And: was he just a bonehead who got a buzz out of the dramatic?

He told himself no. If officers at Redruth, Clare or Peterborough were busy, half a day could go by before Elly Kline's call was attended to.

These thoughts, and a music-app playlist, kept him going as he raced up the highway again. Funny how

'Sultans of Swing' cropped up in all of his suggested playlists, though. What had he done to deserve that?

The pub didn't open until ten, so the place looked shut down from the outside. Hirsch swung around the corner, seeking the driveway access to the yard at the rear, and accelerated onto a blighted half-hectare of weeds, dusty pallets, rusted kegs, struggling vegetable plots and piles of empty beer bottles. And the caravan, parked in the back corner, with four vehicles pulled up to it: a red Corolla, Ed Kline's Holden Colorado twin-cab, a little white Hyundai and David Hillcock's grey VW van. There were three people, too, heaving together and apart in an inhuman dance: Elly Kline, tugging ineffectually on Jacob Maher's arm, which was around Alice McNamara's throat.

As Hirsch braked and piled out, Maher released Alice and drove his black-gloved fist into Elly Kline's lower torso. She gaped, eyes wild, before waddling towards the caravan, holding her stomach. Propped herself against it briefly, then slid down to the dirt.

This all took a couple of seconds. Hirsch called, 'Jake!' sharply, and began to cover the intervening dirt and weeds as Maher glanced at him, unimpressed, and returned to Alice, who had fallen to the ground. She was rolling onto her front as he reached her, levering her trunk off the ground as if to get to her knees, her thin arms just a pair of fragile twigs. Maher booted the nearest arm so forcefully that it snapped. Hirsch heard it. Heard Alice shriek and flop to the ground again as he propelled himself across the final metres rugby-tackle style, shoulder-first into the kid's stomach, wrapping him tight. The momentum carried them hard against the caravan. Somewhere crockery smashed; the caravan rocked; and then Hirsch was on the ground, badly winded, curling against Maher's boots, Maher dancing around him, aiming for his balls, stomach, face, kidneys.

And when the storm passed and Hirsch got his breath back, Maher and the van were gone and Alice was weeping, cradling her arm, with Elly Kline standing over her, shrieking, 'Are you Ed's slut?' while over by the back door of the pub, the morning barman finished a cigarette. He flicked it into the weeds and went inside to open up for the day.

36

THE REDRUTH AMBULANCE had been called to a false alarm in Spalding, only twenty minutes away, so Hirsch asked it to deviate to Tiverton.

Then he fronted up to Kline. 'Calm down, Elly. She's not sleeping with Ed. She came to say sorry for ripping you off.'

Kline turned to him, her chest heaving. Shook her head as if to clear it. 'Pardon? What?'

'The rental-house scam.'

It took a moment to sink in, and then Kline sagged.

Glancing at Alice curled on the ground, quieter now, she said, 'Ed's been really secretive lately, so when she turned up here saying sorry, I went right off, thinking she had him at her place and he was too piss-weak to come and tell me himself.' Pause. 'I've always been a bit jealous.'

Hirsch didn't have time for this. 'I'll help you after the ambulance has been. But just quickly, whose is the red car?'

'Mine.'

'Alice came in the white one?'

'Yes.'

'And that's Ed's ute. Where is he?'

'Look, we had a fight Friday and he went storming off and I went to my mother's and when I came back this morning, there's his ute. He's not at work. I don't know where he is.'

'Like I said, I'll help in a minute. Let's get Alice comfortable.'

Kline dragged a sunlounge into the sun, Hirsch a deck chair. They settled Alice onto the sunlounge, a blanket over her torso, her arm resting on her stomach. She accepted a glass of water and painkillers from Kline gratefully, then said, 'I need to speak to the policeman. Alone.'

Kline's first impulse was to look affronted. Then she glanced at Hirsch, shrugged her big shoulders and went inside the caravan.

Hirsch's mind raced ahead. 'Okay, I'm listening. But I'm going to caution you and I'm going to tape our

346

conversation; do you agree to that? It's for your protection and mine.'

'Do what you like.'

Hirsch set his digital recorder on a second deck chair next to the sunlounge, pressed play and recited the time, date, location, his own and Alice's presence, and finally the police caution.

'What would you like to say, Alice?'

She sank back, and her broken arm shifted minutely. She gasped, recovered, and said, 'I'm sorry Jacob hurt you.'

'Alice, he hurt *you*.'

She looked away, said nothing.

'Let's start with why he came here.'

A minute shrug; another pained gasp. 'Because I want out of everything.'

'I need you to tell me what you mean by "everything".'

'You know, ripping people off. The drugs. Is Brenda still in hospital?'

'She's been moved to a city one. Under police guard.'

'Good. Are you going to arrest me?'

Hirsch considered that. 'Officers more senior than me are likely to do that. Major Crimes. Homicide. You don't have to talk to me, you don't have to talk to them, without a lawyer present. But from what you tell me and what I already know or have guessed, it's likely that you will be charged and maybe taken into custody, so it's best if you're prepared for that to happen.'

She closed her eyes and in a weak voice said, 'Okay.'

'You say you want to get out of everything…Why?'

She glanced at him in surprise. 'Well, Toby. That really upset me. Plus Damien…they didn't have to kill him.'

'Anything else?'

She was silent for a moment. 'Everything was all right at first, then it just got worse.'

'In what way?'

She was silent and when her voice came it was almost dreamy. 'My dad was deported back to New Zealand when he got out of Yatala. Ten years. Manslaughter. Meanwhile Mum had taken up with David. Me and Zoe were only little.'

That rang alarm bells. 'Did Mr Hillcock ever—'

'David? No. He's harmless.'

'And later your mother died of an overdose?'

Alice shrugged. 'Yeah. Me and Zoe were allowed to stay with David. He was like the only dad we knew.'

'And then he met Brenda,' Hirsch prompted.

'Last year. One minute it was just me, him and Zoe, and next minute we're all living with Brenda and Jacob. A bit weird, because I hooked up with Jacob, but, you know, it was okay at first.'

'At first.'

'Zoe started acting out. At home and at school. Got expelled. Brenda said she had to go, so she went to live with our nanna.'

'Alice, did your sister blame Mrs Street for getting expelled?'

Alice nodded. 'I wanted to get back at her for Zoe, you know?' She glanced at Hirsch as if fearing he'd explode. 'I said sorry to Mrs Street. And Kate.'

No explosion, but Hirsch's tone was harsh. 'You said sorry with anonymous text messages!'

Alice adopted the face of someone who wanted to be understood. 'I would've gone to their place to say it in person, but I thought you might be there.' She shrugged. 'Now you got me anyway.'

'I was there, in fact, when the texts arrived. We worked out that it might've been you.'

Alice screwed up her face further. 'I'm really, really sorry. I went too far with the online stuff.'

'Yes, you did,' Hirsch said, but left it at that. He needed her to keep talking.

She said, 'I'm good at computers, you know? IT stuff.'

'Yes.'

'We did a lot you probably don't know about.'

'Such as?'

'Like, Damien's Centrelink payments went to Brenda. She gave him an allowance out of it. I mean, when me and David and Zoe met her, she was already ripping off disability pensions, old-age pensions, Workcover…You name it, she was into it.'

'When detectives interview you today or tomorrow, be sure to tell them all that.'

She shrugged.

Feeling uneasy, Hirsch asked, 'Why did Zoe start acting out?'

'Jacob. He was, you know…'

Hirsch did. 'You saw it? She told you?'

'No. But I'm not stupid. He stopped having feelings for me and she'd be funny around him, you know, all sexed-up one minute and jealous of me the next.' She paused. Said sadly, 'She's the pretty one.'

'Is she doing all right at your grandmother's?'

'Think so.'

'Did you say anything to Jacob?'

'God no. He was off his face on meth half the time and you know how that goes.' Alice looked at Hirsch and raised her broken arm a fraction. 'You saw him just now.'

Elly Kline poked her head out of the caravan, impatient, feeling left out. 'Is that ambulance coming?'

'Here soon, Elly.'

'Do you need more water? Cup of tea?'

'We're fine.'

Scowling, she disappeared inside again. Hirsch said, 'Maybe we should keep our voices down a bit.'

'Yeah, big ears,' Alice said. She was pale, sweaty.

'You said just now that David was okay until he hooked up with Brenda. What changed? The drugs?'

'Plus he was cunt-struck,' Alice said simply. 'Look, he's always been the eager-to-please type, and with Brenda he took that to a new level. She had him at her beck and call. Plus she didn't like it he was close to me when we first moved in. She made it her business to drive a wedge.'

'Brenda was using, too?'

'She was a bit of a meth-head long before we arrived on the scene. But she could control it, you know? High functioning?'

'Yes. And lately? Getting more violent?'

Alice gave him a look. 'Well, yeah, you could say that. She murdered Damien, for a start. And she'd give us all a belt around the ears sometimes. She could be irrational.'

One way of putting it. 'Was Jacob into meth to the same degree?'

'Not at first. He and Brenda bought from a dealer like everyone else, they couldn't afford to be heavy users. But when they got Damien cooking it, there was plenty to go around. They could take a hit whenever they liked.' She shrugged. 'Jake kept saying he was invincible. The cult of the black hand—you saw his glove?'

'Yes.'

'He said he was going to kill fifty people and write a book about it.'

'He helped Brenda kill Mr Pierce?'

She nodded. 'He really got off on it, like, "It was amazing, Al."'

'How did they know him in the first place?'

'We were all in Adelaide then, Brenda doing her thing, hooking up with druggies and Centrelink types, you know, and that included Damien. Then he makes the mistake of telling her his dad bought him a house. She wanted him to sell it at first, but then she thought, you know, it would be a perfect place for a kitchen.'

Hirsch listened to a sound on the wind. It didn't resolve as a siren. Didn't resolve at all. 'Why did they kill him? Greed? He got in the way?'

'First, I need you to know I didn't see it happen, I wasn't there. But yeah, he'd been complaining he did all the work and should get more of a share, so Brenda told him to drive down to talk about it.'

'What car did he come in?' Then Hirsch twigged: 'The station wagon.'

Alice nodded. Delicately wiped the perspiration from her upper lip with her forefinger. 'His aunt let him use it. Brenda faked that receipt we showed you. So Jake could have a car and not keep stealing them.'

'Do you know if he and Brenda did discuss his share of the take?'

'Like I said, I wasn't there, I was at the shops, but when I got back, Jake was all excited and Damien was just lying there with only his undies on and his head bashed in. They'd put their cigarettes out on him! I mean, you can see why I want out, right?'

'Yes. What about David? How involved was he?'

'He was just standing there, kind of sniggering because the others were.'

Hirsch visualised it. Shook his head. 'Didn't it occur to Brenda that she'd just killed her meth cook? Who was going to take over?'

'She probably would've got David to do it.'

'Where is he now, Alice? And where's Jacob?'

Alice paused for a long while. Hirsch tried to guess what she was thinking. Up until now, she'd been unburdening herself, explaining everyone's role. Now she was being asked to reveal information that would drop those closest to her into certain jail time.

Eventually she said, 'Brenda has this old beach shack in Port Germein. Not in her name, of course.'

'The address?'

'I don't know, but it's not a big town.'

'Who cleaned up the Muncowie house afterwards?'

'All of us. Took everything away in the van.'

'What can you tell me about the way Mr Pierce's body was disposed of?'

Alice stared at him warily, registering the more formal note underpinning Hirsch's words. 'Not me, I didn't want to have anything to do with it.'

'The others, then. He was more or less dumped on your own doorstep.'

'When's the ambulance coming? This seriously hurts.'

Hirsch checked his watch: five minutes overdue. 'Soon.'

She winced; wriggled to get comfortable. Her thin face was thinner. 'Really hurts.'

'Alice,' Hirsch said sharply. 'The body disposal.'

'Yeah, well, they were going to dump the suitcase out in the bush somewhere but they saw you outside the police station and kind of panicked.'

'I'd just knocked off for the day,' Hirsch said—thinking what if he'd been five minutes earlier or later?

'Brenda told David to go back for it next day, but there were people around and he got it into his head to burn it.' She looked at Hirsch. She didn't think much of her stepfather's plan. 'Brenda went right off when he told her. Belted him and called him a fucking idiot.'

'She had a point,' Hirsch said—immediately regretting it, since the tape was going to be used in evidence. 'She sent Jacob to check?'

'She sent him to put the fire out. Except you were there. Again.'

'You all seemed pretty relaxed later in the day when I called around.'

'High,' Alice said, 'is what we were. High as kites.'

Hirsch heard a vehicle slowing for the entrance and looked up. The ambulance.

37

INSIDE ELLY KLINE'S caravan, five minutes later.

'He hit you pretty hard.'

'I'm all right,' she said, rubbing her stomach unconsciously.

Hirsch looked around the interior: generic older-era caravan. 'I heard something break.'

She shrugged her heavy shoulders. 'A plate. No big deal.' She looked forlorn, which seemed incongruous to Hirsch, recalling how furious she'd been earlier. On the other hand, she'd just been bashed by a stranger and couldn't find her husband—who she feared had a secret lover.

'So, Ed stormed off after an argument the other day, and you went to your mother's?'

'Yes.'

'And when you got back this morning, you found his car here but you don't know where he is.'

'That's what I said.'

'What was the argument about?'

Another shrug. 'His drinking. His temper. And he'd go out to the pub and stay away for hours so I thought he was sleeping with someone.'

'Did he say where he was going?'

'See his mates, see his slag, I don't know.'

'Who are these mates?'

'I don't know their names.'

'Do they live locally?'

'S'pose.'

'And you think he meets them at the pub?'

Another massive heave of her shoulders. 'Probably the pub.'

'You don't go out socialising with him?'

'I don't drink,' she said primly. 'And we're new here, I don't know anyone.'

What an arid life, Hirsch thought. He tried to think who Ed Kline's drinking mates might be. He pretty much knew all the local men Kline's age—late twenties, early thirties. Married with kids, mostly. They sometimes dropped in for a quick beer after work or weekend sport, but didn't otherwise frequent the pub. The hardcore drinkers were men in their early twenties or much older blokes, divorced or stale.

Perhaps he drank in one of the other towns nearby. 'Was he always a drinker?'

'Not like he is now. It's been wearing him down, this caravan. I mean, look at it,' Elly said, arms wide. 'Like living in a cupboard. Always getting in each other's way. But there's hardly any houses to rent, and they're either half falling down or too dear. A few more places in Clare and Peterborough, but that would mean a long drive to work, and with the price of fuel...'

After a while, Hirsch found himself saying, 'Not sure what I can do, Elly. Wherever your husband spent the weekend, he's back now, his ute's parked outside.'

'Yeah, but he didn't turn up at work today, and no one gave him a lift, either. I rang and checked.'

'I suppose if he was on a bender, someone could have driven his ute back here,' mused Hirsch.

Elly Kline looked at him without animation. As if nothing could surprise her.

'What makes you think he's having an affair?'

'Like I said, he stays out all hours and he's secretive.'

'Secretive how?'

'Calls and texts that he deletes.'

'You thought he might have been involved with Alice? She's a lot younger.'

357

'I got a bit worked up when I couldn't find him and the ute's here with the keys in the ignition, he's not at work, phone goes straight to voicemail, and she turns up and says she's sorry. I thought, what for? Screwing my husband? Then that druggie kid turns up and starts laying into her and screaming. Who is he, anyway?'

'Ex-boyfriend,' Hirsch said. 'Ed's ute: does he usually leave it parked with the keys in the ignition?'

'Not really.'

'Let's go and have a look.'

'Why? He's not there. There's nothing in the glove box. I don't know where his phone or wallet are. I mean, why keep them and not the keys?'

'Is it fitted with a satnav?'

'Yes.'

'Let's check the history,' Hirsch said. 'See where he spent the weekend, at least.'

'Okay.'

'Are you sure you want to know?'

'Yes. It's not like him, vanishing like that.'

Dramatic, Hirsch thought, getting to his feet. She followed him out to her husband's dust-streaked Holden Colorado and stood impatiently beside the driver's door as Hirsch eased his battered bones behind the steering wheel, turned on the ignition and found the GPS menu screen.

No history. Wiped? By Ed, so his wife wouldn't know where he'd been?

'Where did he go?' Elly demanded.

Hirsch didn't reply. He began to get out.

'Tell me,' she demanded.

Shutting the door behind him, he said, 'Sorry, Elly, there's nothing on it.'

'He deleted everything. That shit. Just like with his phone.'

Hirsch was infinitely gentle with her. 'There could be other explanations.'

She was scornful. 'Nah. The prick.'

But Hirsch was uneasy now. 'Elly, it doesn't explain why his vehicle's here and he isn't. Do you know what kind of phone he has?'

'We both got iPhones.'

'Try the find-my-phone app?'

Elly's face cleared. 'Actually, yeah. Come in.'

Hirsch followed her back into the caravan's depressing interior. Waited beside the fold-down table as Elly reached into a wall cupboard above the bed and took out a little MacBook.

'The pub lets us use their wi-fi.' She pressed the start button, entered the passcode and opened the Find My app. Tapped on *Ed's iPhone*.

And Ed—or his phone, at least—was way out east of Tiverton. 'Focus in,' Hirsch suggested.

When Elly did that, with a kind of savage glint, Hirsch saw the words Manna Soak Highway, and, off that beaten track, a location flag and another word: *Ruins*.

—

The trip out east took ninety minutes, on bone-jarring roads. No clouds today, no flowing manes, no red-eyed herd in the sky. 'Just a missing-person lead,' he'd assured Sergeant Brandl, before leaving Tiverton. But he doubted that was the case.

He was on the final stretch now, passing Dryden Downs' impressive gates. If no one lived beyond the property, as Sam Dryden had tried to tell him, then there shouldn't have been signs of recent traffic, yet he saw tyre marks and churned-up dirt and gravel.

Half an hour later, the road dwindled and he found himself at a broad, dented cyclone gate. He got out, eyed the heavy-duty padlock and thick chain that secured it, then read the signs.

Private sovereign property, government-funded agencies forbidden to enter

No entry to anyone working for or loyal to the satanic state

Prosecution will be on-site using common and natural law.

Assuming that prosecution using common and natural law was code for a bullet to the head, Hirsch returned to the Toyota, leaned into the storage compartment and pulled out a pinch bar and a hammer. Started levering, then whacking. Feeling pretty satanic just then.

38

STEERING ONE-HANDED along a badly eroded track that wound through tussocks and stone reefs, the radio handset to his mouth, he told Sergeant Brandl where he was and what he was doing.

'So far it's still only a missing-person situation.'

Her voice scratched from the radio. 'I sense a "but".'

'But the driveway entrance is plastered with far-right anti-government stuff. Pretty paranoid, some of it.'

'Well, Jesus, Paul, stay where you are. I'll get you a STAR squad.'

'Take them hours to get here, sergeant. And Mr Kline could be in strife,' Hirsch said, going on to explain why.

'He might have lost his phone. Left it behind there.'

'He might. I'll soon know.'

He heard the tension in her voice: 'I don't like it. Just scout around, don't blunder in. Don't antagonise anyone.'

'Sergeant,' Hirsch said, completing the call, grabbing the steering wheel with both hands as the rear tyres churned and sideslipped in loose dirt.

Time passed, and then he was accelerating up a steep rise, his gaze fixed only on the central section of the narrow track, not the empty sky or the deep, beckoning ditches on either side. Up and over, hoping no one was coming the other way.

Then he braked, his heart hammering, and took stock of where he was and what he was looking at. He'd reckoned on finding the camp photographed by Pete Aronson as soon as he saw the signs festooning the property's gateposts. And here it was, laid out below him, close now, at a shallower angle than Aronson had achieved in his ultralight plane. But altered in small ways since then: only one tent remained, apart from the mess tent; only one vehicle beside the camouflaged shape that was possibly another vehicle. An air of absence.

Even so, he was a sitting duck up there on top of the rise, and eased his foot off the brake, heading slowly downhill, still following the track, shoulders hunched in anticipation.

That didn't ease until he'd slotted the Hilux between the crumbling stone ruins of the homestead and its outhouse. Collapsed stone; weeds; rusted, drooping corrugated iron. He got out, immediately heard a snapping sound and dropped to the ground. Heard it again.

It was only a flag on a short pole, the red ensign whipping in the wind. He got to his feet and brushed the grit from his palms and knees, still feeling exposed. He hoped he wasn't having another panic attack. Hoped there were no dogs: this crowd would have Rhodesian ridgebacks, probably. Pit bulls. He put his back to the sole remaining wall of the original house and breathed in and out slowly, deeply, habitually, chasing fear away.

He wasn't convinced he was alone. If he was, he couldn't be sure things would stay that way. At the same time, there was a good reason why the place might have been abandoned: someone from here had shot down Pete Aronson and his ultralight, bringing unwanted police attention.

Clearly Ed Kline was part of the insanity. He didn't have a secret lover, he had secret paramilitary pals, and came out here, out of sight, to play soldiers with them.

Hirsch checked his phone, saw that he had an unlikely bar of reception, and called Kline's number. He heard a ringing, very faint, on the other side of the wall. He ducked his head around the corner and saw a battered, old-style aluminium rubbish bin with a dented lid. There was no point searching it. Let forensics do that later on. But why didn't Kline have his phone with him?

A new sound, metal clanging. He edged along the wall, shot a glance across the windy yard and saw a shed door flapping. Like the two portaloos, it looked incongruous in that old landscape: a suburban backyard gardening shed, the kind you got at Bunnings. Checking again that the coast was clear, Hirsch made a fearful, half-crouched run across the open ground.

Into the shed. He shut the door. Would someone register the sudden silence? But the noise had been too distracting, he needed a clear head.

He began to let his eyes adjust to the blanketed light. Drums of ammonium nitrate, which he knew to be an explosives precursor. Beside them was an unopened crate marked Tovex. The mining explosives stolen from the truck parked overnight at the Woolpack? Meanwhile the interior also contained several other crates and cartons, along with ropes and chains hanging from wall hooks, an extendable ladder, a stepladder and three empty jerrycans.

He moved on to a small box sitting on two wooden crates. It was empty, containing only a foam inlay in the shape of an automatic pistol. Of the two crates, one contained rifle ammunition, the other a single automatic rifle.

Where were the other rifles?

In the far corner, a wine carton. No wine, but dozens of federal police badges—fakes, probably.

Then he made a fast check of four plastic crates of a kind sold in Kmart—a creepy little domestic touch, he thought. The first contained multiple copies of back issues of *Red Ensign*. The second was larger and heaped with books. He removed some of them: *Creative Revenge. Happiness is a Confirmed Kill. Improvised Explosives (How to Make Your Own).* And *Encyclopaedia of Historical Accuracy.* Or fake historical accuracy, like fake news, he thought, flipping through it. Hate. Rants about anti-white guilt. Assorted conspiracies.

In the next box was a stack of A4 questionnaires headed 'New Recruits'. He scanned the questions: 'Are you a national socialist?' 'Do you believe Australia's political system is collapsing?' 'Are there circumstances in which armed insurrection is justified?' 'Can you fight? Use weapons?' 'Do you have any traces of Jewish or Muslim heritage?'

And so on.

Hirsch didn't want to spend too much time here. His Toyota might be spotted any minute now. Or someone would wonder why the shed door had stopped banging in the wind. He checked the final crate. It contained a roll of camouflage netting with tan and khaki cotton scraps sewn into the mesh. 'Excellent,' he said aloud.

Heaving the camouflage net into his arms, he staggered to the door, opened it gingerly, poked his head out. Then he slipped into the open air again, shut the door behind him and lumbered like an ox back across the dirt yard to the police Toyota. Dumped the camouflage net beneath the radiator and tugged it along each flank to conceal the vehicle. Psychology, he thought. He was relying on what people like Mia Dryden or her weekend warriors might *expect* to see, given that there was already a camouflaged vehicle in the yard.

A pretty doubtful benefit, though. It might grant him a useful five minutes. Or it might be spotted immediately, a big fat warning to Mia that her perimeter had been breached.

And what if search planes were sent to find him?

Determined not to overthink it, Hirsch stepped across to the security of the stone wall and poked his head out again. All clear, so he dashed to the big, open-sided mess tent. At one end was a large whiteboard. Wiped clean. Facing it were a dozen little school desks; below it, plastic crates similar to the ones he'd searched in the shed. More books. Newsletters. Sew-on cotton patches displaying the bastardised Celtic cross.

He turned around. Two long wooden tables with bench seats took up most of the central area, with two big high-end barbecues, a serving table and a set of empty bain-maries next to them.

There was a creased and fly-spotted photograph sticky-taped to the central pole. He tugged it free for a better look. Fifteen figures dressed in black pants and tops or army fatigues, looking at the camera. Seven on one knee at the front, eight ranged behind them. All sported the Celtic badge on their chests or upper arms and most were masked by balaclavas. The other three were Sam Dryden, standing slightly apart, looking for all he was worth like a commanding officer, Cody Morton and Scott Greig. At least two of the figures appeared to be women. Mia Dryden and Petra Osmak? They were about the right size.

He tried to distinguish who the men might be, but there was no way to tell. Presumably Inspector Cottrell's undercover man, McGain, had names for them all.

Hirsch tried to stare his way into the minds of these kids—he was assuming that most of them were young. The kind to have time on their hands. Unemployed or underemployed. No education, no prospects, ripe for radicalisation. He knew that the federal police—probably every state police force, too—feared a lone wolf like the Christchurch mass shooter, but they'd be concerned about paramilitary outfits like this, too.

He folded and pocketed the photograph and ranged around the rest of the tent's interior. One object was out of place: a wooden chair. Bloodstained. Strips of sliced gaffer tape, also bloody, on the legs. Someone had been bound and injured here.

Who, though? McGain?

He crossed to the cooking and serving area, intending to use one of the big barbecue units for cover while he checked the open ground, and found gouges and drag marks in the dirt, leading to the splintered remains of another wooden chair. Strips of gaffer tape clung to it, too, but there was no blood. He checked the top of the serving table. Little trays of knives, forks and spoons, and a slotted knife block with the handles of two knives sticking out of it. Two people tied up; one cut themself free, he guessed, then released the other one.

He tucked himself in behind the barbecue closest to the open flap and scanned the open ground again. Empty. Check the firing range first, he decided. Pocket as many shell casings as possible. Fingerprints, DNA.

He made another of his crouched dashes, halting where the shooters probably knelt or lay flat on the ground. He found only one shell casing: 5.56 mm, an automatic round of the kind used in NATO weapons. Possibly an M16 rifle or an M4 carbine.

Then he noticed, about twenty metres to his left, a mound of loose dirt tamped down. It looked exactly like a grave. Spooked now, checking in every direction, he dashed across, knelt and began to scoop with his fingers. Sharp stones cut him. He stuck his head up and eventually spotted a shovel and a pickaxe propped against a pile of firewood. Tempting fate, he showed himself again, racing across, grabbing the shovel, racing back to the grave.

He began to shift dirt, small amounts at a time, starting at one end. He uncovered work boots, toecaps facing upwards; started again at the other end and the shovel struck with meaty force against...a skull? He couldn't tell for sure, but that was exactly what it felt like. He teased away the dirt. Found, with a billowing stench of decomposition, the face of Ed Kline.

Hirsch rocked back on his heels, all his energy seeping

away. 'Sorry, Elly,' he murmured.

Fear building, he forced himself to take deep breaths again. Call it in, he thought. But Kline was dead, the urgency was gone. Check the remaining tent first, then the vehicles.

The tent was empty. A bunk-bed mattress tipped onto the ground, a sunhat, a crushed Fanta can. He looked around the camp, spotting one more metal shed. Made another mad run, saw a thick black cable snaking across the ground and realised the shed housed a generator.

Now the vehicles: a dust- and mud-streaked Pajero in the open, a larger vehicle camouflaged. The Pajero was empty but for a rifle case lying across the back of the seats. No gun. No keys in the ignition. *Redruth Motors* on a sticker in the back window. He photographed the rear numberplate anyway, but was pretty sure that Cody Morton owned it.

That left the camouflage net. He lifted one corner and saw that he'd found the Western Australian Land Rover. A sticker on the back window read: *I love my country but I fear my government.*

The windows had been tinted. Hirsch tugged on the front passenger door and poked his head in.

A voice said, 'Please...'

39

JANNE VAN SANT. She was in the back seat with Barry McGain's head cradled in her lap.

'Just a sec,' Hirsch said, withdrawing to drop the camouflage flap to the ground again before settling into the passenger seat of the Land Rover.

Van Sant seemed unhurt, if dishevelled. McGain had been beaten about the face and head: his nose was broken, his eyes bruised, his cheeks lumpen and one ear was torn. He was looking at Hirsch through the gap between the front seats, mouth open, uttering small, panting breaths.

The air was rank: blood, fear, soiled pants.

Hirsch turned away from the pair and leaned across the steering wheel: the key was in the ignition. 'You could have driven away. There doesn't seem to be anyone here—they could be coming back, though.'

McGain's breath came in a succession of weak gasps. 'Tank's...empty.'

And no fuel in any of the drums that Hirsch had found. I need to get them into the Toyota, he thought. 'Did you come here by car, Doctor Van Sant?'

'The same rental car,' she said. 'A young man drove it away from here.'

'Cody,' whispered McGain.

'Mrs Dryden followed him in her car,' Van Sant added. 'I think they mean to hide or destroy my car.'

Or they're going for misdirection again, Hirsch thought. Park it innocuously in the main street of Clare.

'They could be back soon,' he said, starting to open his door. 'I'll bring my car over and get you both on board.'

Dr Van Sant nodded.

Hirsch stepped into the queerly dappled light again, lifted a corner of the camouflage net and peered out. The camp was still quiet—but a quietness he didn't trust, a quietness poised to be violated.

Letting go of the flap, he ran across to the Toyota, tore off the camouflage net and climbed behind the wheel. A brief spurt of acceleration put him alongside the Land Rover. The transfer was quick, McGain settled in the back

371

with Dr Van Sant. Then he shot out in reverse and headed for the track that would take them back to Manna Soak Highway. He kept his speed down; McGain sucked in his breath whenever the tyres thumped into a pothole or skittered over the ridges of stone that regularly cut across the track.

'I can't drive faster than this,' he said, catching Dr Van Sant's eye in the rear-view mirror. She acknowledged that with a nod.

Hirsch worked at his first line of questions as he wrestled with the steering wheel, his wrists on fire. 'You broke your chair to get free, Janne?'

'Yes.'

'Then used a knife to cut Mr McGain free?'

'Yes, correct.'

'Did either of you try to get word to anyone after you untied yourselves?'

A whispery, 'No,' from McGain.

A firmer 'No,' from Dr Van Sant. 'That was my first thought, but they had confiscated our mobile phones and I found no radios or satellite phones. My search was hurried, however: I needed to find a safe place for Sergeant McGain.'

'He told you that he's a federal police officer?'

'Yes.'

McGain interrupted. He lifted his head dazedly from Dr Van Sant's lap, then sat up, his trunk listing, and said, 'Counter Terrorism Command.'

Hirsch knew little about the CTC, except that they

monitored and gathered evidence on extremist groups. Probably Muslim fundamentalists a few years ago. Nowadays, the homegrown far right.

'They tried to extract information from you, sergeant?' Hirsch asked.

There was no reply. 'You, Janne?'

'I was not beaten.'

'How did you come to be captured?'

'I was incautious.'

She went on to explain. Suspicious of the Drydens, she had watched their driveway entrance from a great distance and, when one of the property's Jeeps emerged, had followed it to the camp. 'Mrs Dryden was the driver, and was in a very great hurry. She left the gate open and I waited until she was out of sight before I entered. As I said, I was not careful enough. I came to the top of the final little hill too quickly—I was part of the way down it before I could stop. Of course, I was spotted. The track as you know is narrow, too dangerous. I could not manoeuvre.'

Two men armed with rifles charged up the hill, she said, and piled into her car before she could stop them. 'I managed to lock the doors but one of them shot out the back window, and I thought it best to stop and let them capture me.'

'Did you learn their names?'

'No. They were paramilitary in appearance.' She snorted. 'Recruits for Mr Dryden's white ethno-state.'

The men directed her to park in the yard, she

continued, and she was taken to the mess tent and tied up with McGain. 'He was unconscious, blood everywhere. You can see what they did to him.'

'Did they question you?'

'No. It is my belief that many people had already left. The others were packing up. Clearly, they were panicking.'

No wonder, Hirsch thought. Everything had come at once. Some idiot had shot down an ultralight that was filming them, their great leader had been hospitalised with Covid, and McGain had been unmasked—seen when he was in Tiverton with Inspector Cottrell.

'I found a fresh grave,' he said. 'A man named Ed Kline was buried in it.'

'I know nothing of that.'

'Barry, do you know?'

McGain coughed weakly. Said jerkily, 'He used to hang out with Cody at the pub. Started coming to training sessions. He jacked up when Mia took the plane down so... she shot him.'

The effort depleted McGain. He coughed again.

'Who attended these training sessions?'

'Local kids. Some of the station hands.'

'Petra Osmak and Scott Greig—were they with the crowd who cleared out today?'

McGain's voice scratched with effort. 'No. Mia told them to get lost a few days ago. Too much police attention.'

They're on the run together, Hirsch thought. Probably

pretty desperate. 'If Mia was with her husband the day I called in, who was at the crash site in the Land Rover?'

'Bloke and his girlfriend from Perth. They drove over after they were nearly scooped up in a police raid.'

A lot of networking between these groups, Hirsch thought. 'Was it them who took Kline's car back and wiped the GPS?'

'Yes.'

'They ran with the others this morning?'

'Yes. No petrol. Got a lift.'

'You know everyone's names and histories?'

McGain said nothing.

'Do you check in with Inspector Cottrell regularly?'

Still McGain was silent. Hirsch, checking the mirror, saw Van Sant look down, then meet his gaze. 'He is unconscious again.'

Hirsch was forced to brake sharply for a stormwater trench; McGain gasped as the vehicle rocked forward and back.

'Sorry,' Hirsch said, and checked the mirror. Janne Van Sant was looking down: he heard her murmur to McGain and sensed that she was stroking his head.

Hirsch accelerated again; this section was relatively flat and smooth. 'You weren't questioned at all?'

'Questioned, no,' Van Sant said. 'Mrs Dryden screamed in my face, however.'

Losing it, Hirsch thought, reflecting that, as criminals went, the Drydens were as fucked up and chaotic as

Brenda Maher and her mob of hangers-on. Prestige, wealth and education hadn't made them any smarter, apparently. 'About what?'

'Why had I returned? Why had I doubted her word? That sort of thing. Also, it seems that I represent an old, corrupt and complacent Europe.'

Mia, the intellectual, thought Hirsch. He paused; prepared himself for an emotional minefield. 'Did you learn what happened to Willi?'

Hirsch waited and after a while it came. Her eyes blinked. 'Yes. From Sergeant McGain, not that woman.'

Hirsch continued to wait. He slowed, eased onto a patch of loose dirt and run-off channels. The Hilux pitched about like a little ship in a storm. No one spoke: it was as if they were waiting, scarcely breathing, for calmer seas.

They were rewarded a few minutes later. The track became briefly less rutted and Janne Van Sant was able to say, 'It is such a stupid story.'

'Okay.'

'Willi and his girlfriend were sent to round up ewes that were grazing on a far part of the property and drive them into a sheepyard out there and wait for Mr Dryden to arrive. This they did, but...' Janne paused. He heard her swallow. 'They were alone for some time and maybe they had a little nap, made love, who knows? Unfortunately, they did not watch the dog, which apparently is notorious for being over-vigilant with sheep and had them bunched in one corner of the pen. They were in full fleece, and several of them suffocated. Mr Dryden was of course very angry. He made Willi and his girlfriend walk home. A very long way. Without water or phones or a compass.' She paused. 'And they perished.'

A stupid story. A shitty story. It said more about Sam Dryden than his marriage to Mia, his political ambitions or his army service. Hirsch shook his head, feeling impotent. 'I'm so sorry.'

At the same time, he was also thinking that McGain must have known what had happened to Janne's son. He'd have informed Cottrell. Who had done nothing about it, his eye on a bigger prize: the Drydens' whole outfit.

He wondered about Russ Fanning's dead ram. Pointless trying to speculate who'd shot it. Some weekend warrior playing freedom fighter, tramping around the hills with a rifle.

Catching Janne's eye in the mirror again, he said, 'We'll get them.'

He saw her shrug. Then McGain's voice came weakly, 'Sam and Mia are made for each other.'

'You were with them a long time?'

'Since the beginning of the year.'

'Let yourself be recruited?'

McGain's voice gathered strength as he spoke. 'They advertised for a cook. It was arranged that I'd apply, and I got the job. I was a cook in the army, briefly, so that helped. And I showed interest in their political views.'

'You took a risk coming to see me the other day.'

'Yeah, and Cody spotted me.' He paused. 'The boss's idea.'

'Water?' Dr Van Sant said.

'Thank you,' McGain said breathily.

Hirsch waited, then asked, 'What do you mean, they're made for each other?'

'Complementary,' McGain said, a little more strongly now. 'Mia's the fruitcake element. She's more rabid than Sam, but he's pretty dangerous. Political ambitions— recruiting Young Liberals and Young Nationals, running election candidates. He bought this godforsaken place to be a training ground. He's almost broke, though, and he's been talking about fundraising using fraud, maybe even armed robbery. He's an injustice collector, basically. Afghanistan was the highlight of his life but it seems the main attraction was shooting unarmed civilians...They eased him out of the army quietly.'

McGain lapsed into an exhausted silence. Hirsch concentrated on the gears and steering. They were a couple of kilometres from the main gate.

'How did Sam contract Covid? He does have it, right? It's not a ruse of some kind?'

'He does have it. Bad. Mia too, but only mildly.'

'You?'

'I'm okay.'

Famous last words, thought Hirsch, as McGain added, 'I think they got Covid off a pair who came through from Sydney a few days ago. Freedom Scouts. An offshoot.

They're all offshoots of something.'

'What will Mia do now? Wrap everything up?'

'Doubtful.'

The Hilux continued down the unforgiving section of track, and Dr Van Sant suddenly said, 'Accelerationist theory.'

Hirsch sought her eyes. 'What's that?'

'The use of violence in order to *accelerate* change. In this case, race war and societal collapse.' She shrugged. 'We have it in Europe, too. America.'

Hirsch shook his head. 'They seem small and disorganised to me.'

'Getting bigger,' McGain said. 'Better organised.'

'Was there a plan to raid the camp at any stage?'

That was Hirsch's last question. It went unanswered. As he rounded the next bend, he realised that he'd come to the end of the track.

The gates, fifty metres ahead, were blocked by two vehicles. One was Ed Kline's Holden Colorado; Elly was standing near the front grille. She followed me, he thought. On a mission to find her husband in bed with another woman.

Maybe she thought she'd found her. She seemed to be arguing with Mia Dryden, who stood with Cody Morton beside the other vehicle, a Dryden Downs Jeep.

They've just come from making Dr Van Sant's hire car disappear, Hirsch thought as he braked, the noise and movement alerting the figures at the gate.

He caught the unmistakeable choreography of a rifle being propped and aimed.

'*Duck!*'

The first bullet went through the windscreen where his head had been. The next two took out both front tyres and the Hilux settled with a surprised grunt on its springs. He heard the fourth bullet hit the front of the car. Radiator and engine block, he thought.

There was a moment of shocked silence. Then Hirsch hissed, 'Stay down,' and checked on his passengers through the gap between the front seats.

Dr Van Sant had an automatic pistol in her hand. 'Where did you get that?'

'I found it when searching for a means to communicate. It was in a box.'

He realised he'd drawn his own pistol, as if in sympathy. 'Do you know how to use it?'

'Of course.'

Now a voice was screeching outside: 'I'm going, I'm going, don't shoot me.'

And Mia responding: 'Who are you anyway?'

'I'm looking for my husband.'

'What's his name?'

'Ed Kline. He's here, I know he's—'

Another shot. Then silence.

Hirsch unwound his window and shouted through the gap. 'Mia, put the gun down, federal police are on their way.'

Her reply was another shot. The Hilux shuddered. Hirsch waited, afraid to poke his head up, as she shot out the rear passenger side tyre. She's flanking us, he thought. Circling around us. He was aware of how thin the side panels were. But if she was on the other side of the car, she might not see him slip out to where he could crouch in the shelter of the engine block, he thought; fire at her over the bonnet.

Better still, draw her away. Move out of her line of sight, then veer off in a different direction, near good ground cover, and hope she'd spot him and ignore the Hilux.

Winding up his window, he eased open the door and told Van Sant what he intended to do.

There was no fear in her, just intentness, a vein pulsing in her neck. 'Be careful, of course,' she said. 'And when she comes for you, I shall come in behind her.'

'No! When I draw her away, run for her car and—'

'And the sergeant?' She reached through and touched his sleeve briefly. 'There is really no option.'

Hirsch slid out and ran. And down on the road, Cody roared, 'Mia, the cop's getting away.'

Hirsch chanced a quick look. Mia Dryden was about fifteen metres from the Hilux, standing at an acute angle to it. 'I can see him, you idiot.'

'You're the idiot. He's police. Just let him go and we can get out of here.'

Mia had been tracking Hirsch with her rifle. Now she swivelled calmly and fired at Cody's feet. Not aiming, just

381

telling the kid to mind his manners. He yelped and scurried behind the Jeep.

With Mia distracted, Hirsch raced for the meagre protection of a lichened stone outcrop. Dropped out of sight behind it, then immediately up again, firing two quick shots. This wasn't close quarters; he hadn't a chance of hitting her. But she did need to be reminded that he had a gun, too.

She fired a three-round burst. Chips of quartz broke away.

When he looked again, she was at the Hilux, circling around the radiator, coming in on the driver's side back door. She's guessed I wasn't alone, he thought. He shouted, 'Mia!' and fired another futile shot.

He heard the bullet clang against the rocker panel. It might have been a mosquito for all the effect it had. Ignoring it, Mia pressed her face against the glass of the driver's door, then the rear passenger door. She stepped back—Hirsch thought he could see the smile smearing her born-to-rule face as she tugged on the door handle—and she was still smiling as Janne Van Sant shot her in the forehead.

The shock of it flung her back a step. Then the life dropped out of her and she flopped to the dirt. Hirsch waited for a moment, watching. Just a death twitch. He emerged from the meagre shelter of the rocks. Crossed the tricky ground. Down on the road, Cody was tearing away in Ed Kline's Colorado. A bit more anonymous than a Jeep marked *Dryden Downs*, I guess, Hirsch thought.

With the Colorado gone, Elly Kline was in plain view, a lump on the ground, looking smaller than she had in life.

He reached the Hilux. Peered in and the air was pungent with the graphite-and-nitro smell of a just-fired pistol. 'Are you all right?'

Janne Van Sant was calm. She had dropped the pistol into the footwell and was stroking Barry McGain's forehead again, almost as if he were her child. Hirsch found himself saying, 'Salvation Jane.' A rattly attempt at resurrecting the old humorous connection he'd made with her that first day.

She looked up and said, 'Just so.'

ACKNOWLEDGMENTS

Day's End is dedicated to Sue Turnbull and Graeme Blundell for their many years of championing Australian crime writing. I also owe a debt of gratitude to readers, booksellers, book clubs, the Text Publishing editorial, marketing and publicity staff and all others who have kept Hirsch and my other characters alive and prospering over the years. Meanwhile my thanks to Mandy Brett and Juliane Römhild for making this a better book; and to Sandra Nolan for giving me the nudge I needed to weave Auntie Steph into the story.